For The Love Of The Dame

A Novel

Miriam Allenson

For The Love Of The Dame

This is a work of fiction. Names, characters, places, and incidents are
products of the author's imagination or are used fictitiously. Any
resemblance to actual events, locales, organizations or persons, living or
dead, is entirely coincidental.

Dear Lucia,
Enjoy!
M Allenson

Praise for
For The Love of the Dame:

"A brilliant new voice in contemporary romance, Miriam Allenson writes characters who leap off the page and into your heart, bringing love and laughter with them."
-Nancy Herkness, award-winning author of Country Roads

"Hilarious, sexy, heartwarming—a fabulous debut! Miriam Allenson hits it out of the park in her debut novel, *For The Love of The Dame*. Sofia and Car are proof that when opposites attract, sparks fly!"
-Lisa Verge Higgins, author of Random Acts of Kindness

"I love this book! *For the Love of the Dame* is a charming ride, with every page full of wonderful, warm moments that make you smile all the way through. Miriam Allenson has just shot to the top of my auto-buy list!"
-Lani Diane Rich, New York Times bestselling author of The Fortune Quilt

Dedication

To my two A's, Andy and Aron.

Acknowledgements

Sofia's and Car's story didn't come clear in my head and on my laptop by itself. Many helped shape it along the way. They include Terri Brisbin and Shirley Hailstock, who encouraged me when I had no idea what I was doing, Lisa Kessler who provided invaluable information about the mezzo soprano voice, Jared Max, whose insights about baseball were key to understanding Car's struggle with his injury, Maite Gaeta and Maria Imbalzano for their input on divorce proceedings and custodial rights, Alessia Vittone and Roberta Gesualdo for correcting my incorrect Italian, Gina Ardito, my terrific content editor, Lani Diane Rich and Alastair Stephens for extraordinary graphic design and amazing copy editing, advisors supreme, Beth-Ann Kerber, Kathy Pacheco, and Leigh Raffaele, and my brilliant critique partners, Cathy Greenfeder, Lisa Verge Higgins, and Nancy Herkness. Most of all, I wouldn't have had the emotional strength to keep on without the support of the men in my life: Andy, Mike, Aron, and Herman.

Contents

FOR THE LOVE OF THE DAME

Prologue

Malpensa Airport, Milan, Italy
March 15

Afterward, Sofia de' Medici asked herself why she'd answered her cellphone, but by then, it was too late.

As usual.

"Stupid, stupid girl," he bellowed in her ear. "Where do you think you're going without me?"

She licked her suddenly parched lips. "I'm going to New York."

"I said no to New York. Weren't you listening?"

She began to tremble. "I'm listening now, and it sounds like your leg is broken, but not your voice."

"You dare to use sarcasm? With me?"

She dared. But if she were standing next to his hospital bed in Florence, rather than in the jet way leading to a non-stop flight from Milan to Newark, she wouldn't dare. "When I get to New York I know I can convince Maestro Lupino to give me the audition." She would have crossed her fingers if she hadn't been dragging a carry-on.

"You're too young to sing a role like *Carmen*." His voice grew louder. "When Lupino sees you, he'll know for certain why you can't fill the role."

He was referring to her full-figured body. Sofia cringed and glanced around. Nobody in this crowded jet way could hear his words and if they could, they weren't paying attention. They were too busy with carry-ons, laptops, shopping bags, children, or all four. The only thing they cared about was getting into their seats. "It doesn't matter what he sees. When he hears me sing, he'll know."

"He'll hear that I haven't prepared you to sing *Carmen*," he trumpeted, louder than Roman horns announcing the entrance of lions into the Coliseum.

His jagged words battered her self-esteem. "I know my voice," she whispered. "I can sing this role."

"You're a foolish, impulsive girl, who doesn't think before she acts. No music director will take a chance on you, not after you nearly ruined that performance at La Scala. Lupino won't give you the role. He won't even give you an audition. Do you hear?"

She put a hand to her throat to cover the mad beat of her pulse. He had controlled her forever. Her whole life. No more would she let him do it. "What I hear is I need to hit *end*."

"I'll call you again. And again. Until you understand I'm right."

She clutched her cell hard. Its edges cut into her hand. "I won't answer. Not anymore."

He laughed. Like a donkey.

Funny spots danced before her eyes, tiny black lights, winking and growing. "You've never believed in me. You never will."

Sofia took a deep breath, threw the phone down, and stamped on it until it broke into pieces.

Trembling, she looked up to see people distancing themselves from her. Except for one man. He patted her on the shoulder. "*Brava*," he said. Of course he would say this. He was Italian.

She gave him a half smile, sniffed back tears, and shuffled a few steps forward.

She glanced back at the phone pieces, and whispered, "*Arrivederci, Papa.*"

Chapter One

New York
April 2

It was easy to get a new cellphone. In New York, hundreds of stores sold them. The phone she bought had many more functions than the one that was now scraps in an Italian junkyard. The best part about her new phone was her father didn't have the number. But if somehow he got it tonight, she didn't want him calling and poisoning the moment, which was why she'd left it on the seat in the limo that had taken them from the hotel and dropped them off at the stadium.

"Sofia, why are you hesitating?" asked Chelsea Singleton, her assistant of two weeks.

She couldn't tell Chelsea it was because she'd let thoughts of her father enter her head. In the short time since they'd met on the flight from Milan to Newark, and Sofia had asked if she would be her assistant, she'd found out Chelsea would not let her give in to anxiety. "*Non sto esitando...*"

"Speak English," Chelsea interrupted her. "You need to practice."

That was so true. Her English was awful. "I do not hesitate. I am thinking."

"You need to practice thinking in English. You're in the United States now and it's important for you to get familiar with the language."

"If only it is not so hard," Sofia sighed. She wished speaking this language, with all its odd colloquialisms, was as easy for her as singing in it.

Chelsea patted her shoulder. "We'll work on it. You and I, back in the hotel. Tonight, in fact. In the meantime, we need to hustle up to the field. You're on in less than ten minutes."

"*Lo so...* I know," Sofia said, correcting herself. She gave Chelsea a sheepish smile and looked down the long, concrete-walled hallway ahead of them. There, at the end, was the flight of steps that led up to the field where the New York Federals played their baseball games. It was where she'd sing *The Star-Spangled Banner* for the team's first game of the season. Her dearest Brent, her mentor, had asked her to do it, and she'd agreed for two reasons: he'd asked; and because he'd said it would get her the audition with Maestro Lupino. After two weeks of calling the Maestro, and leaving him messages that were never answered, she hoped this would make a difference. She smoothed her hands down her tight, black wool dress and, in her beautiful Manolos, walked as fast as the dress and the shoes would allow.

"I still don't know why you wore those things," said Chelsea, pointing to her feet. "I'd hate to see you fall on your face. Grass and heels don't go together."

Sofia smiled. Chelsea, who was taller than many men, couldn't understand how important high-heeled shoes were to short women. "Do not do the worrying. It will be okay."

Chelsea didn't look convinced. "And you're sure you're not nervous?"

It was Chelsea who was nervous. Sofia wasn't. To sing a song she'd never sung before didn't make Sofia nervous, any more than breathing made her nervous. "Do not worry, Chels. I have got the anthem down to the patting."

Chelsea pealed a laugh. "You've got it down pat," she corrected.

Sofia was still smiling and thinking of her terrible English when she trod up the steps to the field and ran right into a hard body standing in the way.

"Oof," she said and staggered backward.

Before she could fall back down the stairs she'd just climbed, the person grabbed her shoulders and in a sharp voice said, "Be careful." As if it was not he, the big idiot, but she who should have been careful.

She steadied herself and looked up to suggest standing at the top of a flight of stairs was dangerous and foolish and stupid... and she fainted inside her head.

This person, this idiot... he was the handsomest man she'd ever seen. His eyes sparkled green-blue, the color of the sea during a day of sunshine on the Amalfi Coast. She was blinded. She was struck dumb. As if she were that woman in the Bible who didn't listen when her husband said, "Don't turn around."

Someone said his name. Why? Was it an introduction? How could she know when she heard nothing but crashing sounds between her ears? It was as if she were center stage at the Teatro Communale in Florence, surrounded by one hundred workmen, singing a fortissimo "Anvil Chorus".

He took her hand in his. Surely, it was to shake it. It was a hard hand, with calluses. A warm hand, almost hot. A hand that swallowed hers.

Why, when it was a hand she wanted to hold forever, did she then take her hand from his? And what was it she said to him? Or did she only think she said something? How was it that now it was Chelsea's hand in hers, and they were hurrying up more steps to stand at the perimeter of the stadium's field itself?

The Star-Spangled Banner. At last she remembered. She was to sing it in minutes. She squeezed her eyes shut. The last thing she needed to be thinking about was that man. She needed to heave him out of her mind.

She made herself look around the field, with its grass so emerald green it was impossible to think it real. She gazed at the thousands of people who sat in the seats surrounding it. She stared upward to the stadium's topmost edges, to the parapets above the facades, and the piercing white lights standing like rows of militant sentinels, lights so bright they made a midday of the pitch-dark April night.

Again, she closed her eyes. As if that would help. He was still there inside her head. She couldn't get rid of him, or the feel of his gaze upon her back in the tender place between her shoulder blades, where perspiration glued her too tight dress to her body. She twisted, shrugged, and just resisted reaching behind her to slap away the phantom presence of his fingertips, tickling her overheated skin. "*Maledetto,*" she whispered.

Chelsea squeezed her hand. "Buck up. It's for the audition. You can do this."

Sofia flattened one hand against her middle. Chelsea still thought she was nervous about singing the anthem. Sofia couldn't tell her she had stopped thinking about the anthem. Or the reason she was singing it. She was thinking about that man whose name she hadn't heard, the man who stood behind her in the place called a dugout.

She wiggled her toes. "You are right. I can do this."

"You'll be like Renee Fleming singing the anthem at the Super Bowl, only better. Tonight everyone's going to think you're fabulous."

Fabulous. It was unfortunate that all she could think of was it was *he* who was fabulous.

"Sofia! You're squirming."

How embarrassing would it be to tell Chelsea why. "It is because of this salami dress," she improvised.

Chelsea tilted her head, with its halo of blond, frizzy hair, to the side. The dimple in her right cheek made a quick appearance. "What's a salami dress?"

Sofia hadn't meant to call it a salami dress. She'd spoken without thought because her brain was disengaged. As usual. Now she couldn't take the words back. "It is a dress that fills me with discomfort," she said. At least this was true. She felt a tap on her shoulder and opened her mouth to elaborate on salami dresses, but it wasn't Chelsea. It was one of the men who worked in the Federals' team office.

"Miss de' Medici," he said, puppy-dog adoration fixed upon his shining face. He was young, younger than her own twenty-four. "Time to sing. Are you ready?"

"*Grazie.* I am ready."

"Go, Sofia." Chelsea gave her a nudge.

She smoothed her hands down her dress and took a step onto the grass in the direction of the home place, where two men waited for her by the microphone. She risked a turn of her head to catch a glance of the man in the dugout.

Oh God. She was right. He was staring at her.

"*Merda,*" she hissed. This stupid mooning had to stop. She had a task to complete and one chance to do it. She couldn't let daydreams about a handsome man, whose face should appear on a magazine cover, stand in her way.

As she did before every performance, Sofia took a deep breath and crossed herself. She started toward the microphone, and sank into the boggy soil. Now she knew what Chelsea meant about grass and high heels. "Forget about the bombs bursting in mid-air," she muttered. "If you fall on your face, you'll never get the audition."

Afterward, Sofia rushed off the field as fast as her shoes and salami dress would allow.

Chelsea rushed behind her. "Where are you going?"

Sofia had no idea. The elation in her heart for singing the anthem—and not falling—had driven her to mindlessly sail across the field, propelled as if by the magic of the specter ship in Wagner's opera *The Flying Dutchman*.

"I have sung the *Banner*," Sofia shouted over the roar of the crowd. "I put the nail in it. I will get the audition." She clambered down the dugout's three shallow steps, and further down into the concrete hallway below.

"Wait up, girlfriend." Chelsea's voice caught on a series of staccato breaths.

Sofia didn't slow, not even when they were deep into the hallway. "*Come si dice in inglese...*" She brimmed over with happiness, her heart full as a stuffed artichoke. "The people showed me the love."

"What are you—" *Huff, huff,* "—talking about?"

"I am speaking of the wonderful Americans." She flung the words over her shoulder and kept going. What had Brent said? Meet me in a lighted room, not far from the field.

"What about them... us?"

"They clap for me. Even before I finish the singing." She kept going, looking for the room.

"Baseball fans always clap after the national anthem."

"Yes, but they stand to give me the ovations." Sofia couldn't wait to see Brent and tell him he was right!

"Not that you don't deserve it, but all that clapping is normal at a... oh, never mind."

"*Cosa*?" Ah. Ahead. A room, all lit up. It had to be the one. Her heels clacking against the cement floor, Sofia put on a burst of speed, rushed into the room. And came to an abrupt halt.

It was a large room, no chairs, only wooden benches, with piles of white towels draped over them, some in clumps on the floor. She frowned. This couldn't be where Brent wanted them to meet, could it? "*Al diavolo.*" She sniffed, and flapped a hand in the air in front of her. "Bleach."

Chelsea grabbed her flapping hand. "Um... I don't think we're in the right place. This is a locker room."

"No, no. The door was open, not locked."

"Locker," Chelsea whispered, and turned Sofia to the right. "We're not alone."

They weren't. There, in front of a row of tall, metal closets, stood three oversized men in Federals uniforms.

Sofia felt the flush rise to heat her face from chin to forehead, at last understanding. A locker room was where the team dressed into their uniforms, and undressed from them. She expelled a quick breath. Thank God they weren't undressing. Sofia gripped Chelsea's hand and began to back out.

"Miss? Can I help you?" One of the men took a step toward them. Sofia gripped Chelsea's hand harder, and concentrated on coming up with a correctly-phrased answer. Her English, as usual in these situations, had all but deserted her. "*Sto cercando...* N-No... I am looking for Mr. Brent Mosbacher, the owner of the New York Federals baseball team."

The man glanced at his friends. "Mr. Mosbacher?" They shrugged like a troupe of birdbrained peasants in *L'Elisir d'Amore*.

"*S-Si.* Mr. Mosbacher."

"He's not here. But I'll find him for you." He took up a phone from the wall. "If you'll wait...?"

"*Grazie*. Thank you." Sofia gave the men an awkward smile. Nerves singing, not wanting to look into their eyes, she gaped at everything, including... she sucked in a breath.

Chelsea nudged her. "What?"

"These men, they have the..." The word in English failed Sofia. Until she remembered. "The bulge. They have the bulge."

There was a heavy silence. "My God, Sofia." Chelsea's voice was a barely-stroked bowing across the lowest string of a violin. "You shouldn't say such shocking things."

Of course she shouldn't. But when had that ever stopped her? Like now. She turned to face Chelsea and tried to make it better. "I will tell you a shocking thing. On the stage, in some operas, *The Marriage of Figaro, The Barber of Seville, per esempio*, when the tenor—I do not understand why it is always the tenor—when he makes the first appearance and he is wearing the tights, you look. Because there they are: the parts. The bulge."

The skin around Chelsea's pale, hazel eyes crinkled into laugh lines. "That must make it difficult to sing if you're staring... there."

"I do not stare. When I begin to sing, I do not think about them," Sofia heard herself say, her mind shutting out Lorenzo Latte and his tights. And the shock of what happened that night on the stage at La Scala, when she didn't say, but did a crazy thing.

She couldn't let herself think about that.

A phone rang.

The same man, who made the phone call, answered. He listened a moment and hung up. "Miss?"

"Yes?"

"That was Mr. Mosbacher. He said don't go anyplace. Stay here."

"*Grazie*."

"Excuse me."

Sofia took a few steps forward so a Federals player could enter the room. He carried a dark, brown thing in the crook of his arm. He came to an abrupt halt when he saw her, dropping the thing on the floor with a *thwop*. It settled inches from the tip of her left shoe.

More steps. She felt a touch on her shoulder. "Sofia,

darling. This isn't where I told you to meet me."

Well, yes. Now she knew it, instead of before, when she wished she had. She swung around. Too sharply. The point of her shoe became stuck in the brown thing. When she tried to pull it out, she lost her balance. A hard, callused hand gripped her wrist. In a dizzying twist, she slammed backwards against the body that went with the hand.

With foreboding, she realized she knew the hand.

"You like to run into people, don't you?" The low whisper of the voice brushed against the back of her neck. The hands turned her.

The man from the dugout.

It was fate.

He held her against the scratchy folds of his white on blue pin-striped Federals uniform, against his hard, muscled chest. She breathed him in. He wore a scent she didn't recognize: of lemons and limes. Her knees quivered like unset aspic.

"*Mi dispiace*, I..." She looked up, her eyes traveling the miles to the face above the uniform. She opened her mouth to translate her apology into English. And, once more, lost her ability to think. Or speak.

"You almost fell," he said, this man with no name, his voice a deep, dark, baritone murmur, his big, warm hands cradling her, as if she were as fragile as Violetta, expiring in the last scene of *La Traviata*. Sofia died a little, herself, with the exquisite pain of being held in his arms.

But thoughts of romantic death fell away as she was dazzled, once more, by the green-blue of his eyes, by his golden skin, like autumn wheat in the fields of Tuscany, by the long godlike nose of a Caesar, the warrior's jaw, strong and square. He was as beautiful as Michelangelo's David, so beautiful the great man would, for sure, come back from the dead to sculpt him. Or love him—definitely to love him. Everyone knew Michelangelo loved men.

Someone laughed. Brent cleared his throat. "Sofia, you were magnificent."

With difficulty, Sofia dragged her gaze away from the Nameless One, only to stare like a half-witted loon at Brent. "*Grazie.*" She would have said more, but her tongue was stuck to her palate.

With little movements so as not to offend, she hunched a shoulder and drew herself out of the Nameless One's arms. "*Scusi,*" she whispered. A puzzled frown creased his forehead. "It means pardon me in Italian. I give you the apology because you had to catch me."

"That's okay," he whispered back. Sweetness cavorted in his beautiful blue-green eyes, like ballerinas in the third act of *La Gioconda.*

Sofia's suffering heart struggled not to burst into pieces, the result of gazing into the eyes of this divine being. She had fallen in love. Of course, it was only with his image. She wasn't such a fool to think if he smiled at her, the way he smiled at her now, it meant he loved her. She kept her gaze averted, as one must with a god.

"It wasn't your fault. If Tommy hadn't dropped his glove you wouldn't have tripped."

"That was a glove?" Sofia had lots of gloves. This thing didn't look like a glove.

"Excuse me, my dear. We need to talk about the audition. And soon." Brent gave her a smile that showed off every one of his artificially whitened teeth.

"*Certamente.*" She breathed a sigh of relief, for this was something of which she could speak confidently. "But I no longer worry. I have sung the anthem, like you ask me. Now it is assured the Maestro will give me the audition, and I will be his Carmen."

Brent gazed at her with the affection her own father never bothered to show her. "I know you will be, Sofia."

She sighed, her heart full with love and whispered so the Nameless One couldn't hear, "You are so good to me, Brent. I wish, sometimes, that you were my papa instead of the papa who is my papa."

He looked at her with strange, sad eyes and said, "I wish it too, my dear." But then he added, "Things may have changed. But I have it under control, so don't worry."

Not worry? Now she was worried.

Brent put his arm around her shoulder and turned toward the Nameless One. "Sofia, you two met. Before you sang, right?"

And before she lost her hearing. In the dugout. "Y-yes."

"Let's talk: you, me, and Car."

Sofia blinked. Surely she'd lost her hearing again. She stared into the face of this man, who was called...?

She made an attempt to understand, but gave up. "Do you tell me you are named for an automobile?"

Chapter Two

"It's a nickname, Sophie," Car Bradford said, and smiled.

She cranked her neck back to fix him with the intensity of eyes black as a country night. "You say my name wrong. It is Sofia. The accent is on the next to last syllable."

Car's lip twitched. Mosbacher had pulled him out of the dugout for a reason. He still didn't know why. Not that he cared—he was too busy enjoying this pint-sized Italian, whose body didn't quit. "Sorry. My bad."

"I do not say you are bad." She shook her head. The ceiling's florescent lights cast a shine on her thick black hair. Winched back in a tight knot at the back, he wondered how she didn't have a migraine.

"I only want to know... Car is the nickname for Carlo?"

Now, that was a logical leap. Logical, but wrong. "Not Carlo. Christopher Arthur Robert Bradford: you take the first letters of the three names. C—A—R. That's where you get Car."

"You wish me to call you *Creese-toe-fur*? She pursed her lips.

He almost didn't catch what she said; he was so busy staring at her moist, red lips. Until it registered. "Uh, nobody calls me Christopher."

Brent cleared his throat. "Just a minute." He looked at Tommy, who stood frozen, obviously not knowing how to pick up the glove he'd dropped under the lady's feet without being out of line. Brent saved him by punting it in his direction. Tommy snagged the thing and hightailed it.

Then Brent dealt with the three guys, kids who'd been brought up from Triple A to get a taste of opening night in the majors, and who hadn't vacated yet. Brent pointed toward the door. "Head out now." They left.

Mosbacher turned back to Car. "Okay, so here's the deal. Sofia's not in New York for a casual visit."

Here it came: the reason Mosbacher had asked him to tag along.

"She's trying out for the lead role in *Carmen*. That's a famous opera."

There it was, for a change. The dumb jock thing. "I've heard of *Carmen*."

"She needs to audition for the part, but she hasn't been able to get one." Mosbacher gazed at Sofia, his eyes going all gooey.

Car might only be a dumb jock, but he needed exactly one nanosecond to decide what that look meant. Mosbacher was doing her.

It shouldn't have made him sick. He shouldn't have been surprised. Sofia wouldn't be the first to hook up with a man like Mosbacher, who was the general partner of a major league baseball team, the heir apparent, through his wife Victoria, of the Kirk family fortune, and businesses that stretched into who knew how many areas. Even if he found Sofia interesting—check that, *had* found Sofia interesting—she was now off-limits.

"Here's the deal," Mosbacher said. "Sofia's sung in opera houses all over Europe, but what she's sung doesn't allow her to demonstrate her full potential. She needs to prove she can sing a role like *Carmen*."

"I do not have to prove I can sing *Carmen*. That is the given," she put in, chin going up.

Car shrugged. "Then what's the problem?"

"She doesn't look the part."

Car didn't know about that. What he did know was there was something about Sofia that made him want to look at her non-stop. "Who says she doesn't?"

"The music director and general manager of the Municipal Opera, Antonio Lupino," Sofia said and straightened, which drew his eye right there to her boobs.

Car forced himself to look back at Brent. "Isn't the

Municipal Opera House one of the Mosbacher family businesses?"

Brent nodded.

"So this Lupino guy works for Victoria." Car narrowed his eyes. "All you need to do is get Victoria to tell him to hire her."

Sofia gasped.

Brent said, "It doesn't work that way. Victoria chairs the Board, but she'll tell you she doesn't interfere with Lupino's artistic decisions."

The way Sofia flushed up, Car could see she didn't think this was a fun conversation. Not that it was his problem. "Dress her up in the right costume. That should take care of things."

Brent grimaced. "Well... Carmen's a *femme fatale*. Sofia isn't."

Sofia's chin went up another notch. Now there was a tremble in it. He folded his arms across his chest. He was not going to feel sorry for her.

"You noticed, didn't you?" Mosbacher prodded.

Car noticed, all right. Short she might be—the top of her sleek black head came only to the middle of his chest—but she was curvy in all the right places: that amazing rack, the rounded hips, the suggestion of a waist he could put his hands around, shapely legs, and tiny ankles. Mosbacher didn't have eyes in his head.

"She needs some credibility," said Mosbacher.

All Car knew was she was working damn hard to keep that tremble under control. Yeah, she was all about opportunity. But she shouldn't have to listen to her lover talk about her like that. Car wanted to put his hands over her ears.

"Your face lives in *People Magazine*, and on those TV celebrity news shows," Mosbacher continued. "Paparazzi follow you everywhere. Everyone knows your reputation. They want to read about you in the *NY Post*...that Page, uh..."

"Page Six," Car finished for him. He frowned. Caught himself, tore his eyes away from Sofia, who was trying to hold onto her game face, while Mosbacher talked around her. "What?"

"By the time you and Sofia spend a couple of weeks together, Lupino will think, wow, that girl, she must have something if she's caught Car Bradford. And then bingo; the audition's hers."

This was why Mosbacher wanted him? He glanced at Sofia, whose eyebrows had snapped together. He inclined his head toward Mosbacher. "You want me to pretend she's my...?"

"That's right."

"No," he said.

Brent pointed in the direction of the hallway. "I need to talk to you. Alone."

Car followed Brent down the hallway.

"I'm going to explain." Mosbacher's eyes turned flinty cold. "And you're going to understand."

"No."

"What, you think your latest eye candy's going to have an attack, you being with Sofia for business?"

"Tanya's not an issue."

"Done with her, are you?" Brent barked a humorless laugh. "Then what's the problem?"

"There isn't one." But there was. He just wasn't prepared to talk about it with Brent, of all people. "You need to ask someone else to do this thing."

Brent worked his jaw so long, Car thought they were done, until Brent waved a finger in his face. "How about I make it worth your while? You know those endorsements I ask you to do? Do this for me, I'll never ask again."

"Really?"

"This is a great opportunity for Sofia. Her voice is amazing. She's ready to sing *Carmen*."

Car could agree with Mosbacher on that. Her voice had a smooth sound to it. Like the hum of satisfied honey bees.

"The problem is it's not her voice. It's..."

Car held up a hand. "Stop right there. You don't need me because of my reputation with the ladies. You need me because if Victoria finds out about you and Sofia, oh man, you will fry in hell."

"No, it's..."

"How is it you don't know you can't let your dick do your thinking?"

Mosbacher's face went white. "You can't think Sofia and I are..."

"Please." Car held up a hand to stop whatever was about to come out of Mosbacher's mouth. "Next you'll tell me there are no controlled substances in baseball."

A moment of loud silence stretched between them, until Mosbacher sighed. "I'm not sleeping with Sofia."

Car stared.

Mosbacher's gaze slid away. "According to Victoria, Lupino had a mezzo, but she left him in the lurch. Since then, he's been turned down by everyone he's gone after. He's got three months to find his Carmen. He's running out of mezzos and time. You'd think he'd want to give Sofia an audition. But he doesn't." He sighed. "I think I know why."

"Why?"

"Like I said." Brent shrugged. "It's her looks."

"Isn't opera about the voice?"

"You'd think. I should have remembered. Sofia's always been... she's..." Mosbacher rubbed his forehead and glanced over at Sofia. "Dammit, I hate to say it, but it's her weight."

"Hey, hey. Whatever it is, it's not that. It's that ugly-ass dress she's got on. Makes her look all square-like. Doesn't show off that little waist of hers."

Mosbacher frowned. "What waist?"

The guy didn't notice? Car did a mental eye roll. "The waist you can put your hands around."

Brent continued. "Look, if people think Sofia's hot because she's with you, no matter what she looks like, Lupino will cave."

"You're killing me, Brent. It doesn't matter how much time I spend with her. Nobody'll believe we belong together."

"Well then, act like it. I know you can. Who bluffs a

bunt better than you?"

"That's baseball." Car dismissed the compliment for what it wasn't worth. "This is different. The woman isn't my type." But even as he said the words, they sounded wrong in his ears.

"Oh?" Mosbacher's lip curled at one corner. "Louise was your type. How'd that work out?"

"It didn't. Hooking up with the boss's daughter... not smart."

"Agreed." Hands on hips, Mosbacher turned away and stared up at the ceiling. "Make an exception for me, for Sofia, so she can sing *Carmen*."

Car let the silence stretch until Mosbacher swung around, eyes pleading. It was a look Car had never seen on the man's face. He almost gave in. Until he recalled why he'd said no to begin with and it wasn't because of the endorsements. It was the little fact that he was dealing with someone he couldn't trust, most especially because Brent was the father of his ex-wife and these days, Car didn't need more complications with her, not when the slightest thing could set her off and screw things up royally. "Sorry, the answer's still no."

"I can't get you to change your mind?"

"Nope."

"I mean it, you know. About not doing those endorsements."

Car raised one eyebrow. He shook his head. Slowly.

Mosbacher tapped his lip. "What if I tell you I'm willing to help you out with Louise?"

Car straightened. "Help me out how?"

"I know you don't like the new guy in her life. And Noah being around him so much."

Not like? Mosbacher had no idea. A vein throbbed over Car's eye. "So?"

"While you're with Sofia, Noah will stay with Victoria and me."

"Louise will see right through that."

"Louise will like the idea. It'll give her more time with the new guy."

Car strode down the hall in the direction of the field, stopped, put one hand to the back of his head and rubbed.

Think. He had to think.

Two months ago, Noah's nanny, Helena, called to say she'd come back from a day off to find the boy in the lobby of the building where Louise lived. He was alone. Louise was seventeen flights up in her apartment, sleeping off a night out with the new guy: Pete Jensen.

If Helena hadn't been there, Noah could have walked past the doorman into the street. Into...

Car clenched his jaw against the nightmare he made a point never to relive, which he relived anyway. That afternoon, Car had told his attorney to ask for full custody.

Exhaling sharply, he looked around to focus on something—anything—to wipe from his mind the vision of Noah out in the street... and saw Sofia and her friend standing in the locker room doorway. The friend was yakking. Sofia listened and watched him, alert as a rookie facing a killer pitcher, not knowing what pitch would come next.

In those black eyes of hers, Car could see she knew whatever Brent and he had been talking about concerned her. And her future.

Could he do this thing? If it meant not worrying about Noah being around Jensen for a few weeks, it was worth escorting Miss High Drama around town. Could be, by then, he'd have the custody thing worked out. He turned back. "You mean it?"

Scout-like, Mosbacher raised two fingers.

Very nice. Only Car didn't think Mosbacher had ever been a scout. "If I hear otherwise, the deal's off."

Mosbacher's hard features softened. "I'm sorry I have to ask this of you, son. Sofia means a lot to me."

In a rush of sudden temper, Car said, "Explain, why don't you, how it is she means so much to you that you're willing to use your grandson as a bargaining chip?"

"I love my grandson, but..." Mosbacher shook his head, paused. "I have a debt of honor I need to fulfill. Can you understand that?"

"I guess I have to. For now."

"Thank you."

Car nodded, his gaze fixed on the two women. "Is this everything?"

"Absolutely."

Car turned back toward Mosbacher. "You do know it's going to look like I'm sleeping with Sofia, right?"

Mosbacher's skin whitened. "Jesus."

"You didn't think that far ahead? You don't think people will ask themselves how it's working? You know, man sharing lover with ex-father-in-law?"

"Will you get it through your head?" Mosbacher's eyes fixed on his with a searing ferocity. "I am not sleeping with Sofia."

Car frowned. Maybe it was true. Maybe Sofia wasn't sleeping with Mosbacher. Maybe it was what Mosbacher said: a debt of honor. "All right," Car said, and caved. "When will you get Noah?"

Mosbacher pulled out his cellphone. "I'll make arrangements now."

Car only half-heard Mosbacher's conversation. He was too busy trying to process what just happened.

"Okay. Let's get on with it." Mosbacher shoved his phone back into his belt holster. "I probably should explain what Sofia is up against."

"What do I care what Sofia is up against? The only reason I'm doing this is because of Noah. And the only way I'm going to get through the next few weeks is to think of your girl as a job."

"Brent."

Car was just able to stop himself from jumping. He'd thought Sofia was across the hallway. Not at his elbow. Had she heard him call her a job? Probably.

She stood straight and smoothed her hands down the black dress that belonged on someone else. "When you speak of the Maestro, you speak of *Carmen*. When you speak of *Carmen,* you speak of me. And I?" She firmed her chin. "I will be in this conversation, because no more will I be the spectator of my own life."

Chapter Three

"Of course you're not a spectator, my dear." Brent was all smiles. He took her hand. "We were saying how well-positioned you are to get the part."

Sofia loved Brent. She knew he loved her. But he hurt her today, even as he thought he was helping. To say she wasn't a *femme fatale* and to say it in front of *him*—she cast a quick sideways glance at he of the blue-green eyes—this was complete mortification.

"Did you know the Maestro is a huge baseball fan?" Brent squeezed her fingers. "Of course you didn't. I did, and hoped the Maestro would watch the game tonight. That's why I wanted you to sing the anthem, so he could hear how fabulous you are, and know he had to give you the audition, maybe even the role without an audition. I wanted him to fall in love with your voice the way I fell in love with it that first time I heard you sing."

She'd been little more than a baby—eleven years old—but her father was already having her perform for people like Brent. She remembered that time in the villa high in the mountains above Florence, when she sang *Ave Maria*, and her voice soared through the peaks and valleys of Schubert's heartbreaking music. She remembered how Brent had cried.

He wasn't crying now.

"I'm optimistic it will work." He pretended to cough. "But to be certain, I've been thinking we should, perhaps, take some additional action."

That cough was a signal of something she knew she wouldn't want to hear. What would follow would be as bad as when the storm breaks in the last act of *Rigoletto*, and Gilda is stabbed by her own father.

Except Brent wasn't her father. "Do not worry. Tomorrow I will secure the audition."

"Sofia..."

Drops of perspiration broke out on her upper lip. "I must make more phone calls. I must go to the Municipal Opera House. I must knock down the Maestro's door and make him listen to me. Then he will know I am Carmen."

Brent made placating motions with his hands. "Very dramatic, Sofia. Only you're not ready for the Maestro. At least, not yet."

She stiffened. "How can you say this? It is all the others who are not ready. I am ready."

"Sofia..."

"Some have the voice of beauty," she said hurriedly. "But not the looks of Carmen. Or the fire. I do not have this problem."

Brent cleared his throat again, but she wouldn't let him speak. "Some who sing *Carmen* these days are slender models. Yes, they can sing, but sometimes they have the wobbles and the sharp tones to their high notes because they have no diaphragm, and they have no diaphragm because they do not eat the carbohydrates." This wasn't true, but Sofia said it anyway.

She turned away from Brent and risked another glance at the man beside her, the man who could be a Siegfried, a Radames... this man with the name of an automobile, the name she couldn't say. In that instant, the name she *could* say came to her: *Signore* Beautiful Eyes, for, perhaps, his most beautiful feature, although all his other features were beautiful as well. For an instant, she allowed herself to think how fantastic it would be to die, as Senta dies in Wagner's *The Flying Dutchman*, for the love of such a man as *Signore* Beautiful Eyes.

"See that's the thing, sweetheart," Brent said. "We need to be sure Antonio will be impressed with your stature as a singer."

Sofia blinked her mind away from heavenly death.

Brent cleared his throat. "Despite your..." And he stopped, as if his lungs had seized up.

A shiver raised the hairs on Sofia's scalp.

Signore Beautiful Eyes frowned at Brent.

Sofia's nerves began to sing the Dutchman's theme of doom, just before Senta throws herself into the sea. "Maestro Lupino will be impressed with the stature of my voice. Once he hears me sing."

"Yes, yes." Brent patted her shoulder. "You have the voice. But remember that soprano who got passed over because she couldn't fit into a little black dress? She was much bigger...um...she was big, it's true. You are not. You are...um...you are...shall we say, perhaps..."

Sofia knew how to finish that sentence. Perhaps plump. Big breasted. Bottom heavy.

"It is the voice that matters," she said, "not the body." Except for Carmen, a little voice inside her said, it did. "Carmen does not wear a little black dress," she argued to silence the voice. "She wears big skirts, and frilly white blouses. When Don José sees her blouse and the bosoms beneath, it is one of her parts he falls in love with." She held out her hands in front of her chest.

"Sofia, put your hands down," Brent whispered, and looked away.

Signore Beautiful Eyes didn't look away.

Brent's face turned red. Why? Because she spoke about breasts? Americans, she was learning, didn't like to talk about body parts. Except when they cursed.

"It will take more than... um... bosoms to get Antonio to choose you. He wants to make his stage the place where the best singing is heard. This, without question, you can deliver. He'll want to know you look and act the part as well as be able to sing it." He turned to *Signore* Beautiful Eyes. "Sofia is a wonderful actress."

Brent stopped speaking. Sofia held her breath until, in an undertone, he added, "He'll want you to look seductive. Be thought seductive." He paused. "And sexy."

Sexy. Her breath caught. She never used the word when she thought of herself.

Brent looked down.

She pressed her hands against her lips. "*Dio mio,*" she mouthed against her palms. Her heart plummeted to her feet. She turned away. Did *Signore* Beautiful Eyes know there was a reason why she didn't know how to look sexy?

Brent put his hands on her shoulders and turned her around to face him. "Sofia," he said in a soft voice, "I want you to be the next great *prima donna*."

She looked into his warm, pleading eyes. "Then you must know. It is only when I sing *Carmen*, people will call me *prima donna*."

He squeezed her shoulders just a little and said, "Yes, but until then, I want you to let Car help you. Will that be so terrible? The media loves him. Being with him will help get you noticed as his latest woman. You know, because you... um... seduced him. And it'll get you the audition."

She looked at *Signore* Beautiful Eyes, who was frowning. In disgust, she thought. "He cannot help me be someone I am not." And she didn't want him to try.

"You're wrong, sweetheart. It's all about appearances. Don't fight this. Car's willing, even enthusiastic."

Signore Beautiful Eyes folded his arms across the 17 on his uniform shirt and narrowed his eyes. There was only one reason why this beautiful man had agreed to be with her, and it was the very reason she didn't want to be with him.

"Think about it, my dear."

What she thought didn't matter to Brent. The battle between them was lost.

There was a rustle, some quick steps and a woman's voice. "Brent, I've been looking for you."

Sofia turned, as Brent did, toward the sound of the chilly, feminine tones. "I've been right here, Victoria."

Brent's wife paused in the doorway, staring first at Brent, and then, longer, at Sofia. Her almost transparent eyebrows pinched into one uncompromising line across her forehead.

"*Buona Sera*." Sofia said, before she remembered to speak English and said, "Good evening."

Signora Mosbacher wore no makeup. Her short, neither blond nor brown hair clung to her head in untidy curls. She stepped into the room, and continued to stare, with cool eyes. "Yes?"

Sofia had only met the Signora that once, at a restaurant, soon after she and Chelsea had arrived in

America. The Signora had been cordial and smiling. But then Brent had laughed at something she said in her poor English, and smiled lovingly into her eyes, and the Signora became hostile. Soon after, she made an excuse to leave. She stared, now, at Sofia, as if staring could make her die.

Why? What had she done? Her heart skittered like the snare drums during the soldiers' entrance in the first act of *Carmen*. Her mind went blank, a stage without scenery.

Brent placed a hand on her arm. "Ladies, let's go up to the suite." He turned, then, to *Signore* Beautiful Eyes. "And you too, Car. Join us."

"I can't do that." *Signore* Beautiful Eyes stuck his hands in his back pockets. "Skip may need to play me."

Brent gave *Signore* Beautiful Eyes a slap on the back. "That's fine. Meanwhile why don't you think about where to take Sofia after the game's over."

Before Sofia could tell Brent no, she was too tired, he set his plan in motion. He directed Chelsea to the limo that had taken the two of them from their hotel to the Federals stadium, but now took only Chelsea back. Then he rushed Sofia up to the team's luxury suite, a place she, most assuredly, didn't want to be because she'd be alone and friendless, and worse, in the presence of the Signora.

Miserable, she knew. She was still a spectator. It was *Signore* Beautiful Eyes or nothing. Only by being with him would she get in front of cameras and onto those TV gossip shows. Only by being with him would she get the audition with the Maestro. For a moment she gave in to anger, but only a moment. She had to allow it. For her career.

The luxury box—which was hardly luxurious—was filled to the brim with laughing, drinking men, and a few women, including the Signora, who ignored her. Outside, beyond the box's plate-glass front and overlooking the field, hung a balcony. Three rows of padded seats stretched across its width. Although she would have loved to sink into one of the seats, as some of Brent's guests had, the cold breeze that blew everywhere kept her inside. She eyed the high chairs, pushed up to the equally high tables scattered around the room. No way could she, a woman with short legs, who happened to be wearing a dress that sheathed her like the skin of a salami, lift herself up onto one.

Gazing, hopefully, at the tureens, set on a table off to the side, she realized she hadn't eaten since noon. She peeked into the first tureen. It held mini hot dogs in water with grease floating on the top; the next, chicken wings, drowned in a red sauce, and the third, limp French fries. She sighed. As hungry as she was, Sofia couldn't eat something that wasn't food.

It seemed forever she stood, surrounded by laughter she took no part in. A vision of a lovingly-prepared risotto with asparagus and mushrooms, finished with a rich Pecorino Romano filled her head with unrealized pleasure. Her five-inch heels filled her feet with unremitting agony.

She turned when the door opened.

Brent turned too, and held out his arms to a painfully thin woman, the same height as he. "Ah, Louise honey. You're here. And with my favorite grandson."

With black hair flying everywhere, the woman permitted him the smallest of kisses on her cheek. Brent didn't seem to mind because he'd already bent to hug the little boy beside her.

"Grandpa, I'm not your favorite grandson. I'm your only grandson," the boy said, and giggled when his grandfather tickled him.

Sofia smiled at the play between the two. And when the boy shrieked and bent backward to get away from his grandfather's busy fingers, Sofia saw his eyes and learned something else. Yes, the child's mother was Louise, the Mosbachers' daughter. He had her black hair. But the child's blue-green eyes were all his father's.

The tickling stopped when Louise grabbed the child and pulled him out of his grandfather's arms. He stopped smiling. So did Brent. But Louise, it seemed, didn't care. She began a low conversation with Brent that looked anything but pleasant. It went on until a scrawny man with a head of stringy hair and shoulder-to-wrist tattoos on each arm stepped into the room. The little boy moved closer to his grandfather, and then behind him. Louise didn't seem to notice.

Sofia did. Once she got over the shock of knowing *Signore* Beautiful Eyes had a son who was also Brent's grandson, she tried to notice everything. Years ago, during one of his trips to see her perform in Europe, Brent told Sofia he had a daughter, who was only two weeks older than she. She'd always wanted a sister, and perhaps because they were so close in age, Sofia had dreamt Louise was her sister.

Brent had shown her pictures of Louise as a teenager, all smiles and pretty, curly hair. This woman looked nothing like those pictures. She was pale, with big circles under her eyes, and a mouth turned down in disappointment. She looked like she belonged with the man—with his greasy, disgusting looks—who stood with one possessive arm around her neck.

Now that Sofia saw Louise, especially with such an awful man, she was glad they weren't sisters. But she was fascinated with the boy. Not thinking about the tightness of her salami dress, she bent to him, and whispered, "*Piccolino*, what is your name?" She held out a hand. Her movement drew his mother's attention.

"Hell-lo." Louise smiled with lips only. "Do you speak English?"

Why certain people thought you had to enunciate carefully in a loud voice if you spoke some language other than English, Sofia didn't know. "Yes, I speak English," she said, standing up and sneaking glances at the child.

"Oh, what an adorable accent." Louise forced an off-key soprano laugh.

"C'mon. I'm bored." The tattooed man pulled on her arm, and Louise pulled the child. The three stepped outside onto the balcony. As they did, the child looked once at his grandmother, who ignored him in favor of conversation with some men. He turned back toward Sofia. With solemn eyes and a high, childish voice, he said, "My name isn't peek-o-lee-no."

Sofia's heart melted.

Louise and the boyfriend spent mere minutes on the

balcony, before returning to the suite. Hand held in his mother's, the little one gave Sofia a long look. "It's Noah."

"I am Sofia." The smile stretched wide across her face.

Before he could say anything more, his mother pulled him away. "Your grandfather wants me to drop you off with his assistant. Don't be your usual shitty little self and screw up my plans for tonight any more than you already have." She yanked on his hand. "So let's hurry it up." And they were gone.

Sofia's empty stomach flipped with fear for little Noah. How could any mother speak such cruel words to her child? If Noah were her child she'd hug and kiss him. She'd never pull him like he was a wooden toy on a string.

For the remainder of the evening, Brent stationed himself in front of the plate-glass window, clapped, yelled what were surely curses, and spoke, *sottovoce,* into a phone. Sofia stood, hungry and tired, for the duration, pain radiating up her legs from her beautiful shoes. The agony was so vast, she almost forgot *Signore* Beautiful Eyes, and how the two of them would be together.

Soon.

Alone.

Car returned to the dugout, headed toward the far end by the water cooler, and sat. The worst part about this little caper of Mosbacher's—and there were a lot of bad parts— was he had to trust the man when he said he'd keep Noah away from Louise. Shoving one hand in his jacket pocket, he fingered his MP3 player, and watched the Federals' ace starter, Jimmy Jamison, struggle.

The lawyers, his and hers, were making progress, just not fast enough. Plus Louise kept coming up with reasons why giving Car full custody wouldn't work. He was going to have to figure out a way to get her past that. He or the lawyers.

A moan from the crowd. Car looked up to see a ball arc

overhead and land in the right field seats. Yeah, Jimmy was struggling.

"Why you down here by yourself, Car? And what was up with you and the heifer in the tunnel? With the boss man."

Car cut his eyes toward an approaching Robinson Morales. "She's not a heifer."

"Why you think they ask somebody with that *la la la* voice to sing the anthem?" Robbie shook his head in disgust.

"Everyone knows Brent loves opera. He gets to choose who sings the anthem on opening night. We get an opera singer."

"Yeah." Robbie reached down and gave his boys a quick adjustment. "That is so wrong. Mosbacher, he shouldn't let some foreigner sing the national anthem. It's un-American."

Car grinned. "Says you who comes from Venezuela?"

Robbie huffed. He gave Car one of his ferocious frowns that, often as not, marked his face from shaved skull to meaty chin. It didn't fool anyone. Inside the man was a softie.

He heard Dawg before he saw him. "What's up, Car?"

Dawg Huggins sat on the bench next to Car. "Nothing much," said Car. "Doc clear you to play with the thumb?"

Dawg studied his thumb, jammed during the final game in spring training, like it was a foreign object. "I'm good. I'd be better if Mac was getting the job done catching JJ."

"If Skip decides to take Mac out, you ready?"

"One hundred percent." Dawg grinned. With his big, square body, thick biceps, hefty catcher's thighs, cropped blond hair, and guileless blue eyes, people looked at Dawg Huggins and thought, boy, this guy's a dim bulb. Big mistake. Dawg was one wily master behind the plate, and, yeah, in life too.

Dawg plunked down a two-liter bottle of water on the bench and turned his attention to Robbie, who kept shaking his head back and forth. "What's got you so chapped?"

Robbie hawked a gob onto the dugout's top step. "The

heifer that sung the national anthem? It's good I don't got to see her no more in case she put me off my game."

Car's jaw tensed. "She's a woman, Rob, not a cow, and she wasn't there during spring training when you hit three for your last thirty-one."

"That's a fact. I'm thinking maybe it's some other lady I gotta blame." Robbie wiggled his eyebrows. "If you know what I mean."

"What I know is you're one hell of a ladies' man, Rob," said Dawg.

"Don't you be talking shit to me about my thing with the ladies." Robbie laid the full force of his scowl on Dawg. He hiked a thumb in Car's direction. "Now here's a man who knows his way around the ladies. He's the master. Has them coming and going."

While Dawg snickered, Car wondered whether he should throw Robbie together with Mosbacher so they could compare notes on his love life.

"And you're another one who should be keeping it shut, Dawg," said Robbie. "Not every guy has a fine lady on his arm like that one you got."

"You're talking about the love of my life, man."

Car respected the hell out of the way Dawg talked about Tina and used the L-word. For himself, he didn't get it. Never had. Couldn't imagine it. Only thing Car knew was Tina Huggins was hot. Not that he would ever use that word in front of Dawg to describe her. He liked the shape of his nose and the way it sat straight in the middle of his face.

"Dawg, you may be going in next inning." Skip made his way toward them from his perch down the other end of the dugout. "Something's up with Mac. Go get Zeke to wrap your thumb."

Dawg rose to his feet and turned to Car. "I saw Louise outside in the hallway with Noah. She still making you jump through hoops?"

"It's under control." Car knew Dawg knew better.

Dawg started toward the tunnel. "Don't worry. It'll work out."

"I hope you're right," Car muttered and watched Skip lumber up the steps to the field to go have a chat with Mac. The knee Skip had blown out during the years he played had put a serious hitch in his gait. Car wondered whether someday, he too, would be gimping around like Skip.

Car flexed his knee. The surgery was last November. A success: you have at least three years left in you, Doc said. Even with the therapy, Car hadn't bounced back yet, which was the reason for the rumors of him being traded to the White Sox. Or being forced to retire. He'd toyed with the idea of retiring. Yeah, right. Like retiring was something to look forward to. He couldn't imagine what his life would look like after retiring. Empty, he guessed.

Right now, though, he couldn't think about retirement. What he needed to think about was an undersized Italian female who was an oversized problem.

Chapter Four

By the time the game was over, Sofia's mind had flitted from one anxiety-ridden brain-burst to another. Perhaps her looks would matter with the Maestro. Perhaps her father had called the Maestro and told him about the incident at La Scala. Would he do such a thing? Destroy her chances to sing *Carmen* because he hadn't suggested it? Perhaps she'd sung the national anthem for nothing.

By the time she met *Signore* Beautiful Eyes outside the luxury suite, her mind was a dish of cooked-to-death pasta. Now she'd have to make small talk with him. What would she say? She couldn't talk about opera; he didn't know opera. She couldn't talk about baseball; *she* didn't know baseball. She couldn't talk about the real reason she didn't want to be with him.

He thought of her as a job.

He met her outside the luxury box. He grunted a hello and turned to walk away. She followed, trying to keep up. She took little mincing steps like Madama Butterfly because of the hem of her salami dress. "*Aspetta.*" She sighed in relief when he slowed. "I cannot walk so fast."

For a moment she thought he'd say something. But no. He grunted again, and began to stride away like a god, like Wotan in Valhalla. She firmed her jaw and set out after him.

They got into an elevator. She made conversation about how cold it was for April. He grunted. She followed him through a maze of hallways. She commented on how happy she would be if warm weather came soon, perhaps even this very week. He grunted.

They arrived at an exit, guarded by a man, who broke into smiles when he saw them. "Good game today, huh, Car?" He held the door open. "Can't wait to see you back in the lineup."

"Yeah, Joey. It's strange not being on the field on opening day," *Signore* Beautiful Eyes said.

Sofia squinted at him. Oh, good. He hadn't lost his voice.

"Soon, man. You'll be back," said the guard.

"Thanks for the vote of confidence." *Signore* Beautiful Eyes moved aside for Sofia.

"Thanks for the vote of confidence," she mimicked under her breath, took a step through the doorway, and wobbled.

He shot out a hand to grab her elbow, and she gasped.

Oh God. The feel of his hand, his very warm hand, and the strong bones of his fingers around her elbow made her heart jump like the triplets in the Queen of the Night's aria in *The Magic Flute*.

"What the...? Why do you wear those shoes?"

She took a deep breath to slow the frantic beat of her heart. She needed to get over this silly reaction to the feel of his hand on her body. "With them, I am taller."

He let her go. "The real possibility you might fall in them... that doesn't enter your mind?"

She blinked. She wasn't sure, but was that sarcasm?

They entered a small parking lot. Lined up, like prehistoric monsters, were a bunch of big American SUVs. She didn't understand what Americans saw in these monstrosities. Italians didn't buy SUVs, not when it was difficult, sometimes impossible, to navigate her country's narrow, medieval streets. "Tell me about these vehicles," she said, again attempting conversation.

Silence greeted her.

What was the matter with this man? Did he think this situation was her fault and was angry with her because of it? "Please!"

He slowed and angled his head in her direction. "Please, what?"

"Tell me why you drive them."

"Look at me." He placed a hand on his chest. "You

36

think I should drive something smaller? Squeeze myself into—I don't know—a Fiat?"

Now *this,* most assuredly, was sarcasm. Sofia ignored the twist in her stomach. She glanced once more at the behemoths and tried again. "When before, I am in the locked room..."

"The locker room," he corrected.

"I know." Her patience with him was wearing thinner. "The Federals men, they are all big. Perhaps you are right. They need the SUVs."

"True." He walked away.

Again.

Patience that she had held onto for so long failed her. With a buzz filling her head, she flung it and caution away. Through clenched teeth, she said, "I think baseball players drive the SUVs for more than great height and big muscles."

He kept walking. "Yeah? Spell it out."

He wanted spelling? She'd give him spelling. "I think it is about the bulge."

Mid-stride, he stopped short and turned. Even in the dim lights that looped around the parking lot, she could see his eyebrows rise up to his hairline. "What?"

"I am saying it is because they do not have the big enough bulge."

His mouth dropped open. She'd shocked the hell out of him.

Her mouth dropped open. She'd shocked the hell out of herself.

Her face heated to boiling, and her heart began to thud. She wanted to faint, like when Lucia di Lammermoor sings her aria about throwing flowers into graves. Sofia wanted to throw herself into a grave. What possessed her to talk about men's private parts? She'd done it before. In the locker room. And now again. She was sorry—but after the fact, when it was too late. "I know I..."

"I don't know what you know," he interrupted her, "But if you want to get that role you're after, you probably shouldn't be talking about bulges."

A pulse pushed hard against her temple. "Perhaps I am wrong," she said in a small voice, trying to think what she could say to make amends. "Perhaps it is only what you eat."

He stared into the distance, as if he were looking for help. "What?"

"The Big Macs. The Whoppers." She almost choked on a breath. Too late. Too wrong. She wheeled around, torrents of shame and terror filling her. She began to walk as fast as she could, no mincing this time, to get far away, until his warm hands pressed down on her shoulders, and gave them a squeeze. "Hold up, sweetheart. You're headed in the wrong direction."

Time stood suspended until she wrenched herself away from him, afraid she'd heard laughter in his voice. The laughter, if it was laughter, made everything worse. She pressed her lips together, to keep her traitorous mouth shut.

They continued to walk, both silent, until they arrived at an immense truck, a massive block of metal. It was white, with huge tires, and tiny windows. It was more than an SUV. There was no question; it was his.

She gazed down at the front of his trousers. In the dark she couldn't tell, but surely...no. The image she had of him wasn't perfect. Most assuredly, she was in love with his face, not his private parts. But she'd hate to think his were inconsequential. She took a breath, lifted her head, and focused on the thing. "This is a vehicle for war."

"Some are. This isn't. It's a Hummer." He held out a fist, and it chirped.

Sofia knew the tiny sound came from the remote door opener. But a chirp? It should have been a roar.

He circled around to the passenger side. "Are you coming?"

Was she? Did she want to be in a vehicle with him? Especially this vehicle? Especially when she was thinking about his private parts, even though she told herself she wasn't? "This Hummer. It... it uses a lot of petrol, yes?"

He nodded.

"When you put the many gallons of petrol in your Hummer, the petrol price goes up, and poor people, they cannot afford it."

He stared at her, and she wondered why now, she'd

been reduced to lecturing him on the environment and the price of fuel. Like a self-righteous twit. She knew the answer. Nerves. Singing in front of thousands, she never felt them. Standing in front of this man, she was filled with them. "They cannot, you know. Pay the high price." Still with the nerves compelling her to speak and keep on speaking. She wanted to slap a hand across her mouth. Her hand remained at her side. "Then they cannot drive to work. And so they lose the job."

His hand, the one holding the car door opener, dropped to his side.

"You must drive a vehicle that uses less petrol and does not damage the environment." She was completely unable to shut her run-away train of a mouth.

His one eyebrow went up. "Which am I? A hog? Or am I destroying the earth? Or both?"

"You must get something else," she continued, desperate to prove her point even as she knew she didn't have one. Her voice got louder. "You must get something that is not a *mostruosità!*"

"A what?" He took a deep breath and seemed to swell.

"*Mostruosità,* Hummer. *É lo stesso.*"

"Ay low...what?"

"*Lo stesso.*" She looked into his hard-as-Carrara-marble face. She'd said enough. She'd said too much. "It means the same."

Car knew making her run after him sucked. He was sorry he'd done it. That didn't stop him from wanting to strangle her. "I think we better get something straight. We're going to be stuck together for the next few weeks. Neither of us is too happy about it. But if this is how it's going to be, you complaining and me explaining, you and I are going to be two unhappy pups."

She'd been looking down-in-the-mouth, but that brought a gasp of outrage from her. She planted a hand on her hip. "Pup? You are calling me a baby dog?"

"I did not..."

She stamped a foot. "You did. You called me a dog." She sidled up to him, and got into his face, which seemed weird, since her face was level with the middle of his chest. "I am not a dog."

Car gritted his teeth. Swiveling around, he laid his hands and his forehead against the Hummer, cold in the night air. "I'll make you a deal. I won't call you a pup if you don't..." He gathered himself, remembering how she'd said his name... "Call me Creese-toe-fur."

"I do not understand. Creese-toe-fur is your name."

"It's..." He turned his head to stare down into her eyes that had sucked up the black of the night, eyes that fascinated him, even as he contemplated her murder. He took a breath, and said, "You're not saying it the way most people do."

She raised one eyebrow. "That is because I am Italian."

He took another deep breath, filling his lungs, as if with ballast. "How about you go along with the program and call me Car like everyone else does?"

She tightened her lips. "Now there is a program?"

"Call me Car. Please?" Was that him pleading? He hadn't pleaded with anyone since he was a kid.

"I will think about it."

She would *theenk* about it? Well, hallelujah. He opened the Hummer's door and stepped back. "Okay, then let's go."

She didn't move, looked at the seat, looked up at him, and back at the seat. Not the seat. The threshold. Which is when he got it. With those short legs, that tight skirt, and those ridiculous high heels, there was no way she could get in without help.

On an exhale, he put his hands around her waist. With one motion, he lifted, and plunked her down on the seat.

Which was when he knew he was in trouble.

"Why did you lift me? I am too heavy! I weigh too many kilos!"

He stood in the lee of the door, stunned, like somebody had clobbered him upside his head with a bat.

The ugly dress didn't matter. The hair, vised back in the no-nonsense old-lady bun, didn't matter. The crazy talk didn't matter. He pulled out the seat belt so she could fasten it. "You're not too heavy," he said over the wailing, which had gone from a mixture of English and Italian into full-blown Italian.

His hands weren't on her anymore, but he could feel the heat of her body imprinted upon his palms. The scent she wore, like the roses that bloomed outside Chicago's Wrigley Field, drifted around his head. He wanted to pull her off the seat, out of the truck, into his arms, and bury his face in the juncture between her shoulder and her neck, the better to take her scent deep into him.

He began to sweat.

She was still at it when he threw the stick into gear and wheeled out of the parking lot. "How else did you think you'd get in?"

"*Avresti dovuto prendere la mano e aiutarmi.*" She was fanning herself with both hands.

"What?"

"I wanted you to take my hand to help me."

"Well, I didn't." Pressing his arm to his forehead to blot the perspiration, he negotiated the late stadium traffic and headed for the highway. When he'd put his hands around her waist—when he'd *spanned* her waist—he'd wanted to slide his hands under that ugly dress, and smooth his fingers over her warm flesh.

As he accelerated into the center lane, he scrambled for something to say. "I liked the way you sang the national anthem."

"*Grazie.*"

He waited for a flood of words. Nothing came. "We don't often get opera singers at Federals' Stadium."

"I know."

He slid a hand under his seatbelt and let it snap back into place across his chest. "There are different voice categories in opera, and you're a mezzo-soprano, right?"

"Yes, a mezzo-soprano."

Jesus. He was pulling teeth, fucking pulling teeth to get her to answer him. He gripped the steering wheel, tore into the left lane, and floored it. For one gratifying moment, he saw her clutch the edge of her seat. "Did you find it difficult to sing the anthem?" he asked, voice raised.

She threw up her arms.

He jumped.

"*Grazie a Dio*! Somebody recognizes!"

"Recognizes what?"

"The words, they make no sense. How do ramparts stream? Ramparts are walls." She made a grand, circular motion with her right hand, almost hitting the window. "First it is dawn."

He smiled.

"The next minute it is the twilight's last gleaming. Twilight is night. Dawn, twilight—I know these meanings, because I look in my English-Italian dictionary. The composer, he should decide it is one or the other."

Damn, she tickled him. "I remember when I was a kid in school how the words didn't make sense."

"But I am not a school kid. And I do not understand the part about proud hail. Hail is ice."

At last, he laughed outright. "You are one funny lady."

"It is better I am a funny lady than a job, yes?"

The laugh died in his throat. Of course she'd heard. "I shouldn't have said that."

Silence.

"It's just that..." Yeah, and how was he going to explain the deal he'd made with Brent without her getting crazy on him? He rubbed a hand across his mouth. "You're not the job. What we have to do together: that's the job."

Silence.

"Why don't we go back to your hotel, find a table in the lobby, and talk?"

She shifted a little in her seat.

"We'll put our heads together; decide what we're going to do to get you noticed. Maybe we'll think about hitting a high-profile club downtown."

She turned a fraction toward him.

"We can have a few drinks, hang out," he said, warming to the subject. "We can watch everybody, let them watch us, maybe dance some."

Those black eyebrows of hers arched, and then turned down at the center. "I do not dance."

"Okay. What about we watch? Or do a dinner at a popular restaurant."

"I would like to go to Cinque Terre. Maria Torelli says Cinque Terre is the good place to go."

"Who's Maria Torelli?"

"She is a soprano, famous in Europe, but not so famous in America."

"Cinque Terre isn't an in place."

She churned on that one. "What is an *in* place?"

"Where the beautiful people go." He took his eyes off the road and gave her a pointed look. "Hasn't Brent taken you to Cinque Terre?"

She stared at him. "Why would he?"

Because he wasn't her lover. That puzzled look on her face said it. What was the matter with him that he hadn't seen it? It was—and had been—as clear as the Plexiglas wall fronting the bullpen at Federals Stadium. If he hadn't been driving, he would have banged his head against the steering wheel. What a blind jerk. Why had he ever thought it? Hah. He knew why. When it came to this woman, he hadn't had many straight thoughts, not from the beginning.

"There's a Japanese restaurant, Noro. It's been getting media attention lately because a lot of high profile people have been going there. The chef makes great sushi."

"Sushi?" Her head whipped around. She speared him with a look of horror. "I do not eat the fish that is not cooked."

She didn't, huh? "Well then, you can get salmon or steak in a sauce. That's cooked."

"But I will have to eat with the..." She floundered. *"Come si dice in inglese..."*

"What?"

She huffed a frustrated sound. *"Come si dice,* how do you say? In English?" And she lifted her hand to make a grasping motion with her fingers.

Light dawned. "You mean chopsticks."

"Yes, the chopsticks. I do not know how to use them. I will drop the food, make a mess, and be to myself a big embarrassment."

A lime green Saturn cut in front of him, almost clipping his right front bumper. He slammed on the horn, kept his hand on it, letting it blare way longer than needed, since by the time he lifted his hand, the Saturn was five car lengths ahead. Between his teeth he said, "Then you can use a fork."

"But I will look silly when everyone else is using the chopsticks."

His brain was exploding. "I guess we'll have to come up with some other idea."

"That would be good. Thank you." She paused. "Car."

Chapter Five

She'd said his name. Finally. And wasn't he a pathetic sap because it made him happy? "So what do you do at night while you're waiting for your audition?"

She gave him a sideways glance. "I make the parties. I would invite you, but you would not like my guests."

"I like most people."

"*Mi dispiace...*" She paused. "*Mi dispiace* means I am sorry. These people you would not like."

They were some of her opera friends. Or some literary types. Of course she'd think he wouldn't fit in with those types. "It's all good, Sofia," he said and told himself not to get too insulted. "We'll go out tomorrow, okay? Go to Cinque Terre."

The smile bloomed wide on her face. Her eyes lit up like the Federals centerfield Jumbotron when someone hit a home run. "I do not tell you but Vittorio della Rovere—he is the chef of Cinque Terre—he has also the restaurant in Florence. I have eaten there many times. He makes the most sublime ox-tails. And his *Penne Arabbiata*, this I have not tasted, but I have heard it is *eccezionale*." She made a kissing sound.

Car slewed his eyes in her direction. Her fingers were pressed against her plump, puckered lips.

His hands twitched. His dick, too.

He shifted in his seat and listened to her drone on about foods whose names he didn't recognize. As he listened, he imagined it was *his* fingers, not hers, pressed against the moistness of her lips. He glanced at his speedometer. He was doing 75. He lifted his foot from the accelerator, and let the Hummer slow.

She jabbered on about pasta and sauces and stuff. He didn't understand her whole food-love thing. He liked a good roasted chicken, a thick, bloody steak. Yeah, he ate sushi. He could identify salmon and tuna by color. He liked pasta, kind of. But ox-tails? He knew what an ox was, but Jesus, he didn't know people ate their tails.

"So we're okay with things now?" Car cruised to a stop at a traffic light.

Clapping her hands together she gave him a big smile. She looked like a kid in a candy store. Well, maybe not candy, but whatever it was Italians ate when they were in a good mood. Her cheeks were pink with pleasure. Her eyes sparkled a shiny black. She leaned toward him, looking young, fresh, innocent, untouched, like she'd never slept with anyone, least of all Mosbacher.

A terrible thought came into his head. "How old are you?" He hoped she wouldn't say twenty, or God forbid, younger. Yeah, he'd made a deal to be seen with her, but for people to think he was a damn cradle robber, that messed with his head.

The smile faded, those black eyes flickered. "Twenty-four."

He let go of the breath he hadn't known he was holding. There were ten years between them. Not a deal breaker. "We're almost at the hotel. Let's talk about what time I'm going to pick you up tomorrow, okay?"

She tipped her head to the side. "Yes, okay. But perhaps when you come, you can bring another automobile?"

She almost smacked herself. When would she ever get the sequence right: brain in charge of mouth, instead of mouth in charge of brain? He loved his Hummer, even if she didn't. And where before he hadn't been kind, now he was trying.

46

From beneath her eyelashes, she glanced at his hands resting loosely on the steering wheel. They were lovely hands, so large and strong. She'd felt the heat of them through her dress when they slid around her waist and lifted her into his Hummer. Oh, the dizziness. The thrill. The tragedy. Now he knew she weighed the equivalent of a small hippo.

He brought the Hummer to a halt in front of her hotel. It didn't take a moment for Sofia to spot the paparazzo, lurking like Mephistopheles in Act One of *Faust*. No paparazzo had ever followed her, but Maria Torelli told her stories about the ones that haunted her. From the way this one tried to hide, Sofia knew he was up to no good. *Signore* Beautiful Eyes—Car—did not see him yet.

When Car swung her door open, she put out a hand, but he pushed it aside to grab her around the waist. She gasped.

"Chill, Sofia." His breath tickled her ear, abrading the sensitive skin of her throat. He set her down and curled one hand around her arm. She felt all of him, the hard muscles, the harder bones of his arm and his chest, his powerful thigh against her hip. Her poor heart threatened to burst, but her eyesight still worked enough to see the paparazzo, slithering his snake-self in and around the crowd of people lingering about. It wasn't she who interested him. It was Car. But the paparazzo *would* be interested in her, if she were Carmen. Perhaps Car would be interested also. If she were Carmen. Perhaps he would think she was no hippo, but as desirable as other women he had in his life. Perhaps she could show him and Brent that she could help her own case to get the audition with the Maestro.

She closed her eyes, channeled Carmen, and knew what she needed to do: stick out her more than ample chest, and wiggle her equally ample rear end. With one eye on the paparazzo, she arched her back and pressed her breasts against Car's lovely cream-colored linen shirt, and the muscled chest beneath. She blinked as many times as she could without blinding herself with her thick-with-mascara eyelashes, reached up, and ran the backs of her fingers across his cheek.

Car drew back, surprise clear on his face.

Sofia—Carmen—tossed her head. A small frown flitted across Car's tanned-golden-by-the-sun forehead. She almost wilted. But no, there'd be no wilting. "Darling, you cannot leave. I want you to come with me." She pitched her voice so the paparazzo would hear. "Up to my room, yes?"

Afterwards, she remembered the strange silence that preceded the uproar.

"Car, turn your head; look this way," the mosquito rat yelled. He was so close she could smell sweat, like day-old garbage, on his body, and his breath, stale garlic, every time he panted. *Snap-snap-snap-snap-snap.* "Honey, you too. Keep up with the eyelashes. Give me a smile, yeah. And kiss Car."

He snapped one blinding shot and then another and another, his lens inches from her eyes. She gulped and pressed her forehead against the rough fabric of Car's jacket. The camera flashed with the same beat as her heart. If only she'd known this would happen—the odors, the sounds, the glaring lights—she never would have pretended she was who she wasn't.

Car put a protective arm around her shoulders. He shifted and took something from his pocket. "Watch the truck for me," he said to someone, *the doorman, her muzzy brain decided.* He shifted again. She heard a clink, and then he was drawing her with him into the hotel. Once through the door, she wrenched herself out of his arms, and tore across the hotel's pale gray marbled floor. He, with his long legs, kept up with her.

"What was that about, Sofia?"

She could hardly talk, she was so ashamed. "You will think I am foolish." How could he not? *She* thought so. What kind of trick had she thought she could pull off this time? She kept going toward the elevators, he, right behind.

"Try me."

"I wanted to help my career." This was true. "But I did not do so well." This was so true.

"By help, do you mean your plan was to get that guy to take pictures of us?"

She dared not look him in the eye.

"Because if you did, it worked. One of them's going to be somewhere in print or online, maybe both, by the latest tomorrow morning."

"I did not know he would take so many pictures. I did not know the flash would be so bright." *And now you not only don't want me, but you think I'm crazy.*

At last at the elevator, she mashed her finger against the call button. "*Grazie*, Car, for taking me to the hotel. I will go upstairs by myself."

He pulled her hand away. "That's not going to bring the elevator any faster, and forget it. I'm going up with you."

She opened her mouth—and closed it. What was the point of saying anything, maybe making it worse? When the elevator door slid open, he stepped in with her.

"What floor?"

"The Penthouse," she said, her eyes on his long-fingered hand, hovering over the buttons.

As the elevator cruised upward, they stood in silence, his arm around her. At last he was holding her the way she'd wished him to hold her, but this was with pity. She stared, dry-eyed, at the floor. Pity wasn't what she wanted from him.

The elevator door slid open. Hand at the small of her back, Car guided her into the quiet hall. "Which is yours?"

She hurried toward her suite, where Chelsea stood, waiting, in the doorway.

"They called me from downstairs to let me know you were on your way up," Chelsea announced, and stepped aside for them to enter.

Edging in the direction of her bedroom, Sofia forced herself to smile. "I must be rude and leave you now. I have the exercises to do for the audition when I will get it with the Maestro." She fled across the suite's living room and let herself into her bedroom, closing the door gently behind her.

Eyes closed, she pressed her back against the coolness of the door, and thought about how he'd protected her against the paparazzo. Out of pity. She couldn't bear pity. She groaned. If only she could get the audition without him. If only she wasn't so stupid to think he could possibly see her as a desirable woman, and not a small hippo.

Car watched the door shut behind Sofia, before turning his attention on her mousy assistant.

She narrowed her eyes at him. "What did you do to her?"

He held up his hands. "Not a thing."

"Really? She angled her chin toward the door behind which Sofia had disappeared. "You could have fooled me." She backed away from the door, pivoted, headed toward a sofa in the middle of the room, and sat.

He followed her, not that he'd been invited. "Chelsea, isn't it?"

She nodded, eyes wary. She didn't trust him.

Too bad. He had questions needing answers. "Sofia... she's different." He settled into a chair perpendicular to the sofa.

Chelsea stared at him, unblinking. Hostility radiated off her, hot as the glare of the sun on a Texas ball field in July. "Why the interest?"

"You don't remember I'm supposed to help her get that audition? You were standing there, right? At the stadium?"

She stared. Gave him nothing.

"If I knew something more about her, I could do a better job."

She cleared her throat. "It's true. Sofia's different. She marches to a different drummer."

"A whole different band."

"Orchestra." What passed for a smile nicked the corners of her mouth. She folded one slender leg over the other and narrowed her eyes at him. Again.

Car had been given that squinty-eyed look before—when he had a bat slung over his shoulder—by pitchers whose job it was to intimidate him. If he got what he needed from them, he had faith he could get what he needed from this skinny blonde. "How long have you been working for Sofia?"

"A few weeks."

"How'd you meet?"

As good as he was at reading faces, he almost missed the cue, the millisecond she decided there was no harm in answering that one.

"The same day I decided it was time to come home to the States, having spent the last couple of years lazing around Europe, was the day I found Sofia at a self-service kiosk at the main train station in Milan." Chelsea pushed the mop of her hair back behind an ear. "She was trying, with no success, to buy a ticket for the airport bus. I was in line behind her, me and a dozen other not-so-happy campers. I showed her which buttons to push, and what slot to put her credit card into. Then we happened to sit next to each other on the flight. We bonded. She asked me to be her assistant, help her with the day-to-day. I thought why not?"

"Would it be safe to say you know her long enough to understand her?"

The squint was back. "What, you think I'm okay with..." She made air quotes, "telling tales about her out of school?"

"No, but she and I have to spend..." He made his own air quotes, "quality time together for the next few weeks. I need a Sofia dictionary to help me."

He didn't think she was going to reply. But then, "Sofia is very good at acting."

She grudged him that one.

"Care to elaborate?"

"No."

"No?"

"Hmm." She gave him an assessing stare, before rising to pace over to the window.

While she pulled the curtain aside to look at whatever, he glanced around. To his right was a room with a dining table made of some dark wood. It had seating for a cool dozen people. Hovering in the air was a sharp scent of spices, the kind that made him think of Italian restaurants. Which was damn strange for a hotel suite, even one with a table.

He opened his mouth to ask what was up with that,

when Sofia began to sing. He half-turned toward the room into which she'd disappeared. Her voice rose and fell in a wave of golden, bell-like sound. Her exercises, she'd said. Those were some exercises. They made the hair on his arms stand at attention.

"Her whole life, Sofia's been on the opera fast track."

Car brought his mind back to Chelsea, who must have decided she could elaborate after all, and was just sitting down again on the sofa.

"Oh, yeah?" The sound of Sofia's voice reached through the door to surround him. What Chelsea had to say didn't interest him so much. Not while he was listening to Sofia.

Chelsea pushed the sleeves of her loose black turtleneck above her elbows. "She has an unusual voice. It's the kind that comes along once every century. Even she doesn't know how really good she is."

Sofia began to sing a dark melody with notes that hesitated, descended down, stopped, and began again. The song curved and twisted through his head. *What was she singing?* He searched through the drawers in his mind where he kept memories of tunes, and came up blank.

"The place Sofia's most at home is onstage. It's her reference point for most everything."

"What?" Oh yeah. He'd been pumping Chelsea for information. Trying to figure out the scene with the paparazzi guy and why Sofia melted down after.

Before, when he pulled up to the hotel, he'd purposely come around to her side of the truck to lift her down from her seat. He wanted his hands around her waist again. He wanted his hands on her lush body. He wanted to touch her everywhere. Fill his hands with her breasts. Press himself against her. But after that moment with the paparazzo, everything changed and now he wanted... what? She made him think of... what?

Well, hell, he didn't know. "I don't understand."

Chelsea nodded. "Hopefully, someday you will. Right now I have a piece of advice. Get her to tell you about her father and how she grew up. That'll help you understand her."

So. A story about a kid and her parent. He shook

himself out of the spell Sofia's voice had woven around him, the memory of his bitch of a mother, dead these last ten years, making a rude intrusion. "She's not the first person with parent problems."

"No, she's not."

Sofia stopped singing. The air echoed with her silence. Car shook himself and rose. "Listen. Tomorrow's a day game, so I'll pick up Sofia and take her to dinner at that place she's hot to try. Tell her to let me know when to pick her up."

Chelsea rose with him. "I'll call. Sofia doesn't do phones."

Car shook his head in disbelief. "She doesn't do phones. That makes no sense. It's so..."

"Crazy, right?" Chelsea said, finishing for him. "But it's kind of charming, isn't it?" Finally, at last, a smile.

"I don't know about that." But he did. And it was. "What's that song Sofia was singing? It was amazing."

Chelsea nodded. "It's from *Carmen*. It's called an aria, not a song. It's one of the most famous in all opera: the *Habanera*."

"Yeah?" He paused. "It was like a siren song."

Chelsea's face broke into a wide grin. "Exactly like a siren song. When Carmen sings the *Habanera*, Don José hears it, and he falls for her like a rock."

Chapter Six

He couldn't stop thinking about her. Not during the night when the memory of her voice woke him, not the next morning on his way to see Noah, and he marveled how it had been just one day since she'd blown into his life. As he headed downtown on the East River Drive, he remembered standing in the dugout, watching the pre-game first-of-the-season antics on the field, and how she'd steamed up from the clubhouse, almost knocked into him, only stopping when one of the front office guys introduced them.

"Good luck," Car said, like he would anyone going out to the field to sing *The Star Spangled Banner*.

She'd reared back on those ridiculous heels, black eyes open wide in horror. "Do not wish me luck."

Watching her stagger up the steps to the field, he finally knew what it meant to be struck dumb.

He was still reliving that moment when he pulled off the highway, slowed down, and looked for a space—any space—on East End Avenue, somewhere between the Mosbacher's luxury high rise and the small park opposite. Luck was with him. He found one at the end of the block. Backing in, he locked up, and headed into the park, where he knew, this time of day, he'd find Noah and his nanny, Helena. He hadn't seen the kid in a couple of weeks.

Wanted to now.

He set off on the pathway that wound around to the slides and swings, the bag in his right hand knocking against his leg. It held a soft cloth, olive-green stuffed animal he'd bought earlier. Noah, according to Helena, was into monsters of all kinds these days.

"Daddy!" Noah shrieked when he saw Car coming toward him. He launched himself against Car's legs, winding his arms tight around his knees.

Helena said, "Noah, don't knock your dad over."

"It's okay." Car stooped down so he was eye-level with the little boy. It shocked him every time he looked into Noah's clear blue-green eyes, identical to his own, that by some miracle, he'd reproduced this small being. He ruffled Noah's hair. "What's up, sport?"

But Noah only had eyes for the bag Car held in his hand. "Did you bring me a present?" He lunged at the bag and, ripping the paper, yanked out the alligator. Holding it in both hands, he turned it around and around, finally clutching it to his chest. "This is my alligator." Noah looked up at Car, who had risen to his feet. "His name is Larry."

Car glanced at Helena and raised his eyebrows.

"We've been reading a book about alligators in the Okefenokee Swamp," she said, with her faint Polish accent. "The father alligator's name is Larry."

Noah went dashing toward a tree down the path, and circled back to Car, coming to a halt in front of him. "Can I come to your new house?"

Car knelt again. Car had moved a month ago, and he'd not brought Noah over to his new place yet. "Not for a while. I'm out of town for a few weeks."

"Then when you come back?"

"We'll see. But you know you're coming to live with me soon, right?"

"When is soon?"

Car looked helplessly at Helena. He never knew how to deal with questions like this when Noah asked them. She shrugged.

"Soon."

Noah stamped his foot. "I don't like soon."

Car stood and picked Noah up. He fastened an arm beneath his little butt and brought his face close to his. "I know you don't, but soon will be here...soon."

Noah laid his head on Car's shoulder, wound his arms around Car's neck. The alligator, clutched in one of Noah's hands, flopped against Car's shoulder blades. "Okay, daddy."

Closing his eyes, Car pressed his face against Noah's sweaty, little boy hair. His son. His child. He'd wanted him when he was born, in spite of all the bad between Louise and him. He'd imagined sharing custody with her. Then came that time ten days later and the panic, the fear, and the terror. After it was over, he couldn't give Louise custodial rights fast enough.

What a mistake that had been.

He took a deep breath to calm his hard beating heart and unknot the clench of his gut. He tightened his arms around the boy. No way would he let anything stand in the way of fixing that mistake.

"Daddy, you're squeezing me," complained Noah.

After one last convulsive hug, Car put him down. "Go with Helena now." He turned to the nanny. "How are things at the Mosbachers?"

"Don't worry, Mr. Bradford. It's all fine. We're fine."

"Any word on the visa situation?"

She made a face. "Not yet."

"Keep me posted." To Noah he said, "You make sure you hold onto Helena's hand when you cross the street, and don't let go, okay?"

Noah rolled his eyes and took Helena's hand. "You always say that."

Car watched the two leave the park and cross the street. He watched them until they entered the Mosbachers' building. Only then did he get in the truck, and ease out of the parking space to head downtown for his first date with Sofia.

She was ready when he pulled up in front of her hotel. He helped her into the Hummer, wondering what the next few hours with Miss Opera Singer were going to be like. He expected some snarky comments. He was sure, for starters, she'd hike up those judgmental eyebrows and remind him she'd wanted him to pick her up in another vehicle. Like a

Fiat. But she didn't, much to his disappointment. Which made no sense. Why the hell would he be disappointed that she wasn't making comments about his *mos...* whatever that Italian word was she'd used for the Hummer.

The moment they walked into Cinque Terre, Sofia brightened up. It was obvious to Car the restaurant owner—Vittorio—was crazy about Sofia, bowing and kissing her hand. He took them to a table in the middle of the narrow room. The middle was his least favorite part of a restaurant, but hey, it wasn't about his comfort or his privacy. He was here for her. Doing his job. Even if he'd apologized. Even if he was beginning to think she was fascinating in an odd way, truth was truth. This was a job.

On the table stood a vase of big-headed, wildly-colored flowers. While Sofia and Vittorio jabbered in a whole lot of enthusiastic Italian, Car eyed the flowers, and thought even they looked enthusiastic. At the next table sat two couples who gave him a look. Great. They recognized him. He nodded their way, opened his menu, and hoped he didn't have to deal with them.

Sofia's pleasure and excitement radiated out from her in waves. It was catching in a weird way. "So what's good?"

"Everything is good, but you must try the *Tagliatelle al ragú di coniglio*. It is fantastic." She closed her eyes and shuddered.

"Sorry. Not for me." There it was again. That crazy business of hers about food. "I don't eat things I can't pronounce." And didn't get too excited about any food, whether he could pronounce the name or not.

She narrowed her eyes at him.

"It probably has some kind of sauce on top."

"It has sauce. Good sauce."

"Yeah, but what's underneath?"

"*Ovviamente*, the pasta."

"I know that." He buried his face in his menu. "I mean what else?"

"The rabbit."

He dropped the menu on the table. "You want me to eat a rabbit?"

Her eyebrows met in the middle of her forehead. "What is wrong with rabbit?"

58

"Maybe I don't want to eat the Easter Bunny?"

The eyebrows twitched. "*Cosa?*"

"Never mind. At least you're not telling me to order ox-tails. I don't think." He ran a finger down the left side of the menu. "Which one is a plain chicken dish?"

She looked at him like he'd whomped her with a bat. "You want plain chicken?"

"Yeah." He leaned back in his chair and folded his arms across his chest. "I want plain chicken."

For a moment, she stared at him, eyes unblinking. Then she cocked her head to one side. "You do not like the adventure?"

"I like an adventure as well as the next person." That wasn't entirely true.

Devils with little forked tails began to dance in her eyes.

He frowned. Was she teasing him?

She pointed to an entry midway down the menu page. "Try this chicken. It will be plain, but also give the adventure."

He looked where she was pointing and read '*Cotoletta di milanese*'. "You sure that's not chicken innards, or chicken half-cooked?"

She said nothing, but in her eyes lurked those devils. Oh yeah, she was teasing him.

And he liked it. "Okay." He closed the menu. "That's what I'll order."

"*Bravo,*" she crowed and clapped her hands.

By the time they ordered, Sofia decided *Signore* Beautiful Eyes truly did deserve the *bravo* she'd given him. He was playing his role to perfection. And he was charming her to pieces. His eyes, which before this evening had seemed cold and flat to her, sparkled with a special blue-green warmth. Could it be he was something besides his beautiful physical self? This would be problematical, if true, because then she'd have to like him instead of just foolishly desiring him. Whichever it was, tonight she was committed to pushing aside her feelings and playing the game with him so she didn't have to face what was really between them: the job.

Over his protests, she ordered an appetizer for them to share.

He curled his lip and stared at his plate. "The glop on top...it's the truffles, right?"

"Yes." She forked two slices of the thinly sliced flank steak onto his plate. Drizzled over the top was a creamy truffle vinaigrette.

He drew back and held his hands up, palms out, two determined stop signs. "Truffles are what pigs sniff for under trees in forests. I'm not eating something a pig digs up with its snout."

The giggle rose in her throat. "Do not worry. They wash the truffles first."

"That's not what I..."

"I know." She smiled. "It is your suspicions."

He took a breath and attacked the plate with a vengeful fork and knife, stuck a piece in his mouth and chewed. Closed his eyes. Moaned.

Sofia knew why. It was the piercing pleasure of eating such divine food. Pigs' snouts, indeed.

By the time the main course came, Car had abandoned his seeming disgust of Vittorio's food. "This chicken is outstanding." He turned a piece around on his fork. "Somebody must have taken a hammer and pounded the crap out of it." He popped the piece in his mouth and chewed. "It's crusty on the outside, really tender and juicy on the inside. I like it." He cut another piece. And another.

Dessert came, a lovely zabaglione. "What's this stuff?" He fixed his blue-green eyes on the fluted glass in which perhaps the juiciest, glossiest, reddest strawberries Sofia had ever seen were bathed in the delicate foam of the zabaglione. He lifted his head and gave her one of his charming smiles. "You think anybody'll mind if I stick my tongue in the glass and lick?"

"No, I do not think so," she breathed and thought, if he smiled at her like that, he could put his tongue anywhere. On her. She wriggled in her seat before she reminded herself. For him, this was a job.

He had just signed the credit card slip when it happened.

"Excuse me, Car?"

There stood one of the men from the next table. "I knew it was you," he said, and whipping his head around, raised a thumb to his friends. "I said to myself, if that's really Car Bradford, I'm going over there and asking for his autograph." He stuck a pad under Car's nose.

Car scooted his chair back, and took the pad. Scrawling his name on the page, he said, "I'm making this out to...?"

"Your name's enough." The man hovered over Car, waiting, greed plain on his face.

Car handed the pad back. "There you go."

The man turned the pad around and studied what Car wrote. "So, Car." He lowered his voice. "My friends and I have a bet going, and if you'd give me some inside information, I could maybe make a couple of bucks in Vegas." He winked as if they were conspirators, and leaned down.

Car leaned away.

Sofia would have leaned away more.

Loud enough that Sofia could hear, the man whispered, "Rumor has it you're going to be traded. Rumor has it the White Sox want you. Is it true?"

The sparkle in Car's blue-green eyes disappeared, but the smile remained on his face.

"I also heard you might retire instead of letting yourself be traded. Or, until your knee's better you'll be playing for the Triple A team in Allentown."

"Wish I could tell you, man. But I can't talk about any of that. Lawyers, you know." Car stood and reached across the table. "Sofia, let's go." She took his hand, glad to get away from this man who had dampened the pleasure of the evening.

"C'mon, Car." The man got in their path. "You're not afraid of any candy-ass lawyers."

Car grabbed Sofia's elbow. "Sorry, bud." He stepped around him in the direction of the restaurant's front door.

As Car moved them toward the front of the restaurant, the two couples moved along with them. People at other tables stopped eating and stared. They were almost at the front door, where a couple with two little ones was waiting to be seated. The little girl took a step behind her mother. But the boy—surely he was no more than six or seven— stood in place.

At once, Sofia knew he recognized Car. Eyes bigger than Vittorio's pasta platters, he reached into a bag his father had hanging from one hand, and pulled out a pad of colored paper and a marker. He held up both.

Suddenly a skinny woman inserted herself in front of Car. She was so close, Sofia could see the make-up line on her jaw. "Car, sign this." Backing and backing toward the door, she waved the paper in Car's face.

Sofia tensed. The two couples, moving along with them, had eyes only for Car. The woman wasn't watching her steps and was about to collide with the boy. "Car," Sofia whispered. "*Attento!*" As the word came from her mouth, she realized it was useless. She'd spoken her warning in Italian.

Whatever the language, Car still understood the danger. He slid his arm from Sofia's shoulder. He blocked the two couples and took a step around the woman. He stooped in front of the boy, scribbled his autograph on the paper, straightened, and moved him behind his father. Then he grabbed Sofia's hand and pushed the restaurant door open. "Let's go," he said, his words cutting scissors-sharp.

The door slammed behind them.

Car saw giving autographs as part of his role as a major leaguer. Every once in a while, though, he'd come across someone who didn't know how or when to stop. Like this jerk tonight, and out of nowhere, it became a situation. Sometimes it involved a kid, which frightened Car in ways no one but he understood.

Car was halfway down the street before he realized Sofia was yanking on his hand and saying something that sounded like 'expect.' He forced himself to slow. "What?"

"My legs, they are so short, I cannot do the running. I ask you to wait. But you do not listen and you do not wait!"

He slowed, looked at her feet. She was wearing crazy shoes again. This pair were gladiator-looking, the heels almost as big as she was. "Sorry."

She waved a hand behind them in the direction of the restaurant. "It is like this always with the autograph seekers?"

"Not always. Sometimes. It comes with the territory."

She scrunched up her face in distaste. "If this territory comes with such disgusting people, I never get used to this thing."

He had. "You'll have to get used to it. It's the price you pay if you want to be a star." Finally his heart rate began to slow.

"That pig who comes to the table and disturbs you, and then makes his stupid friends like the rabble, and the...the...I do not know the word in English, but in Italian I say she was *un' asina*. She does not look where she goes, the fool. She would perhaps fall on the boy and smash him flat if you do not rescue him."

He came to a stop, a zing of pain knotting his forehead. "Yeah, that's me. The rescuer." He took her by the arm and kept going in the direction of the parking garage, wishing she'd drop the subject.

"You must always give the autographs to little boys. You are a..." She waved a hand in vague circles and muttered, "*Come si dice...*" She was silent for a moment. "You are a model of the role."

"Role model. I even give autographs to little girls."

She squinted her eyes at him. He guessed she wasn't impressed with his commitment to gender equality, or distracted by his attempt at making a joke about something that was, to him, the furthest thing from funny.

"This is nonsense what you speak."

They rounded the corner, arrived at the garage. Car handed the ticket to the attendant.

"I know you give the autographs to little boys and to little girls. You need not explain. But something disturbs you. Something you do not say."

"Something disturbs me? No." He laughed as proof, probably would have had to say something else to get her to believe him if his Hummer hadn't been brought up right then.

They were making their way uptown when she spoke into the silence. "It was something about the boy, yes?"

He pushed out a laugh. "You never let up, do you?"

"No."

"It wasn't about the boy." *No, it wasn't. Not this one.*

"I saw a little boy with the adoration for you in his eyes, a little boy who loves you. I saw your face become white with fear."

He took a deep breath and held it for a long moment.

"Perhaps little boys scare you."

It was getting hot inside the Hummer. He slid his window down. "Not hardly."

She adjusted her scarf around her neck. "No?"

"How could they? I have a son." He took another deep breath, if possible, even deeper than the first. "And I had a little brother."

She got a dreamy look on her face. "To have a brother, or a sister, to have a family, it is something I have always wanted because I do not have it. You are so lucky to have a brother."

She'd completely missed what he said: had, not have. A spasm of nausea rose up in his throat.

"When he was little, did your brother adore you, the way little brothers do?"

"He did." Car fixed his eyes on the traffic ahead and gripped the steering wheel tight.

"Did he follow you around, perhaps go to the ball field to see the big brother play beautiful baseball?"

The lump in his throat was so big, he could barely answer. "He did."

"Does he come to watch you play now? Can I meet him?"

He opened his mouth. Nothing came out.

"Car?" She said his name, hesitant.

"You can't meet him." He exhaled soundlessly. "He's dead."

At first it didn't penetrate that she'd put her hand on his arm. "*Mi dispiace,* Car," she whispered, a catch in her voice. "I am so sorry. My heart breaks."

He swallowed hard, and cleared his throat. "No need to be sorry. It was a long time ago and I've come to terms with it." The heat of her palm warmed his skin through his jacket. He didn't pull his arm away.

"Tell me about him." She squeezed, kept squeezing. Gently.

"Stevie. He was ten years old."

"Truly a little brother." She ran her hand up to his shoulder and down. Again. And again.

"Yeah. I was kind of like a mother to him." He smiled, a grim upward shaping of his lips.

"What does this mean: kind of?" Her hand was lodged, now, at his elbow. He didn't tell her to move it, even if it meant he had to work a little to turn the steering wheel.

He cracked a laugh. "Our mother was one of those women who shouldn't have had children."

"But if she did not have children, I would be driving your Hummer."

He gave her a quick sideways look. Her black eyes glowed with honeyed, teasing warmth, a sweet smile curving her lips upward.

"That would be a bad thing, no?"

She was comforting him. With humor. He felt his mood ease. "We'd have to get blocks attached to the gas pedal and brake so you could reach them."

Sofia leaned toward him across the console. "Will you tell me more about you and Stevie?"

"What's there to say? I..." And his throat closed up. He couldn't have said more, right then, if he tried. How could he explain how much he loved his little brother? How could he explain how much he loved the time they spent together, all of it, even walking him to school in the morning and picking him up after school in the afternoon?

Sofia kept rubbing his arm. Her hand spread warmth on his skin that penetrated all the way to bone.

"How did he die? Was he sick?"

Car took his foot off the accelerator. They began to coast. "No, not sick. It was after school. He was by himself and didn't see the car veer up onto the sidewalk where he was standing. He was thrown across the street. They said he died right away."

Chapter Seven

The next night at the game, the seventh inning stretch came and went. Car was resigned to his ass being planted on the bench for the duration. Then, in the bottom of the eighth, with the game tied at two, Skip's eye roved down the length of the dugout, looking for a pinch hitter for Jelevic—Jelly to everyone. That eye landed on Car. Car's pulse kicked up.

Skip's gaze slid past him to Chip Fox, who'd been a hair away from getting a starting assignment in the outfield—the kid had been so hot in spring training—and motioned for him to grab a bat. Foxy failed to advance the runner. The Federals won anyway when, in the bottom of the ninth, Dawg lined a single off the Oriole's closer, driving in the winning run.

Afterwards, Car headed downtown to pick up Sofia for their first evening out clubbing. The season was all of three games old. There were plenty of games ahead, and he'd play in a lot of them. "Yeah, you tell yourself that, Car," he muttered.

He'd have been ecstatic if all he had to think about was his future in baseball. But last night with Sofia: *that* was what he couldn't get out of his mind. What the hell had he been thinking? How could he have opened himself up to her that way? He'd told her things he never told anyone. Why? And why didn't he feel embarrassed, even angry at himself that he'd let his guard down so far as to tell a woman who might as well have been a stranger about one of the darkest, most private parts of his life?

She was the oddest woman. She had a lot to say, half

of which he didn't understand. She made scenes. She was All-Star Game irritating. But that she had such warmth and comfort in her?

He drove on, smiling a little, remembering how she'd whispered a whole lot of nothing words to him in Italian, none of which he understood. But he hadn't stopped her, or pulled his hand away. He replayed that moment when Sofia had lifted his hand off the wheel, and kissed it. "*Che cosa tremendo,*" she'd whispered, her warm breath bathing his knuckles. "*Mi dispiace, mi dispiace.* I did not know. You will forgive me for bringing up the bad memory, yes?"

"There's nothing to forgive," he'd said. And he'd meant it. For her. For him? Forgiveness was something he would never have.

By the time he drove up to the hotel, he couldn't wait to see her. What she'd been doing to him... it felt like a blessing. No one in his life had ever done that for him. Only she. Only Sofia.

When the woman herself swept out of the entrance, his heart leapt. As usual she was all in black, wearing a high-necked dress, which covered up her beautiful breasts, her best feature. Although he had to say there sure as hell was nothing wrong with those hips of hers. Around her trim waist, she wore a shiny black belt, and on her feet a pair of shoes—excuse the hell out him—stilts. Smiling, he hopped out of the Hummer, intent on helping her down the shallow steps.

The baby-faced doorman got to her first. He was all up in her personal space, hand in hers. "Here you go, Sofia."

"*Grazie,* Edward," she said, like she was some kind of queen... and gave him the smile of an imp.

Edward got a look on his face that reminded Car of the one on Foxy's face when Skip handed him a bat.

"It's okay for tomorrow night?" Edward asked.

"*Certamente.*"

What the hell was this? Was she planning a date with the big, strapping kid, who was what—twenty, maybe twenty-one? That look on the doorman's face, the broad smile on Sofia's, twisted up Car with something he never experienced and didn't like to put a name to.

"I've got you, Sofia," Car said, and grabbed her arm from Edward's with a little too much force.

She angled a curious look at him, then turned her head. "Ciao, Edward. *Ci vediamo*." She stepped up to the side of the Hummer, hesitated, and looked at Car, one eyebrow raised.

Ticked about the doorman, Car couldn't think why she stood there. Until he remembered. Oh, yeah. He slid his hands around her tiny waist. Beneath the black dress, her skin was sunlight warm. He lifted her and breathed in her scent: roses, sweet, sweet roses. In the millisecond before her butt hit the seat, he had the strangest thought: Sofia was his. Not Mosbacher's. Not Edward's. *His*. Which was why he nailed the doorman—Edward—with a look that said *you watching, dude*? He barely heard the intake of Sofia's breath, so focused was he on the doorman.

Lifting himself into his seat, he clicked the seat belt in place. Through clenched teeth, he said, "What was that chee thing you said?" He shoved the stick into drive.

"*Ci vediamo*. It is what you say to a friend when you will see him later. In this case, it is tomorrow."

"So you two are friends? You have a date?"

Into the loaded silence that lasted and lasted, she finally spoke. "Not a date. A party. I tell you the other day. You do not remember?"

He remembered, all right. Remembered how strange it seemed. He came to a jerky halt at a red light. "You going to party with the doorman?"

"I..." Her lips creased together. "You do not understand."

That was an understatement. "Try me."

"You and I, we must pretend in public. In private we do not need to pretend you have the attraction for me." She hesitated. "And so there is no need for the jealousy."

He accelerated when the delivery van behind him blasted his horn. "Yeah, you're right. I'm sorry."

Not sorry. An ass.

"Where do we go now?"

Good. A change of subject. "A place called Pitti Palace."

"We are going to Italy? To Florence?"

He took his eyes off the road, glanced at her, felt irritation wash over him again. "What are you talking about?"

"The Pitti Palace. It is a museum. In Florence. In Italy."

Jesus. How did she come up with this stuff? "It's a club, Sofia. Downtown. Big hot spot. We're not getting on any planes to fly to Italy." The air felt thick around him. He smelled the stench of his very own green monster.

She cocked her head to the side. "You are angry?"

"I'm not angry." Just stupid.

But she didn't believe him. Why should she, when he didn't believe it himself? "What did you do today?" he asked. "Your exercises?"

"We are having a conversation, no?"

On a heavy inhale, he said, "Yeah. We're having a conversation." He hoped it wouldn't be about her partying. That was not the subject of any conversation he wanted to have.

It was her turn to sigh. "Yes, I did my exercises." She tapped her bottom lip with one finger.

An uncomfortable silence.

He gripped the wheel, his mind cycling through something—anything—to say.

She beat him to it. "Did you win the game this afternoon?"

No way could she know this was the number two off limits subject. "We won."

"*Bravo.* And how many hits did you make?"

"I didn't play."

"Why you did not play? You are the star."

"I've been out of commission since an operation I had last year."

She made a clucking sound. "I do not know what commission means, but they are fools they do not send you to the home place to hit the ball and help the team win the games."

She leaned toward him. "Chelsea and I, last night, we are watching the TV about the sports because I want to learn. Two very loud men, they speak about you."

He stiffened. She'd been watching ESPN: *The Bob and Rob Show*. He'd heard about last night's show today in the clubhouse. Bob and Rob weren't admirers of his. Not lately. "And?"

"And I am angry because they say you are..." She floundered. "Done."

He flinched.

"Chelsea, she says that means you do not play baseball anymore."

"Thanks for reminding me."

"I do not remind you. It is what *they* say."

"Thanks for reminding me what they say."

There was a pause. "I am making conversation about something you do not like. I will try to think of another conversation."

Dammit all to hell. Something collapsed inside him. He was a bastard. It wasn't her fault Skip hadn't played him. She wasn't a big mouth on ESPN. For sure her name wasn't Car Bradford, a grown man who should know better than to be jealous of a doorman who hadn't yet grown a real beard. He was acting like a five-year-old, ticked that a little girl whose hair he liked to pull wanted to play with another little boy. "Don't worry about it," he said, voice softened. "I'm just in a mood, acting like a jackass."

With a feather-light brush across the back of his hand, she touched him. "It is okay."

She rested the tips of her fingers on his forearm. His muscle flexed involuntarily. Damn, her hand was driving him crazy. "Didn't anyone ever tell you you're not supposed to touch the driver?" He forced a smile.

"Oh!" She snatched her hand back. "This is a driving rule in America?"

"I was joking." And he wanted her hand back, right there on his arm, or anyplace else she chose.

She folded one hand over the other and rested them in her lap.

He sighed. Dumb-ass that he was, he wasn't getting

either one of her hands back.

After a long, uncomfortable moment she said, "We can listen to the music on the radio, yes?"

Calling himself all kinds of names, he wondered if there was a way he could rewind the last few minutes and delete. "Sure." He pointed to the power button on the dash. As she reached out, he remembered what was cued up in the CD player. Her CD. He'd been listening to it. Now it was too late. Her music filled the space around them.

He glanced at her across the console. Her pale skin had gone all rosy. "This is my recording," she whispered.

"Yeah, it's yours." Embarrassed, he shifted in his seat, the little boy caught making nice to the little girl whose hair he'd just been pulling.

"Do you like?"

Did he like? He couldn't pronounce the name of the song—excuse him, the aria. But he knew it was one from a boy part she sang: Cherubino, from *The Marriage of Figaro*. He'd been trying to imagine her as a boy. It wasn't working for him. But her voice? Yeah, that worked. Big time. He canted his head toward her. "I like. Very much."

"I am glad." Once more she put her hand on his arm.

Okay then. She was touching him again. "Why don't you tell me how come you're playing a boy's part in this opera." He shifted, giving his fellas room while they swelled without his permission.

"It was written for a woman, a woman with a voice that can go lower, almost like a boy's."

"How does that work?"

"Like this."

He turned his head towards her at the moment she pressed her hands against her breasts in an attempt to flatten one of the most beautiful parts of her body.

He winced and because he couldn't help it, laughed.

"*Mi dispiace*! I am sorry, but this is funny?"

"No, it's not funny," he said, laughing harder at the look of affront on her face.

"Then why do you laugh?"

"B-because I'm t-trying to i-imagine it, that's why."

"You try to imagine what must be done with my bosoms when I sing Cherubino—or the voice?"

He sobered in an instant. "Never the voice, Sofia. Never the voice." He rotated the volume knob to the right and took her hand into his. The amplified sound of her music filled the Hummer.

"That is good then." After a moment she added, "That is very good, Car."

Car maneuvered through mid-town traffic, not letting go of her hand. He decided he was glad Brent had forced him to do this thing with her. When she was out of his life in a few weeks, he'd still have this recording to listen to. And that business about her being his?

A demented thought, already passing.

Chapter Eight

Right away Sofia hated Pitti Palace, with its higher-than-a-cathedral ceilings and an interior dark as the devil's intestines. "This is so..."

"Appalling?" Car finished the observation.

Appalling: that was a good word. She'd have to remember it. This Pitti Palace, like the museum of the same name in Florence, was crowded, not with paintings, but with women who wanted to be seen and men who wanted to be seen with them. Until she no longer could, Sofia held her breath to keep from breathing air tainted with the smell of headache-inducing perfumes.

Being jostled back and forth by the constantly shifting crowd, the demanding, percussive music pounding against her breastbone, Sofia hoped one evening here would be enough to get her the audition. She had no desire to come back. Ever.

"It's places like this we want to be seen in. Everyone knows who's here and talks about it afterward," Car said, voice raised, one hand at the small of her back.

Sofia leaned against the hand and the comforting warmth of his body.

"These people need to hook up with as many people they think can help their careers. We need to also," he added.

Sofia studied the faces of the people as she and Car inched past. One man was prettier than the next. Daily shaving seemed not to be important for them. Many wore their hair in a funny up-fluff at the front. She glanced into their eyes, roving everywhere, focusing only for a moment before moving on. The women, all beautiful, some dark-skinned, some blond—but not necessarily blond when they were born—wore outfits that showed off their breasts, slender waists, and long, long legs. They were all taller than she. Much taller. And thinner.

It was clear to Sofia that none of them understood how she could be in the company of *Signore* Beautiful Eyes. They—the models and the actresses—didn't see her as "someone." Like horses, they tossed their hair so it swished across their backs, and slid their eyes away from her to fasten on Car.

"Hi Car," one said, very low and whispery. Like a cat.

"Car, I looked for you today at the game," said another.

"Car, there's a party later at the Woodstock. Are you going?" This one had sharp, heavily-kohled eyes and long, black-painted fingernails. Sofia didn't know about the Woodstock. But the invitation was for Car, not her. She grabbed his wrist, as if she could keep him from going.

As nice as he was, as much as he paid her compliments for her voice, and bought her CD, which stopped up her heart with joy, she knew he'd go where the models and actresses went. Perhaps not tonight, but soon. When he was through with her. And then she would never again feel the shock of pleasure when he took her by the waist to show poor Edward that she was his. His! How heavenly it would be to be possessed by him. Like Tonio in *I Pagliacci* with his Nedda—but without the stabbing.

She wondered what it would have been like if, when he had his hands on her waist, by accident, they slid upwards to her breasts. One time she let Gregorio dell' Apulia touch her breasts. She didn't like it and thought, surely, since she found it distasteful, there was something wrong with her. In the romances she read, it did seem a wonderful thing, with the surges, the releases, the soaring to Heaven, and all the other exquisite expressions which had no meaning for her because she was a virgin.

She felt the women's hostile eyes on her back. They didn't wish her well. What they wished her was away from Car. She wanted to say, 'I'm with him because he wants me to be with him.' That was ridiculous. It couldn't be. Even if he did love her singing. Even if he did buy her CD. So she tossed her head like they did. Even if her hair was in a neat bun at the back of her head, and the tossing lost its drama.

She was still tossing when Car pulled her to a stop. Confused, she gazed up at his face, exquisite even in the darkness of this hellish place. "What?"

"My ex. There, across the room with..." He bared his teeth. "Her boyfriend." He pointed. "She's waving at us to come over." He followed this with a curse. She would have to learn all the American curses.

"Victoria too. Perfect. Let's get this over with." Car took her hand in a firm grip, and eased his way through the crowd, past the men who slapped his back, as if they were truly friends, and the women who simpered at him like little girls.

He continued to pull her toward the table where Louise stood with her boyfriend, and where *Signora* Mosbacher sat, smiling at a man seated next to her, a man whose bald head glistened in Pitti Palace's meager light.

Why, Sofia wondered, was the *Signora* in a place like this with men and woman half her age? And with her own daughter too. Perhaps she thought being with people half her age made her seem half her age? Quick, before the *Signora* could see that unkind thought show on her face, Sofia smiled. It was the kind of smile Maria Torelli adopted when she realized a director wasn't going to give her a role she wanted, but she needed to seem pleasant in case there was a role to be had from him in the future.

"Victoria, good to see you," Car said, stooping to place a kiss on the Signora's cheek. He glanced once at his ex-wife, who was moaning because the tattooed boyfriend had begun to bite her neck.

Sofia stared, fascinated.

"Good to see you, Car," the *Signora* answered in a cool voice, her eyes not on Car, but on Sofia. They travelled from the top of Sofia's head to the tip of her shoes.

Sofia kept her Maria Torelli smile in place.

At last the boyfriend raised his head, and threw Car a grin, exposing a set of ugly, uneven teeth. He planted a hand on one of Louise's breasts. Eyes, not quite focused, Louise leaned against him, and beamed at Sofia. "Hi, singer from Italy."

"Louise," her mother murmured.

"Oh, Mother. I'm not going to embarrass you. Too much." Louise grated a laugh, and looked up at Car. "You should come with us. Back to my apartment. We could have a really good time."

Car's eyes fixed hard on hers.

She stuck out her bottom lip and put one of her hands on top of the hand her boyfriend had on her breast. "You could watch, see what you're missing."

Louise was foolishly using the boyfriend to taunt Car, thinking she could make him jealous, when anyone could see Car had no interest in his ex-wife. Sofia wanted to feel sorry for Louise. But she couldn't.

With jerky movements, Louise tore out of her boyfriend's arms, and began to dance to a song so loud it could deafen the world. "I love Lady Gaga," she shrieked, stumbled, and fell. The boyfriend bent to pick her up. When Louise was back on her feet, she locked eyes with Car, and swiped a trembling hand across her nose. "I know what game you and my father are playing."

Car stiffened. "Think what you want."

"Oh, I will."

"Louise, enough," the *Signora* warned.

"I'll tell Noah about you."

Car's eyes burned with fury. "What will you tell him, Louise?"

"I'll tell him you didn't want him."

"That would be a lie." Car stabbed a finger in Louise's face. "I didn't want you."

Louise grabbed her boyfriend's hand and tossed a wary glance at him. Then she gritted her teeth and turned flashing eyes on Sofia. "You bitch. You better not try to take my husband away from me."

Car's mouth curled back in a snarl. "Ex-husband."

Louise she swung back towards Car. "I don't care. If I see you with her, I'll challenge the case." She screeched the last words, louder than Lady Gaga.

He tensed. Sofia put a hand on the steel-like muscle of his arm.

He looked down at her, took a deep breath, and

nodded once. He understood. She sighed in relief.

Louise took her boyfriend by the arm. "Let's go."

As he and Louise were swallowed up by the crowd, the *Signora* said, "That girl is a drunken disgrace. She sickens me."

Sofia didn't have to wonder how the *Signora* could say something terrible about her daughter, even if true, in front of others. Her father said terrible things about her, in front of others, all the time.

But her concern wasn't for her father. Or the *Signora*. Her concern was for Car. She looked around. "No one pays attention," she said to him. "Everything is okay." Sofia was sure, in Pitti Palace, gossip was secondary in importance only to being seen. If Car had done what he wanted to Louise, he'd be sorry afterward, especially if it affected his custody case.

The *Signora* shifted in her seat. "So, Sofia, I assume you still haven't spoken to Antonio?"

Sofia put her Maria Torelli smile back in place. "No, *Signora*, I..."

"You understand I don't interfere with Antonio's decisions." The *Signora* paused. "Even should I want to."

To smile was becoming a struggle. But Sofia knew she needed to continue the act, as if she were a fawning courtier in Act One of *Rigoletto*. "For sure I understand. For sure."

The man with the *Signora* took that moment to clear his throat. "Victoria, aren't you going to introduce us?"

"Certainly." The Signora held up a graceful hand. "Gareth, meet Sofia de' Medici. Sofia, this is Gareth Silver. I'm sure you know of him."

Of course she knew. *Signore* Silver was one of the world's most feared opera critics. "*Buona Sera*." She held out a hand.

"*Piacere mio,*" he said, taking it and giving Car a sidewise glance.

"And this is Car Bradford," the *Signora* said. She turned to Car. "*Signore* Silver is the music critic of the *New York Morning News*."

Signore Silver lifted his chin and smiled at Car down his nose. "What do you do for a living, Mr. Bradford?"

"Car is a famous baseball player," Sofia said. How did he not know Car? Everyone did. It took a mere second for her to realize *Signore* Silver lied. He knew.

Car gave *Signore* Silver a toothy grin. "Sofia, I wouldn't expect someone like Mr. Silver to know anything about baseball."

Was this another lie? Had it become, in an instant, a battle of male wills?

"Gareth is a highly regarded critic, Car," the *Signora* said. "He doesn't have time to watch baseball games."

Signore Silver lifted her hand and, like a lover, placed a kiss on her palm. Sofia's stomach did a flip of disgust.

The *Signore* leaned back in his chair and swung one leg over the other. "And so, *Signorina*, I understand you want Maestro Lupino to engage you to sing *Carmen* for the Muni's re-opening. You've never sung it, have you?"

"I have not, but I have prepared myself to sing the part. Also I have performed the big arias in concert, the *Habanera* and the *Seguidilla*."

"Singing arias and singing all four acts of such a massive work are two quite different things. You know that, I assume." The leg kept swinging.

She did know, but the arias were not all she'd learned of *Carmen*. She shivered with apprehension.

Car slid his hand around the nape of her neck.

"To sing *Carmen*, this is something I have the confidence to do," she said, the feel of Car's warm hand calming her, while she tried to steel herself against Signore Silver's words, which were spoken in a too kind voice.

"You are twenty-four, is that right?" More swinging.

She stiffened. "Yes."

"Ah."

Sofia's heart skipped a beat. She knew what his *ah* meant. He, who knew the world of opera better than almost anyone, had little, perhaps no faith in her ability to sing *Carmen*.

"My age is a mere number," she said in a small voice.

He leaned forward and dismissed her with a wave of his hand. "Your Cherubino is adequate. The role of that pre-pubescent page fits you nicely."

"Pre..pre... Sorry?"

He uncrossed his leg, and gave her a pitying look. The *Signora* laughed as if she found Sofia's ignorance of the English word too funny.

"One can picture you as Cherubino—pre-pubescent means a young teen, dear—with a crush on every pretty woman he meets. That's the kind of role you should play for the foreseeable future."

Sofia didn't like his idea of her future.

With one long finger, *Signore* Silver tapped the table. "Antonio won't consider you for *Carmen*. At twenty-four, your voice is not mature enough. More important, Carmen is a woman with whom men are obsessed. They look at her and they want hot, dirty sex with her. Men will do whatever they must to have her. I look at you and see a girl: Isabella, from *The Italian Girl in Algiers*, Dorabella in *Cosi Fan Tutte*, and yes, Cherubino." He clucked his tongue. "These are your roles. Not Carmen. Don't feel bad, my dear."

Sofia's head filled with bits and pieces of confusion, dashing about like the Furies in Act Two of *Orpheus and Eurydice*. Everyone stood against her: her father, *Signora* Mosbacher, and now *Signore* Silver.

"So Gary," Car said, soothing Sofia with a slow caress the length of her spine. For a moment, the Furies weren't so furious. "Maybe you can answer a question for me."

"Which question would that be, Car? And you know I've been a little curious myself. Where did you get such a ridiculous name?" *Signore* Silver pressed the tips of his fingers against his chest. "The name's Gareth."

"Gotcha, Gary. 'Scuse me. Gareth." Car's hand stilled on Sofia's back. "You get a name like Car if you make things happen, as opposed to writing about them."

Signore Silver gasped.

The *Signora* said, "Gentlemen, please."

Car said nothing. Instead he kept his eyes fixed on *Signore* Silver, his jaw hard like the stone wall of the Duke of Mantua's castle in *Rigoletto*.

At last he said, "I'm curious how you know, Gary, that Sofia can't play Carmen because she's not... uh, hot enough?"

Now the *Signore* hardened his jaw. "It's *Gareth*."

Car began to caress Sofia's shoulders, his hand so big,

so strong, so hot, Sofia's bones began to melt. She stilled, when he began to play with her ear lobe.

"Car!" The *Signora* stared first at Car's hand and then at his face. "You cannot be serious."

Car's fingers flexed against Sofia's skin. He slid his arm around her waist and turned her against his hard chest. Before she could think, he was bending his head to hers. "I've never been more serious," he whispered. And he kissed her.

Sofia forgot her confusion. She forgot her past. And her future. She sank into the cradle of his arms. She didn't know a mouth could be so soft, or that lips could move so gently. She didn't know a man's breath could be so sweet and still carry a man's scent. She didn't know the rasp of the stubble on his chin could scrape against her mouth and she wouldn't mind. She didn't know because she was lost.

Then he let her go. And she remembered. She was in Pitti Palace, assaulted by its deafening sounds slamming against her eardrums. She stumbled and put a hand out to steady herself against the warm, strong muscles of Car's chest. "Why do you...?

"Ssh." Car pulled her close again, his tongue curling around the rim of her ear. Her knees threatened to give way. Her heart beat so loud she heard its thumps, over the raucous music, inside her ears.

"Don't you know who this woman is, Car?" demanded the *Signora*. She came to her feet. "Don't you know what being with her makes you?"

The *Signora*'s words knotted lines of anger on Car's forehead. But before Sofia could wonder what the *Signora* meant, *Signore* Silver stood too. "Let's go, Victoria. There's no reason for us to remain and watch this nonsense."

He turned to Sofia. "Young woman, I wouldn't attempt that role if I were you. Unlike your caveman boyfriend, I have some expertise in the matter of what it takes to sing *Carmen*. I'm planning to write a piece about young mezzos who attempt roles that are too big for them. I would hate to make you a laughingstock on the printed page." He patted her hand. "Know your limitations, my dear."

Chapter Nine

For Sofia, time stopped. Her breath closed up inside her chest. Her ears pulsed. "I do not understand. What does this mean what the *Signora* says?"

"She thinks something that's not true. She's an angry woman. Don't listen to her." Car rubbed small circles on her back. She concentrated on the circles.

"*Signore* Silver, he wanted to hurt me." Sofia was surprised her voice sounded so normal.

"Yes." Car's hand shifted to the back of her neck. She focused on the warm comfort of his hand.

"I can sing *Carmen*," she said, her voice stronger. "*Signore* Silver is wrong. He does not know my voice. I am ready to sing many primary roles, not just *Carmen*."

"You know what I'd like?" He slid his hand down to the small of her back, and pulled her hips close to his. "I'd like you to tell me the story."

"What story?" She began to shiver from the hate still swirling like sulfur in the air.

"Of *Carmen*. Tell me."

She swallowed once and tears filled her eyes, but they were tears she wouldn't let fall. She took a deep breath and began the story. "Carmen is a beautiful gypsy, who works in a cigarette factory in Seville. One day, she has a fight with a girl inside the factory and stabs her. The soldiers drag Carmen out. The one, who is in charge, orders a very young soldier from the country, Don José, to take Carmen to jail. There, she sings to him, and foolish boy, he lets her escape."

Car eased Sofia's head to his chest. Any other woman

would be having hysterics about now. Not Sofia. Damn, but she was one tough little cookie. She hadn't let any tears fall before in front of that bastard, Silver. The whole time she'd had that game face of hers on. "Don't listen to that son of a bitch, Sofia. He's got a stick so far up his ass, he wouldn't know good singing no matter what he does for a living."

Her chin trembled. But she giggled.

"Is that the whole story?" He palmed the satiny smoothness of her hair.

"*Certamente*, no. Don José has the obsession for Carmen and when she grows tired of him, he refuses to give her up and he kills her."

"That's it? She dies?"

"Yes she dies, but there is much beautiful singing about this."

Finally one tear escaped. He blotted it with his thumb.

"*Signore* Silver is not right about my singing. But perhaps he is right about... me?"

Car cut her off. "You know he's not right." He held her tighter.

"Carmen would not be like me. Even if she wears the white, frilly blouses and the big black skirts, she would not be fat."

"You're not fat." She wasn't. Her curves, her rounded arms, her sweet hands, her ankles, her generous breasts, her tiny waist, and hips that flared gently, he'd been fascinated by them from the start. When he thought of her, fat wasn't the word. Luscious? Yeah. Tempting? Oh, yeah. His groin tightened.

"It is also how I dress. I do not have anyone to help me understand, not even Chelsea. We both like to wear black."

He held her away from him and looked down. "How to dress is something you can learn, Sofia."

"I try. I study Maria Torelli. This is how she dresses." She took a step back, and swept her hands over her black dress, with its high neck, severe cut across her breasts, and thick leather belt at her waist. The skirt fell to the middle of her leg.

Car squinted at her get-up. Suddenly it hit him. She was too little for the dress. "How tall is Maria Torelli?"

"She is the height of Brent."

In other words, a head taller than Sofia. "You know," he began hesitantly, "I think you've got the proportions wrong, kind of like you're going up to hit with a bat that's the wrong wei... uh, length. Maybe you need to buy things meant for a smaller woman."

Her eyes brightened; the frown on her forehead disappeared. "*Davvero*? You will help me to shop?"

Now there was a question guaranteed to shrink his dick. "I'll be on the road for the next two weeks, and you need to get that audition clinched soon. So the sooner you start..." A thought jumped into his head. "I'll call Tina Huggins. Dawg's wife. There's a woman who knows how to shop. When she finishes with you, you'll be a knock-out."

Car hadn't had to do more than state the situation before Tina declared herself up for the project. Still, Car hoped Tina wouldn't make too many changes in Sofia. All Sofia needed was a little... something. He had faith Tina would figure it out.

He was still thinking about it the next morning as the team sat in the lounge at Newark, ready to board their flight for Seattle. He couldn't help thinking about Louise's childish, stupid threat. Louise could be a vindictive, unpredictable bitch. Would she follow through and tell Noah some made-up story about him to cause the kid anxiety?

Thank God Sofia had stopped him from lashing out at his ex, and compounding the problem. In Pitti Palace of all places. Who knew how Louise might have reacted, if Sofia hadn't placed that one hand on his arm? Maybe Louise would have walked away from their negotiations.

He didn't think this had anything to do with why he'd kissed Sofia in front of Victoria and Silver. It was more that he wanted to stop the poison from spewing out of Silver's mouth. But when he'd taken Sofia in his arms, the why of it hadn't mattered. Because of all the women who had ever been in his life, including Louise, everything clicked when he held Sofia in his arms.

What a complication.

In the beginning he was clear; Sofia de' Medici was a pain in the ass. A complication. Then he fell in love with her voice. An odd complication. Which was followed by him getting jealous because she smiled at a rookie doorman. A stupid complication. And now? Now he thought she was what? Sexy? A strange complication. No doubt she was stacked. But sexy?

As the team boarded and they took off, as the pilot circled around to get on a north by northwest heading, Car decided having Sofia de' Medici in his life was, by the day, becoming a bigger and bigger complication.

"I am not ready," Sofia wailed when Chelsea came rushing into the bedroom the next morning to tell her Tina Huggins was in the living room.

"When she tells me she will come at the noontime, I think she means five minutes before the noontime, not ten o'clock," complained Sofia, struggling to fasten the snaps on her black calf-length skirt. The night before, when she had put it out to wear, she remembered Car's words about proportion and thought perhaps the skirt was a problem of proportion. But what if it was? Everything she had in her closet was a problem of proportion.

"Let me." Chelsea pushed her hand away to fasten the last, difficult snap. "Do you know who that is in the living room?"

"*Certamente*. She is the wife of Car's teammate."

Chelsea took Sofia by the shoulders and brought her around so they were face to face. Chelsea's corkscrew-curly hair stood out in every direction, her hazel eyes were wide and shining with excitement. "Yes, she's Dawg's wife, but before she got married, do you know who she was then?"

Sofia patted Chelsea on the shoulder. "*Calma ti*. I

know she is somebody who knows how to dress to make the good impression."

Chelsea huffed her frustration. "Before she gave up modeling, married Dawg, and had four children, Tina Huggins was Cristina Alvarez, *the* top model in the world."

Sofia put a hand out to find the edge of the bed so when she sat it would be there and not on the floor. "*Dio mio*. What does she look like?"

Chelsea sighed. "Beautiful. Stunning. She's tall. Her hair is this dark brown. She has it up in a top knot, and her clothes..."

"No, no, I do not want to know what she wears. I want to know about her face."

A look of confusion crossed Chelsea's features. "Her face?"

Sofia pressed her fingers to her forehead. "Is it all squashed up with a sulky mouth because her husband says she must do this for his teammate? Will she look down at me and hate every minute we spend together?"

Chelsea's face cleared. "Stop. The first thing Tina wanted to know was how long it would take you to get ready."

"Aha! She is impatient to be finished with me."

"Because," Chelsea continued, "'I can't wait,' she said. 'This is going to be so much fun. Tell Sofia to hurry.'"

"Oh."

With her last snap snapped, her sweater smooth and perfect, her hair pulled back in her usual neat bun, Sofia straightened and stepped out of her bedroom to meet Tina Huggins. Or Cristina Alvarez.

In that first moment Sofia saw Cristina—no, she needed to think of her as Tina so she didn't melt into a puddle of insecurity—her heart almost stopped. There she was, tall and slender, faced away and looking out the window.

At that moment the most famous model in the world turned. "Sofia!"

Tina Huggins was ravishing. In her white, high-necked sweater, and white trousers, with dark brown hair flowing in ringlets, cascading down from the crown of her head, golden skin glowing, light, brown eyes sparkling, this woman was everything Chelsea said she was, but more.

She came swiftly across the room, both hands held out. "When Eric said Car wanted me to help you do a makeover, I was so excited I could barely contain myself."

Sofia frowned. "Who is Eric?"

Tina threw back her lovely head. Her curls bounced and she smiled with her beautiful, sparkling white American teeth. "If you're around baseball players long enough, you'll find out they can't call each other by their real names. Some of them go by initials, or a short form of their last name. Or in Eric's case, a nickname. His teammates call him Dawg. I won't."

"That is good to hear," Sofia said, warming to this woman and forgetting she was the most famous model in the world. "Already I did not like that I must call Christopher an automobile, but it would be terrible beyond terrible for me to call your husband an animal."

Tina rolled her eyes. "Can you imagine if I called Eric 'Dawg' in front of the kids? It's bad enough they hear him called that in school."

"Oh, I love children. Yours, they are boys? Girls?"

"Two of each, the little devils. Eric brings our two oldest, Brianna—she's eight—and Joshua, he's the six year-old, with him to practice on Saturdays when the team's at home. One of these days, you'll meet them. But we can talk about my kids later. Let's get going." She hustled Sofia out the door, with Chelsea just behind.

Tina Huggins would teach Sofia how to dress so she'd get the audition. But Sofia knew she needed to be honest with herself. After last night, when Car held her in his arms—yes, it was for pity, but she chose not to think of it that way—what she wanted, even more than the audition, was to learn how to dress for Car, so he'd look at her and think she was as beautiful as Cristina Alvarez. Sofia suppressed the dreamy smile she knew was on her face, and followed Tina into the taxi, there to pick them up in front of the hotel.

It was quickly apparent Tina knew what fashion advice she would give Sofia. "Jersey and chiffon, soft materials. Nothing cut and severe, no stiff fabrics that fight with your natural curves." Tina eyed Sofia, shoulders to knees. Sofia felt her hips and her rear end swell under Tina's roving eye. She tightened the muscles of the latter.

"We have to use intense colors."

"Red?" Sofia ventured.

Tina snapped her fingers. "Jewel tones, and of course red. But with red, it can be many shades: scarlet, crimson, ruby, they're all your colors." She tapped a finger against her lower lip, continuing to study Sofia, but, now, thank God, just her face and hair. "I think not orange red though."

"Not orange red," Sofia parroted. On stage, she never minded being the object of everyone's attention. But in the hushed atmosphere of this little store? With Chelsea and Tina, and even the lady who worked in the store— Jacqueline was her name, she was French, of course, and very chic and sophisticated—here it wasn't so wonderful to be the object of everyone's attention.

"I know what you're thinking, Sofia," whispered Chelsea, standing just behind her.

Of course. Chelsea always knew what she was thinking.

Sofia looked at Tina. "Do you also know what I am thinking?"

Tina laughed. "You're thinking 'what did I get myself into?' You're thinking 'how will what I wear, whether it's ruby or scarlet red or any other color, change what people think of me? I'll still be little Sofia de' Medici.' That's what you're thinking, right?"

She was thinking that, but little was not the word in her mind. She sucked in her midriff, which wasn't big, and her back end, which was. "I look at you and see beauty and elegance and then at me..."

Tina hooted a laugh. "You haven't seen me without makeup; otherwise, you would never say that. And you don't know about my temper. When I lose it, my face gets all nasty, and I'm one ugly thing."

"That is in private," Sofia said, dismissing what she knew was Tina's way of making her feel better. "For the men who see you and want you, even though you are the wife and mother, you are their dream." She swept her hands wide and looked down at herself. "I am not you."

"Thank goodness for that. You are you, a goddess in miniature. Now they worship you for your voice. After we transform you, they'll worship you for your body. Car, too."

Sofia blushed. She wasn't sure which shade of red, but it was red. "I do want that," she said, in a tiny voice. "How did you know?"

Tina patted her on the shoulder. "You wouldn't be female if you didn't want Car to worship you." She grabbed Sofia by the arm and propelled her toward a dressing room. "Now, enough of that. Jacqueline, bring everything we discussed."

For the next hour, Jacqueline did. There were dresses, there were skirts that went with long blouses that caressed the tops of Sofia's thighs and settled lovingly against her skin. There were even trousers, which she never wore, for she was afraid they would show off too much of what she didn't want seen. They had wide legs that swished around her ankles...well, they would swish if they weren't so long, she tripped on them as she shuffled out of the dressing room to the mirror so everyone could lay their critical eyes on her.

Tina crouched down and gathered together a big handful of material. "Even after it's shortened, I think less width." She looked up at Jacqueline, who studied Sofia's leg as if she had never seen one like it before.

Jacqueline tipped her head to the side. "But of course," she said in her reserved voice. "She is too short for so much leg."

"Perhaps I do not need the leg at all," Sofia suggested.

Tina stood up. "Don't be silly. We'll just take it up and you'll see. You'll be a knock-out in this outfit."

Sofia looked down at her trouser-covered legs. "But I

do not understand. They are black. Why not red or the other colors you tell me are mine?"

"Black is one of your colors too," Tina said. "It just depends on how you wear black."

When she was back in the dressing room—for the three hundredth time—Sofia fumbled with the side button, and prepared to have another outfit sail in with instructions for her to put it on. "It just depends on how you wear black," she mimicked under her breath. "It is black or it is black, I am thinking. But no, I am wrong."

The door opened a crack and Tina peeked in. "Why are you taking that off?" She pushed a handful of something soft, silk-like, and bright white into Sofia's hands. "You need to put this on with the pants." She shut the door with a loud crack.

It weighed nothing, this thing she was to put on over the pants. There was a precious delicacy about it. She opened her fingers a bit and let it flow downward.

It was a blouse. But how could she wear it? It was so sheer, everyone would see through to her brassiere, which was like all her brassieres; meant to hold in her melons. Who'd want to get a glimpse of such a brassiere?

She glanced at the closed door. At some point, she'd lost what awe she had of the top model in the world. Sofia's hand was on the doorknob, preparing to tell Tina to come get the silly white thing, when there was a short rap. The door opened a fraction.

"Don't bother to put that blouse on unless you put this on first." Tina thrust another bundle of white at her, this time something much smaller and very lacy.

Sofia stared down at it. A brassiere. But one like she'd never seen, except on shapely women, like Maria Torelli, with whom she'd dressed and undressed in changing rooms all over Europe. The cups were all over gossamer tracings of lace. Except for where the nipples would be. There they were satin.

She held the bra in her hand. It would never fit right. Too much of her would spill over the top and she'd shake like pudding when she walked.

She let the thing dangle by its straps. It swayed in the still, quiet air of the dressing room. Perhaps it was her size.

Perhaps it would fit. Perhaps there'd be no lasting harm if she put it on. She could always take it off and put on her own brassiere before she opened the door, before Tina or the just-a-little-snobbish Jacqueline in her little black dress with her necklace of lustrous pearls could see her.

With a sigh, she took off her neutral-toned—so it would go under everything—brassiere, and slipped on the delicate thing. And looked.

In the mirror her face was still her face. All big Roman nose, sharp slashes for eyebrows, too full lips, and high forehead. But her breasts. She caught her breath. Her brain stopped working. The word that came to her mind was not one she'd ever said about them. They looked...

Beautiful.

The lacy, so-nothing-it-weighed-a-mere-ounce confection shaped her perfectly. Yes, they were still there: her melons. Unless she did plastic surgery, they wouldn't go away.

Without thinking, she laid her palms against her breasts. The lacy fabric covering them felt slightly rough beneath her fingers. She shifted one hand over the satin at the center. The nipple beneath stiffened to a sharp point. Would it stiffen the same way if the hand was not hers, but a man's?

If it were Car's?

She swayed, light-headed. Her breasts seemed to swell. She thought of Car's beautiful mouth. Would he lean down from his great height, press his mouth to the little bow at the center of this lovely thing, and run his tongue over the lace to the satin covering her nipples? A sharp pain prickled between her thighs. She took a shuddering breath and pressed her thighs together against the insistent throbbing.

Only on the dimmest level did she realize she was rubbing her fingers back and forth. There was a loud bang from somewhere in the back of the shop and sudden raised voices. She snatched her hand away from her breast.

"Sofia, what's taking so long?" came Chelsea's voice.

Sofia grabbed the blouse from the bench where she had dropped it and slipped it over her head. "*Che imbecille,* Sofia," she muttered. "*Che sta pensando?*" She stepped out into the dressing area. All three ladies looked at her. Sofia took a deep breath and stood up straight.

Tina was the first to speak. "I knew it; I just knew it." She took a step toward Sofia and placing both hands on her shoulders, turned her around to face the mirror.

Sofia caught her breath at the vision. The silky blouse, with its sheer sleeves, the deep side slits showing the black satin pants beneath, the deep plunge of the jewel neckline that hinted at her now divine bosoms, it was exquisite. She was...

Exquisite.

Her heart rollicked with elation.

Tina patted her on the back. "Hmmm, let's get that scarf, Jacqueline."

Sofia's heart stopped rollicking. To have dreamed, if for an abbreviated moment of time... it had been wondrous, those few seconds of bliss, looking at herself in the mirror, thinking she could be beautiful for Car. But naturally, her too big breasts must be covered up. "You think if I put the scarf around my neck it will make the thing better?"

"Not around your neck, Sofia. Your waist."

Chapter Ten

Car came back from the road trip hurting bad. Skip had finally started him, and Car delivered like always. True, Seattle's pitcher held him hitless, but in the field, Car had robbed Seattle's Aron Percival of his first homer of the season, which if Car hadn't hauled some serious ass and reeled that bad boy in would have won the game for Seattle. But Car hadn't come away unscathed. He'd banged up his shoulder colliding with the right field wall reaching up to snag Percival's long fly.

In Kansas City, Skip put him in as Designated Hitter in the last game of the three-game series, because he was one of the few who could hit their fire-thrower, E.M. Kelly. First time up, he got himself a screaming line drive triple down the left field line, It cleared the bases, earning him his first hit and his first three ribbies of the season. Woo-hoo.

He'd been icing his shoulder ever since Seattle, had held his breath until Zeke and the whole damn bunch of trainers had looked at it and said it would be okay. Thank you, God. What he didn't need was a new injury.

After they left Kansas City, he'd talked to Skip and Skip said what Car thought he would; he'd play him regular when it was time to play him. Which is what guys, who were thirty-four and didn't play like they did when they were twenty-four, got used to hearing. That was when he dredged up the question he'd been asking himself a lot: what was he going to do with the rest of his life? He still didn't have an answer.

On the plane ride back, Car sat by himself, not up for

conversation. He rubbed his shoulder, stiff and cold from the ice pack, and wished the trainers hadn't stowed the big ice blankets. He was aching in places where he didn't think he could ache.

"You okay there, Car?"

He looked up. Naturally, it was Dawg asking.

"Yeah. I'm chilling."

Dawg's gaze lit on the ice pack. His eyes widened. "Good one." He laughed and left.

Car laughed too. The pun was unintentional, but lightened his mood anyway. His eyes were closed when he felt a nudge on his shoulder.

"Wanna beer?"

Dawg was back. With refreshments, at least.

Car took the offered Molson and twisted off the cap. "You the designated scout? Somebody send you up here?"

"Nah, I'm here on my own." Dawg eased himself into the empty seat across the aisle and took a slug of his own Molson. "So, how you doing?"

Car laughed. "I'm fine. Just dealing with the usual. The career. My kid."

Dawg shoved his seat back almost prone. "Season's early. You got time to worry about your career. And there's nothing to worry about with Noah. He's with his grand-pop." He raised the bottle to his lips and took a swallow. "Tina called me before we took off."

"Tina calls you all the time. What's new about that?"

"She called to tell me about Sofia."

Car straightened. "So?"

Silence.

"So?" Car said again, this time with an edge in his voice.

Dawg smiled. "At least she's one problem you don't have to think about anymore."

"She's not a problem."

More silence from Dawg.

"You going to tell me what's going on or do I need to get up and yank it out of you?"

Dawg laughed. "Nah. I like giving you a hard time."

"You did. Now talk. What did Tina tell you?"

"That your idea of dressing Sofia up worked. She's out

showing off her new self, and getting reaction. Tina says she was on Access Hollywood last night and she was slammin'."

"That was fast." A worm of unease crawled through Car's gut. "Is she doing the showing off by herself? Or with someone else?"

"Not by herself. With Rex Bellamy."

"She's been with Bellamy?" Car gripped his Molson hard.

Dawg folded his hands across his stomach and closed his eyes. "Yup. He and Tina have the same agent. Tina asked the agent to get them together."

Car lifted the ice bag off his shoulder. He stared straight ahead at the seat back in front of him, his brain seething with wild and crazy thoughts about Sofia with the cross-town New York Stars hot-shot third baseman.

"You got nothin' to say?"

Car shrugged. "What do I care who she's with?"

"Tina didn't say she was *with* him. So to speak."

"Being with Bellamy, it makes her look like one of his airhead babes."

"Makes her look hot. And wasn't that the idea? For her to look hot?"

"Yeah well, somebody should tell her she shouldn't be flaunting it with a guy of Bellamy's reputation."

"I repeat. Wasn't that the idea? Get her a bad girl rep?"

"Not that bad."

"Dude, we a little exercised?"

"Bite me."

"Nah, I don't think so." Dawg snapped the seat back into its upright position and hauled himself to his feet. "I'm gone." He pointed at the bottle Car held in a death grip. "That's so you can cry in your beer all by yourself."

"Fuck you." For a crazy moment, Car thought about standing to deliver the suggestion.

"Nope." Dawg put up a staying hand. "I am loyal to my wife."

Car squeezed his eyes shut and gave his head one good shake. "Look, I appreciate it, man." If Sofia was hitting her stride, he'd done his job. "Thank Tina for me, okay?"

"Sure thing." Dawg left, this time Car hoped for the duration of the flight.

Car knew he should be happy, even relieved. Without doing too much with Sofia—one dinner, and a part of an evening at Pitti Palace—she was on her way to getting noticed and getting that audition.

He rubbed hard in the middle of his forehead where the mother of a headache had come on him like he'd been beaned by one of Kelly's heaters. He closed his eyes. Snapped them open almost at once because of what he saw behind his lids: a vision of Sofia with Rex Bellamy. In bed.

The idea of Sofia with her pretty, cream-tinted skin—which he could only imagine because he hadn't seen any of it—her little waist, those beautiful breasts and lush hips, naked, with Bellamy—Car shook in a rage so intense it was a wonder the bolts holding his seat to the fuselage didn't snap in half.

Car fumed until it came to him clear as a sunny day in May at Denver's Coors Field. Maybe Brent had blackmailed him to be with Sofia. Maybe Sofia really was with Bellamy. God, he hoped not. But if he was jealous of Bellamy, he was feeling something for Sofia he hadn't come clean with himself about, and it was more than him loving her voice.

Car blinked himself back to the now. He estimated they'd be landing at Newark in twenty minutes. He gathered up his playbook, his audiobook on the Galapagos Islands, and his MP3 player, and got himself ready to make an exit the moment the plane's doors opened at the gate.

He needed to see her. This woman, who he'd wanted nothing to do with. This woman he now wanted *something* to do with. God knew what; Car didn't understand it.

But tonight? Tonight he was going to do his damnedest to find out.

Sofia opened her closet doors over and over again in the days after she shopped with Tina. There they were. The clothes that would change her life: the dresses, the trousers, the jersey and silk tops in jewel tones of every shade. They spoke to her of the new Sofia, the new, sexy Sofia.

Of all her new outfits, the one she knew she'd wear when Car returned from his long 16 days' trip on the road, was the bright, white blouse and the black trousers. And the lacy bra. She hung the blouse and trousers on a hanger on the outside of her closet and stared at them every day.

She hadn't given a thought to wearing this outfit on her supposed date with Rex Bellamy. She didn't feel the need to be sexy for him. In the limousine they took to the party, the one the agent arranged for them to attend, Rex said, "You know Car's going to beat my...uh...beat me up when he finds out we're together." He smiled at her with his too-white teeth and his bright-as-the-sky blue eyes.

"But we are not together, Rex. It is only for the *paparazzi*." Sofia knew women loved this handsome man for his charm and his beauty.

Rex patted her cheek. "Believe me, sweet thing, if Car got a look at us, he'd be plenty ticked off. He doesn't like to share his women."

"He does not?" Her smile fled. Now that she was transformed into the new Sofia, she did not like to be reminded of Car's women.

"Nope. Not while they're with him."

Sofia had made herself forget Car thought of her as a job. But being honest with herself, she reasoned there was little difference between him calling her a job and she making use of Car's reputation to get the audition.

She forced a bright smile like Adina's in *L'Elisir d'Amore* when she thought Nemorino didn't want her as he had before. "Well, I am with him now." Thinking she shouldn't insult Rex, she added, "And also you."

Rex gave her a melting smile Sofia was sure caused thousands of women to indulge themselves in fainting spells. She wasn't one of those thousands. Still, she was surprised when he brushed a soft kiss across her lips. "If I didn't like Car so much, I might think about moving in on him."

Sofia didn't understand why Rex thought he could

move into Car's apartment. But she did know she had almost let Rex see her weakness. She wouldn't do that again.

Though she'd known when Car was to return from his road trip, she didn't expect him at the hotel the night his plane landed. Now he was downstairs in the lobby. Her party, although almost over, was still going on in her suite. How could she explain why he couldn't come up? She knew she had to tell him someday. But not tonight. She couldn't stand it if, tonight, while she wore her beautiful new outfit for him, he laughed.

Taking the elevator down to the lobby, she worried over what story she would tell him. When the doors opened, that worry fell away. There he stood, filling her vision. His blue-green eyes glowed in the light of the crystal chandeliers. His brown-blond hair had lightened and grown. There was a funny peak at the center of his hair line. His face was the rich color that comes from spending much time in the sun. He was dressed in jeans and a dark brown leather jacket, open over an olive-colored tee-shirt. The jeans were worn and a little frayed; the jacket scuffed. He was the handsomest man she'd ever seen.

She hurried toward him. "You are back. *Bene!*"

Car was still trying to figure out why Chelsea had told him to wait in the lobby when the elevator doors opened and Sofia stepped out. His mouth opened. And closed. Her hair was not in its usual bun. It cascaded freely over her shoulders, down her back in darkest brown, runaway waves and curls. He took a step back. And saw what she was wearing. Took a step forward. And found himself staring down at her... cleavage.

He swallowed and continued to stare. If she hadn't made a sound, he might have continued to stare until next spring training.

Reluctantly he lifted his eyes. There was a blush on her

amazing face, stars shining in her black eyes. He looked down again. She wasn't wearing black. Well, the trousers were black, of some shiny material that shaped her rounded hips. He couldn't describe the blouse. The lacy bra beneath? *That* he could describe. There were things the lace did to her breasts, things his hands wanted to do. He glanced to his right and left. Was anyone looking?

No.

Good.

Because no one but he should be able to look down at Sofia's lace-covered breasts and see what he saw. He crowded closer.

"What do you think, Car?" Anxious eyes appealed. "My ensemble: it is pleasing?"

Pleasing? No. It was hot. *She* was hot. Everything about her was hot. "Yes, very pleasing." His eyes roved over her outfit, imagining the body beneath.

"We think perhaps a scarf around the waist, yes?" She put her hands there. "But we decide too much material. A belt is better. Do you agree?"

Car had never been asked for an opinion on scarves as opposed to belts, but he was ready to offer one now. "Hmm, let's see." He slipped his hands under hers to encircle her waist, the heels of his hands resting on her hips, the fingers of each hand practically touching at the small of her back. Oh man, what a waist; what a perfect waist. "I think the belt," he said, having to clear his throat to get his tongue off the roof of his mouth.

"That is good then." She laid her palms flat on his chest and began a slow, sweeping motion, smoothing her hands over him, from his nipples to his navel and back. Her hands made a shushing sound against the fabric of his tee-shirt. The feel of her hands on his body arrowed straight down to his dick, which appreciated the torture. But his dick had to stand in line and take a number. First things first. He pulled away.

"So what's going on upstairs? Is Rex Bellamy there?"

Her lips twitched. "Rex is not upstairs."

Car relaxed. A little. "When I called before, it sounded like you had a party going on."

Her hands stopped moving. She stepped out of his

arms. "It was what I tell you. A party. But not a party."

"Which is it then?"

She stiffened. "*Non é niente.*"

It was nothing? She wasn't going to tell him? No problem. Car Bradford didn't have a lifetime batting average of .311 striking himself out before the ump pulled the string.

"How's it going with this guy, Lupino?" he asked, switching gears—or seeming to. "Has he given you a time to sing for him?"

She took another step back. "No."

"That's not good."

"No."

"I think I've come up with a solution." He had. Just now.

Curiosity replaced wariness in those fathomless black eyes. "What is the solution?"

"We need to concentrate on getting people to think we're lovers."

She slapped a hand over her mouth. "*Dovremmo essere amanti?*"

Gently he tapped her nose. "English, Sofia. English."

She licked her lips with a pointy little pink tongue. Thinking its number had at last been called, his dick once more came to attention.

"I am asking: do you say we must be lovers?"

"That was kind of the idea at first. Remember?" She looked everywhere but at him. "But we let it go. So now I have to ask you: would *you* like us to be lovers?"

A feverish red colored her cheekbones. "I am a virgin."

For a moment he wasn't sure he'd heard right. It wasn't every day women blurted out that particular piece of information. Naturally, Sofia would. He'd thought it was the case way back when. All the evidence had been there. He put his hands on her shoulders and drew her against him. She was trembling and his heart melted. She was his very own sweet, trembling virgin. He held her away from him, looked down. Beneath the lace of her sinful bra, he could see the rapid beat of her heart.

Would you like us to be lovers? He was very serious about this. But as with everything else with Sofia, he knew the path to them becoming lovers would have a lot of curves, detours, and red lights. His virginal Sofia was going to need tender, loving care. And romance.

"Do you want me to show you how it would work?" he whispered, warning his dick to relax. Not that it was listening anymore.

Head bent, she was busy rubbing one thumb against the other. She nodded, a quick jerk of her head.

He took her hand, looked around for a place where no one would see them, and led her to one of the half-moon alcoves on the periphery of the lobby. The alcove held a chair and a ridiculously small table, just big enough to hold a cocktail napkin. He dispensed with the table by hooking a foot around one of the spindly legs, and pulling it out of the way.

He put his arms around her, brought her up against his chest, leaving not one fraction of one inch between her white blouse and his olive green tee. He ran the backs of his fingers across her baby-soft cheek, and bent toward her. Her eyes widened. Her mouth opened. It gave him the perfect opportunity.

Which he took.

He bent, angled his head first one way and then the other, ran his tongue across her lips, and rubbed his mouth against hers. He nipped at her full lower lip, insisted upon entry, pulsed his tongue against hers.

At first she stood stiff within his arms. But by the time she put her arms around his neck, by the time she pressed her breasts against his rib cage, by the time her trembling legs strained against his thighs, he forgot what he was doing.

Panting, gasping, her fingers kneaded the fabric of his shirt. She arched and thrust against him. Where before she'd passively received his tongue, now she did some fencing of her own. She wasn't good at it. He didn't care.

When Sofia began to pull away, it didn't register. Not at first. Not until she said, "Car, *per favore*. Please. We must stop. People, they look."

He let her down, making an effort to control his breathing. "Then I guess we better take this somewhere private."

Chapter Eleven

This was Sofia's best dream. *Signore* Beautiful Eyes and she, lovers. She didn't try to control the tremble in her voice or the overflowing joy in her heart. "Yes, let us go," she whispered, thinking how strange; these were the same words Zerlina, the foolish peasant girl, said to Don Giovanni in the great Mozart opera, after Don Giovanni convinced her to go to bed with him.

Dizzy with Car's lemon-lime scent, she'd lost herself in the feel of his mouth on hers, where it grazed the corner of her eye, and whispered against her neck in the shivery place behind her ear. He'd crowded her, the furnace-like heat of his palm running down the outside of her thigh scalding her with his intent. "I'll get a room," he murmured.

Muzzy with rioting emotions, she didn't understand. "But I have a room."

He took her hand and started toward the front desk. "Yeah, and a party going on."

She had forgotten. She pulled back. He stopped and turned toward her.

"We cannot do this," she whispered.

"Why not?"

She pulled her hand from his. "I must go back." She looked up at Car, hoping he would understand.

His eyes narrowed, and he shook his head.

He didn't understand. Her heart beat fast, but it was no longer in anticipation of becoming his lover. Now she'd have to do what she didn't want to: tell him about the parties.

Car knew Sofia wanted him, maybe even more than he wanted her. But what this blowing hot and cold of hers was: that he didn't understand. Maybe it was about her virginity. Maybe it was about the audition. Maybe it was about some god-awful secret she was afraid to tell him. Whatever, he needed to know because he wasn't going to let anything stop him from having her. Not now. Reaching down, he linked her hand with his. "Okay, let's get this mess straightened out."

He led her into the bar, where it was cool and quiet, and guided her over to a corner table. They sat; he shifted his chair next to hers. "What's going on?"

Sofia wouldn't look at him. Instead, she pretended an interest in the pianist, who was playing Sinatra's *My Way*.

A waiter stepped up to their table. Car ordered a dessert wine. When he left, Car gave Sofia a nudge on her shoulder.

She turned away from the pianist and gave Car a weak smile.

He prodded. "Maybe Bellamy is really upstairs?"

She giggled.

"C'mon. Time to come clean. What's up with the parties?"

The waiter arrived with the wine.

"It is hard to tell you, but I will try," Sofia said, once Car poured her a glass. She took a sip. "When I travel to different opera houses in Europe, I am often by myself at night. My papa leaves me to go out with the music directors, and the opera house managers."

She twisted the stem of the wine glass. "You do not know this, but I love to do the cooking. When I am in the hotels, I ask always for a suite so there is a kitchen and I cook for myself. And sometimes for others. Since I am in New York, I cook, and I make some parties. I invite certain people to come and eat my food."

"That's why your suite smells like an Italian restaurant."

Her chin came up. "I give myself pleasure when I cook. And them too."

He touched his knee to hers. "Don't get huffy. That's not criticism."

After a moment, she took another sip of wine. "I do not have real friends; only work friends, like Maria Torelli. And Chelsea. So I make friends with the people who work in the hotel. The men who hold the doors open, the ladies who make the beds, the nice ones who stand all day and night at the reception desk and give you the room key after you have lost it every day for two weeks." Very carefully, she set the glass down. "And when I do this, I am not lonely."

Car sat back, floored. He remembered when she first talked about her parties and how he was annoyed she didn't think he was good enough to mingle with her friends, the opera types, who, undoubtedly, were who she'd invited to her parties. How wrong he'd been. She was no snob. She cooked for people who worked in the hotel, who even though it was their job to smile at her, gave her that gift of friendship she craved.

"And..." She spoke so softly, Car had to bend forward to hear her. "I know this is not normal what I do. But with my parties, it is like I am normal. With real friends, just like everyone else."

A rush of compassion washed over him. She wanted what everyone else had, what they didn't even think about because they had it. It explained so much more about her than he knew before: how she'd grown up. Which was when he remembered what Chelsea had said to him. *Get her to tell you about her father.* There: the answer was there. Never taking his eyes from hers, he moved both glasses and the bottle aside, and reached for her hands. "You're a special person, Sofia de' Medici."

She tried to pull her hands away, failed, made a face. "I am not special."

Squeezing her hands, he said, "Yes, you are. Tell me about your father."

Her hands spasmed. "Why?"

"I want to know about the Sofia who has such a beautiful heart, how she grew up with it living in the house with her father."

"He is my father. There is nothing else to say."

"I think there is."

Resistance, whatever little there was, went out of her. She slumped. "All my life I try to be a good daughter, but he tells me I do not succeed."

"It's hard for me to believe you've ever been anything but the best." Car ran a finger down her arm. "Except maybe when you ask crazy questions."

The tiny smile she gave him was as fleeting as the Chicago Cubs' annual quest to win a pennant.

"I am a big disappointment to him."

"Why?"

Her eyes, always so intense, went unfocused. "My papa married my mama when he had more than fifty years, so perhaps he did not want a child because he was old. But when he got me, he realizes he wants my voice." Her jaw tightened. "I take voice lessons from when I am six. He likes how I sing, except when he does not, and then he punishes me. He sends me to my room, which is small and dark. He locks the door. There I wait. Sometimes I wait until the next morning."

"Alone? What if you had to go to the bathroom?"

She jerked her hands from his and flushed a dark red. "That is part of the punishment. I must use a..." Her voice trailed off.

She had to use a bottle. Or a pail. Sofia's fucking father had treated her like a dog. Car's head filled with white-hot rage. He pressed his lips together and breathed deeply through his nose. The last thing she needed was to see the violence inside him, even if it was directed at her father.

"When he unlocks the door, I cannot stand the light for a time, and I am very hungry and very thirsty."

"I guess so." He took her hands again. She didn't realize he had. He firmed his grip, hoping the heat of his hands would penetrate into hers, now cold as winter. "But I don't understand. What was he punishing you for? It couldn't have been your voice."

"He says..." She squeezed her eyes shut against

remembered pain. "He says my body is too fat and so he must keep me from eating food like pasta."

Now Car understood. Sofia's fixation with food. He shifted closer. Her father's savagery... he had no words. He pried her hands apart and took both in his. He squeezed. Gently. "Did he ever hit you?" he asked, his voice just above a whisper.

She swallowed hard. "No, he never punishes me this way."

He sagged in relief. One small thing: her father hadn't taken abuse to the next monstrous level. "How long did the starving business go on?"

"Until I begin to perform. After I start my career, he can no longer do this because we are in hotels and I can order room service." She opened her eyes. "There are many things I can do now and he can no longer stop me."

"Like traveling to New York to sing *Carmen*. You escaped."

She nodded. "It rained much in Florence this winter and spring. One day, my papa, he is in a big rush to meet the music director of the *Teatro Communale* and make more arrangements for my career. He falls on the wet pavement and breaks his leg in many places. He goes to the hospital. I am sorry for it, but not so sorry I stop myself from going to the airport in Milan."

Car's mother had had her own cruel way of punishing him. Guilt was her specialty. But she'd never starved him, or locked him in his room and made him pee in a bottle. He wondered if de' Medici was out of the hospital. He wondered how it would feel to be able to put him back there.

Or the morgue.

Two nights later, Sofia sat next to Car, in the Hummer on their way up to Vauxhall on the Hudson. Quiet. Not Sofia. Was she sorry she'd told him about her father? He couldn't tell, because she didn't say. He hadn't slept too well last night or the night before, unable to get what she'd told him out of his mind. Now he understood the odd combination of Sofia's great confidence in her voice and the overwhelming anxiety about her body and yes, the business with food. He could almost picture the lonely child she had been, and how she longed for friends, any kind of friends. He couldn't make it up to her for her crappy childhood. But he could be there for her now.

He risked a sideways glance at her. Tonight she wore a deep pink dress of some soft stuff, like wool, but softer, with a thin gold belt that fell across her hips. She was wearing her hair loose. It fell over her shoulders and down her back. He couldn't wait to get his hands in all those curls.

"You know where we're going, right?"

She sat a little straighter. "I do not know."

A couple of years ago, Car went to one of these fund-raiser gigs at Vauxhall on the Hudson, which was a ways upstate on the Hudson River, and his date, a blonde, almost as tall as he, squealed in his ear the whole time about how romantic it was. Which was why he'd thought it a perfect place to take Sofia. "It's a place you can't get into unless you know someone."

She unfolded her hands. The shadow of a smile threatened the corners of her mouth. "You know someone, yes?"

"I *am* someone," he answered, thinking a joke was in order.

"It is good to be famous." She turned toward him.

Those eyes of hers almost swallowed her face. It was dusk; the street lights blinked on. He opened his window to let in the sweet, spring air. "Vauxhall doesn't open until July, except for this VIP thing they do in early May." He pointed to the thick white throw in her lap. "You'll need that shawl for the musical performance, which will be outside."

"There is a musical performance?" A note of curiosity entered her voice.

"Some group called the Camera Bonn."

"Ah. You mean to say the Camerata Bonn. They are a

wonderful ensemble that performs baroque music. That is the music from when Louis the Fourteenth was king of France."

"Louis the Fourteenth?"

"Yes, the one who had all the hair and many mistresses."

Car knew about Louis the Fourteenth. He'd just borrowed an audiobook about the Sun King from the library. Still he'd wanted to hear what Sofia-like thing would come out of her mouth. Hair and mistresses—vintage Sofia. "So how do you know about this Camerata Bonn?"

"I sing with them."

"Maybe you want to say hello to these guys."

"Ladies."

"Yeah, ladies."

Right away Sofia could tell Vauxhall on the Hudson was beautiful. Even as they circled the gravel driveway, stones crunching beneath the wheels, Sofia felt its magic. Shaded yellow and red lanterns cast warm light across a drive filled with Jaguars and Mercedes. No Hummers though. People alighting from their vehicles gave Car's Hummer haughty stares, as if it didn't belong, as if its presence was offensive. She wanted to tell them to mind their own business.

As Car lifted her down, Sofia caught the eye of a woman with Botox lips and bleached white-blond hair, worn girlishly long. She was of the *Signora*'s age. She stared at Sofia, cool as the *Signora*, before she turned her gaze toward Car and smiled. Was this woman wondering how Car could have chosen her as his date? Sofia felt a tick of anxiety wash over her and stared down at her shoes.

For two whole days, since her discussion with Car about her parties—and her father—she'd done nothing, not even her exercises. Chelsea kept asking if there was something wrong. It was better to lie and say she had a two-day headache than to admit she had disgusted the handsomest man in the world with her pathetic story of how she grew up.

He'd wanted to sleep with her. She might be a virgin, but she knew what an aroused penis felt like. She had felt his through his trousers. Now? Now, the way she kept wrecking everything, she had as much chance of feeling that penis in the flesh as getting the audition.

A spurt of temper overrode her anxiety. What was the matter with her? When would she stop letting others—her father, the *Signora*, and *Signore* Silver—make her feel she was a failure? When would she let women like the Botox lady think she wasn't worthy of Car's attention? Hadn't she had the evidence of Car's penis saying otherwise?

She tossed her hair so it swished across her back, just as the disdainful models did at Pitti Palace. She challenged Botox Lady, with her own cool stare. At last the woman looked away. Sofia kept her satisfied smile to herself, took Car's arm, and walked with him into Vauxhall on the Hudson.

They came to a high arch, a white-latticed canopy of spring flowers—deep blue, almost purple hyacinths, white snowdrops, and yellow daffodils. "*Bellissimo,*" Sofia said, now both hands clutching his arm.

"I wish you'd speak English. And watch where you're going. Those shoes of yours..." Car pulled away from her and looked down. "Do you own any without foot-long heels?"

She stopped, lifted one shoe, and wiggled it. She did not understand dresses and trousers and blouses and gold link belts. But she understood shoes. "Yes, they are high, but they must be. The world is tall and I am short."

"I did notice you're short. But there's nothing wrong with short."

Whatever she might have said to his teasing grin, was lost as they crossed into the clearing. She came to a stop. "*Ancora piu bello,*" she breathed. Before them, the path divided into many paths, all leading to little tents, which were trimmed with tiny, winking lights along their bottom edges. The tents were open on the clearing side, and inside each, a round table. It was a landscape painting come to life.

A woman in a long skirt and glasses with black frames took their tickets and led them to one of the smaller tents. Inside, a table set for two. In the center of the table, which was covered with a white cloth, sat a squat, rectangular, glass vase with more hyacinths and daffodils. To the side, a floor heater to cut the cool evening air.

"Good evening." A waiter stepped into their tent. He gave them each a menu and began to recite a list of added dishes.

Sofia heard him from a distance, her focus on the menu with its selection of sandwiches and salads. She looked up. Interrupting the waiter's litany, she said, "*Pranzo.*"

"Huh?" The waiter's mouth fell open.

"*Pranzo*, lunch, I am saying this is a menu for the lunch."

The waiter's mouth closed. "Oh no, ma'am. We don't have a lunch menu."

"Sofia," Car interrupted. "This place is about the atmosphere. The food is secondary."

She ran her eyes over the right side of the menu. "But the prices, they are not secondary."

With one long finger, Car tipped the top of her menu down. Sofia found herself staring into his serious blue-green eyes.

"I don't care what this night costs, sweetheart. It's all for you."

Leaning toward him she whispered, "It is enough you take me here, Car. I know you do not want me anymore and it is okay."

Car had known he was going to have to navigate through many curves with his shy, virginal Sofia. He reached across the table to take her hand in his. "Don't want you?" Car wanted Sofia with a fierceness he'd never before experienced. He didn't care if the waiter or anyone else knew. Or heard. He wanted to declare himself so the world understood how he felt about her. "You could not be more wrong."

Sofia glanced at the waiter and colored up a fiery red.

She'd seemed more sure of herself, before, after he'd lifted her from the Hummer. But here, again, she was showing him an anxious smile. Yup. Twists and curves. He wasn't going to let them matter.

Satisfied, sitting back, Car said, "We can talk about this later. Meanwhile, why don't we order? I think you won't mind it's just Panini by the time's the evening's over."

She looked back at the menu. "*Allora*, I will have the Panini Tapenade."

The waiter stared at her, blank-faced. Car knew the feeling. "That word, *allora*, it's Italian. It means *then*, as in, 'then she'll have the Panini Tapenade.'"

Her black-as-the-Vauxhall-night eyes smiled her approval.

"I'll have the ham and cheese," Car said, returning her smile with one of his own, no longer looking at the waiter, who went away.

"You learn the Italian just by the listening." Sofia bowed her head to him. "*Bravissimo*. You are a very smart man."

"Nah. I'm what's called a dumb jock."

She turned her head to the side. "A dumb what?"

"Jock. Athlete. In school that's what they call kids who aren't good at academics but are good at sports. I'm good at sports—baseball—but not good with learning."

She made a face at him.

"Now if I want to know something, I've got to listen to it," he explained. "I go to the library, borrow audiobooks, or get downloads." He flipped his MP3 player out of his pocket to show her. "I have to do something to keep from being a dumber jock than I already am." He laughed. He'd been laughing at himself for years. Before anyone else could.

She angled her head to the side and gave him a serious once-over. "Because you find another way to learn? No, no. That makes you smart. Anyone can see how smart you are. If they are smart themselves. I think the ones who say you are the dumb jock? They are the ones who are the dumb jocks."

"Right." He leaned away from her, and studied his fingers where they drummed a mindless beat on his knee.

She tapped the table. He looked up. "I have the admiration for you to solve this problem of learning that is not, to me, a problem."

He said nothing. Couldn't. But he blushed. Blushed!

Their order came quickly, which was fine with him. His struggle to read, the taunts he'd had to listen to all his young life, he'd made it a point never to think of them, and especially not to talk about them. And yet he'd opened up about them with her? Just like he'd opened up that night at the restaurant about Stevie? When had he become such a blabbermouth?

He was relieved when Sofia started to talk about wine.

"We will order a Valpolicella. It goes well with my tapenade and with your prosciutto."

They shared the wine. They shared conversation. They talked about politics. Sofia became animated. He found out she was a lefty, which had nothing to do with which side of home plate she stood on. She was anti-war. She was angry because women didn't earn the same salaries as men. She believed in family leave, unions, cradle-to-grave health care. She was for solar and wind, but not nuclear power. She was a crazy tree-hugger. He was completely the opposite. It gave him one big charge.

They talked about baseball, of which she knew next to nothing, but had a thousand questions. He finally got her to call it home plate, not the home place. He laughed his head off at the look of shock on her face when he told her what she'd been saying.

She gave him a translation of the *Habanera*.

"The soldiers in the square are in love with Carmen when she sings the *Habanera*, right?"

"*Certamente*, but they are a little afraid of her also." Sofia waved her glass at him. The ruby red liquid sloshed back and forth. "They know they cannot control her."

She went on with details of the story she hadn't told him, demonstrating with her knife how, at the start of the opera, Carmen stabs the girl in the factory. People in a nearby tent eyed her nervously.

Car eyed them back.

"When that *disgraziato*, Corporal Zuniga, makes Don José take Carmen to the jail, when she sings the *Seguidilla*, that is when finally Don José gives in to his hunger for her. This is very seductive music." She patted her chest. "I sometimes seduce myself when I sing the melody."

"What's that word? Diz ...?"

"*Disgraziato*. Pig, fool. It depends how you say it, what it means."

He wanted to laugh, had to be careful how he drank his wine in case she ambushed him with one of her observations and he spit all over his shirt. When the waiter cleared the table, Car said, "How do you feel about meeting up with your friends?"

She paused, her napkin halfway to her mouth. "My friends?"

"Yes. Camerata Bonn."

"*Fantastico*." She clapped her hands.

He didn't need a translation for that. He stood, the chair making a scraping sound against the tiles. "Let's go before the crowd gets in the way."

Chapter Twelve

The five women were overjoyed to see Sofia. Car stood to one side while they did the two-cheek kissing thing. He still couldn't figure out what was with these Europeans and the double-tap.

They all spoke German, even Sofia. "So, ladies," he interrupted. They stopped mid-word. "Can you share with the one person who doesn't speak the language?"

Sofia clapped a hand across her mouth. "I am so sorry." She introduced Berta, the nearest of the women, a tall, lanky brunette, and then the rest. They gave him no-nonsense handshakes.

"We have been telling Sofia about our tour in the States," Berta said.

"And we talk about next year," Sofia added, "When we think it is possible for us to perform together."

"Yes," said Berta. "I was about to tell Sofia we're performing tonight with a colleague of hers."

Sofia's face brightened. "Who?"

"Lorenzo Latte."

Sofia stilled. "Lorenzo is here in America?"

The other women continued to chatter. In German. Car barely listened. He was too focused on Sofia's reaction—not a positive one—to Berta's news.

"He's in the States to meet with someone, I don't know who," Berta explained. "He arranged to join us before returning to Europe."

Sofia sighed. "Ah."

One sound, lots of meaning, Car thought. He opened his mouth to ask who this Lorenzo was, when someone—a man—from somewhere beyond the tent began to laugh. It was dramatic and, if Car had to guess, staged.

Sofia patted her hair and smoothed down her dress just as a man burst into the tent.

He was short, stocky, wore gray slacks and a striped, dark pink and white shirt with a collar that stood up above the lapels of his black jacket. The shirt was unbuttoned a good ways down his torso, revealing a mat of black and gray hair.

The moment he saw Sofia, he stopped mid-stride. A look of dismay passed across his forehead. He took a big breath and said, "Sofia! Darling! What a surprise."

"*Salve*, Lorenzo. *Come stai?*" she said.

"I am very well, but we must speak English for your friend, who does not have the look of someone who speaks Italian." He smiled at Car, all teeth. "She asked how I was."

"That's okay. I understood." Which he didn't.

"You are the new boyfriend?" Latte raised his eyebrows. "I am the old boyfriend."

Sofia inched, if possible, closer to Car. "*Che imbecille,*" she muttered.

Car slid one hand under the curls at the back of her neck and held out the other to Latte. "Car Bradford, the new boyfriend."

"Lorenzo Latte, and I am happy to meet the great American baseball star." Lorenzo's hand was silky-soft, not a callus or rough spot anywhere. "You have heard our Sofia sing?"

"I have. Even though I'm just learning about opera, to my way of thinking, she's got one amazing voice."

Lorenzo nodded his slick, black head. Car would have bet his place back in the rotation he was looking at one helluva dye job.

"Amazing, yes." Lorenzo chuckled again. "The mezzo voice can be a wonder." He pantomimed a shiver, threw his hands out, and looked heavenward.

Asshole.

"And the mezzos who sing *bel canto*—the Rossini, the Donizetti, the Bellini—this is music that our dear Sofia sings so wonderfully well," Lorenzo said, continuing with the blah-blah-blah. "She has such a rich, low register."

Lorenzo patted Sofia on the shoulder.

Sofia stiffened, her smile frozen in place.

"Our Sofia has great technical control, but perhaps not..." Latte's voice trailed off, leaving off the rest, hanging it out in a deafening silence.

Car waited a beat, turned to Berta, and said, "You know, you guys need to be alone to do whatever you do before a performance. Practice, maybe." He slid his hand down Sofia's arm, took her hand, and steered her toward the exit. "Why don't we leave them alone, Sofia?"

As Car pushed the flap aside, Lorenzo said, "If Sofia should tell you what happened at La Scala in February, you must understand she could have picked up the patch and the—umm—without a problem."

Sofia's hand tightened like a vise on Car's fingers.

Lorenzo tapped Car on the shoulder. "Afterward I tried to explain..."

Car was already ticked at Lorenzo for slamming Sofia. He'd resisted the urge to retaliate in front of the women. No more. "When were you an item?"

Lorenzo's eyes opened wide. "An item?"

"Yeah, a couple." Car made a circular motion. "You know, together. Boyfriend and girlfriend. Although, calling yourself a boy..."

It took Lorenzo a moment to gather himself. "You're right. It's silliness to speak this way." He swerved around to the Germans, who had been listening with undisguised interest. "We should go over the Strauss, yes? Just once more."

Car didn't hear the rest. He was steering Sofia outside.

Only when they got back to their little pavilion did she speak, her jaw clenched, temper burning black in her eyes. "I did not pick up the patch, although it was there on the floor."

"But you picked up something."

"I had to."

"What?"

"His teeth."

For one moment Car was still. And then he exploded into laughter. Except for the way irritation marked Sofia's face, he might have laughed until morning.

She flopped into her chair. "It is not funny."

"Sofia, sweetheart, I'm sorry. I shouldn't have laughed." He eased into his chair, and leaned his elbows on the table. "Tell me about February and that boyfriend of yours."

"*Che mascalzone*, he is no boyfriend of mine. He tries to be once, but does not succeed. He does succeed in spreading the rumors about me to the music directors everywhere, perhaps even Maestro Lupino."

"What, that you sing like an angel?"

She waved his compliment away.

"What happened? Other than Lorenzo dropping his teeth?" Car moved his chair closer.

For a moment her eyes took on a faint sparkle, but almost at once, the sparkle disappeared.

"C'mon now," he said, his voice firming, as if he were speaking to a rookie who'd just dropped an easy pop-up. "Open up. Talk. Stop holding back."

She sighed. "In La Scala in February, we perform *Marriage of Figaro*, and I play Cherubino. Lorenzo plays Count Almaviva. The Count is cheating on his wife. He thinks this is okay. But for his Countess to cheat, especially with the boy, Cherubino, who is perhaps fifteen and only dreams he is doing the cheating, this would not be okay."

"Cherubino has a crush on her."

She nodded. "In the scene, the Count is furious with Cherubino—that is me. I am hiding and—how you say—the position of the body when it is bent with the knees up to the mouth...?" She said, the last word gliding up in a question.

"Crouching," Car supplied.

"Yes, Cherubino—that is I—crouches behind a chair. At last, the Count—that is Lorenzo—finds me and pulls me out and that is when it happens."

She twisted her hands in her lap. He grabbed her hands, and wouldn't let them go. "Tell me, Sofia. I promise it's not as bad as you think." He hoped that was true.

She took a deep breath and said, "That is when his teeth fall from his mouth as he opens it wide to sing the big note. The teeth fall in front of me. The patch, the one the wardrobe mistress puts on his cheek, also falls because Lorenzo has too much sweat. I leave the patch." She faltered. "But I pick up the teeth."

With iron control on his laugh reflex, Car said, "Why didn't you leave them?"

Her eyes widened. "But Car, I cannot do this, even though Lorenzo is the rat to me, and there, while we are singing, he is spitting and sweating, the saliva is falling from his mouth onto my face, and he smells."

She looked at him to see if he understood. Oh, did he ever. "And so you picked up his teeth and handed them over."

She threw her hands in the air. "If only that is what I did, but I know people will laugh if I do that, because then Lorenzo must stop and put his teeth in his mouth, and how will that look? The audience will laugh and the next day there will be terrible blogging and tweeting, perhaps people will read about it in the newspapers. Lorenzo will not go anywhere, even to walk on the street, without people opening the mouth wide and pretending to let their teeth fall out. I do not like Lorenzo, but I do not wish him such a bad thing."

"So you...?"

"I pretend to hit him in the face and that is when I push the teeth back into his mouth. Then I turn him so his back is to the audience and he can make the adjustment. This is even though Cherubino would not dare to hit the Count, because the Count would chop off his head."

Car made like he was coughing.

She sighed. "The teeth, they do not fit the right way. Perhaps the glue did not work and that is why the teeth fall to the floor? I do not know. But he does not sing so well because he must continue to adjust the teeth.

"After, Lorenzo cannot admit this embarrassing thing. So he says I try to upstage him, him the star, and my punch is so powerful he cannot support his vocal line. He says his bad singing is my fault."

Car tried to imagine how Sofia felt, shaking in Cherubino's boots. "He kept saying you were the one who was the screw-up?"

"Most assuredly, yes."

"I have one question."

She raised an eyebrow.

"How does the man sing these days without his teeth?"

Sofia waved a dismissive hand in the air. "He does what he should do long ago, but he did not because he fears the dentist. He gets the implants."

"I guess you'll never have to pick up his teeth again."

With one hand, she covered the smile that threatened.

"I wouldn't worry about Lorenzo anymore. He's just one person, Sofia. He's said what he's going to say. Let it go."

"But his mouth is more than one person. It is so big, the story of what I did is in all the opera houses of Europe. Nobody believes me when I try to explain. Why should they? I am only a new mezzo. Lorenzo is a star. My papa believes Lorenzo. When I return to the hotel that night, he yells. Am I a whore? Do I want to destroy all my chances doing something stupid? Now I think the story is here in America. My reputation is ruined before I can prove it is not my reputation."

Car sat back, his brain grappling for purchase on this new, unwelcome thought. "Are you saying after everything we've done, the new clothes, the paparazzi, it's not your looks, or your voice, or even your age? It's this business with the teeth? That's why the guy at the Municipal Opera House won't see you?"

The corners of Sofia's generous mouth turned down. "Yes, I need the paparazzi to take my picture, and yes, I must wear different clothes, clothes that Carmen would wear if she is living now. But how is Maestro Lupino so busy he cannot make one phone call to me when I call him many dozens of times? Do you doubt Lorenzo's lie has not reached him? Do you doubt the Maestro thinks I will do something bad that will destroy the production of his beautiful new *Carmen*?"

Sofia's body was stiff with frustration.

"I'm not buying it. Lorenzo could have explained the teeth thing away, said you saved him. Lorenzo has it in for you. Or Lupino. The question is what?"

She paused and looked away. "About Lorenzo perhaps I know." Another pause. "You will think it is a stupid reason."

Car doubted it was stupid. "What?"

She got smaller. "I would not give him me."

He frowned. "Are you saying what I think you're saying?"

She nodded.

Car folded his arms across his chest. "That's definitely not a stupid reason." He tipped his chair back, casual-like, when casual was not how he felt. "What happened?"

Eyes filled with anxiety, Sofia said, "You are thinking I should tell you what happened when Lorenzo wanted my virginity and I would not give it to him?" Sofia didn't want to tell this story. "You will not understand how a person who should say no did not say no."

He brought his chair's front legs down with a loud rap. "I'll understand."

He could say he'd understand. Sofia wasn't so sure. But she'd tell him, because she already knew she could trust Car not to judge her. "From books, I know what it means to have a lover. But only from books."

Car began rocking again.

"When I am older, my papa hires a keeper, *Signora* Griselda Tucci, and I do not get boyfriends, because the keeper goes everywhere with me. She takes my wrist in her bony fingers when we cross the street. She stands outside the door when I go to the ladies room. She watches my lessons. She watches when I dress for the performance. She does all this with unsmiling eyes. I cannot ever escape."

He kept rocking.

"But one day I do escape."

"How?"

"*La Signora* Tucci—the keeper—has the *bronchite*."

"Bronchitis?" His eyebrows rose.

"*Esattamente.* She has the bronchitis and she cannot go with me when I sing my first Rosina."

"Which opera is that?"

"*The Barber of Seville* by Rossini. It has the 'Figaro-Figaro-Figaro' aria. It also has a part for the Count Almaviva. The Mozart opera does too."

"I'm confused. I thought we were talking about Lorenzo."

"Yes, okay. I distract myself." She took a breath. "I am just turned 21. Lorenzo is still in good voice and in demand all over Europe. He has not yet grown the two chins. He is almost handsome."

"He's singing...?"

"He is singing the Count to my Rosina. They are in love. In the opera, Rosina and the Count—Lorenzo and I— must be clasped together. It is like..." She paused for a beat. "It is like if you play the baseball game and it is hot and you are sticky and you must hold Eric—I mean Dawg—close to your chest, and press him in his sweaty uniform against your body and be too close to his underarms. You do not like it, but you do it because you must."

Car brought the front legs of his chair down and clapped a hand to his forehead. "I got the picture."

"When Lorenzo brings me close, I feel everything, even the main part—you know, the big one, although later, I find out from some of the women, Lorenzo's is not so big."

Car turned away. Sofia saw a suspicious sparkle in his eye. She faltered.

Car knew he should have controlled the need to laugh. Now, because of his lack of control, she was thinking she shouldn't tell him the rest. He reached across the table and gave her hand a reassuring squeeze. "I'm listening."

She eyed him with suspicion and paused, but only for a moment. "It is then I think to myself, tonight I have no *Signora* Tucci. I am filled with the curiosity. Lorenzo sweats too much, but perhaps after he bathes, he will not smell so bad that I must breathe through the mouth. I can do the experiment and touch his main part."

All flushed, she folded her hands in her lap. "Lorenzo knows this. When we take the calls at the curtain, he whispers in my ear to come with him to his dressing room.

"What happened then?"

She sighed. "There is no bathing. He cannot wait and he takes me with him."

"And you go."

"Because of the curiosity." Her eyebrows came together. "You see? You have doubts of my intelligence that I would be so stupid."

"That's not what I think. I think you were young and curious."

She shrugged. "He pushes me against the door and

touches my..." She began to lift her hands, but dropped them back into her lap.

Car made a fist and tightened it against his knee. Despite the business of the teeth, which was hilarious, this had never been much of a funny story. It was getting less funny.

"He pushes so hard, I cannot breathe. With the breath I have, I say to him, Lorenzo, perhaps we should take the bath? He likes this suggestion and tells me we will take the bath together. I tell him we should take one for him and one for me. He tries to kiss me, but I do not like this either. His mouth is more smelly than his body. Like garlic that is rotten and teeth that want to fall out."

"Which they did."

"Yes, but that night he still has his real teeth. Again he puts a hand to my breast and he squeezes so hard I feel the pain, even between my eyes. It is then I decide I do not want to feel Lorenzo's main part. It is then Lorenzo begins not to like me so much."

"Because..."

"Because then I yell *aiuto*."

Car had wanted to hear this story. Now what he wanted was to rearrange Lorenzo's face. Keeping it to himself, he said, "Which means?"

"Which means help. Suddenly people are running. When they push down the door, Lorenzo tells everyone he is an innocent man who has been tempted."

Car snorted. "You were twenty-one and he was how old?"

She paused for a moment. "I think perhaps forty-three."

"Pervert." Car pushed his plate away. "This is what Lorenzo has against you. He was embarrassed."

"I did not mean to embarrass him." She was playing with her napkin, folding it into little squares.

"You didn't. He embarrassed himself." Car leaned forward. "That business at La Scala? That was Latte being jealous of you. Deep down, he knew, even then, he didn't have it anymore, and you're the rookie who's going to make it big like he never could."

"He can still sing. Some roles."

Maybe because he was contemplating the end of his own career, Car thought he understood what Latte was going through. Thought. It didn't mean he could sympathize. "Maybe he can, but he'll never be what he once was. Instead of manning up, he takes it out on people who he thinks can't get back at him. Like you. You're the real deal, Sofia. He isn't."

Car didn't know if others thought this was true. But he'd listened to her CD and loved it. So that's what he went with. He raised her hand to his mouth and pressed his lips to her fingers.

She stared at their joined hands, at his lips against her skin. "Thank you for saying this, Car."

He placed her hand on the table and began caressing the flesh at the base of her thumb. "What happened to the keeper?"

"My papa fires her, and hires a guard. The guard goes with me everywhere with his wire in the ear and the folded hands in front of him and the unsmiling mouth and eyes. My papa tells him to make sure I do not try to find out about a man's main part."

Car's mouth dropped open. "Your father said what?"

"He did not say those words," she added hastily. "But they were the words he meant."

"You got rid of the guard too, didn't you?"

"So I could get away from my papa and come to America?"

"Yeah, that."

"It was simple. When my papa goes to the hospital with his broken leg, the guard goes to see him to be paid, but my papa yells that he will have to wait."

"Don't tell me. The guard didn't believe your father would come up with the cash."

"My papa is—how you say...?" She held up her hand and rubbed her fingers together.

"Cheap."

"*Esattamente.*"

"So you go to the airport and meet Chelsea, get on a plane for New York, and the rest I know."

For the longest moment she stared at him, black eyes getting blacker and bigger, saying nothing.

"What's the matter?"

She looked away and then back, sighed and said, "Before. You kiss my hand like a lover."

"Sofia." His hand tightened on hers, pulling her towards him. "It's a promise of things to come."

Chapter Thirteen

"A long time I have hoped you will be serious," Sofia whispered.

"Oh, I'm as serious as a heart attack."

She pressed a hand to her chest, against her own pounding heart. Once more she'd trusted Car with a terrible story. Except for that moment, when she thought he was laughing at her, she knew she was right to trust him. Now, to find out he still wanted her, after everything, it was almost more than she could bear. "A heart attack is serious."

"Yes." A little smile lingered on his mouth. His eyes, so green and blue, sparkled like the waters of the Aegean Sea. "Are you afraid?"

She stiffened. "Me? I am not afraid." But she couldn't look into his eyes.

He grinned. "Can you prove that?"

Even in Italian she couldn't. "*Merda*," she mumbled.

For a moment not even the air breathed. His eyebrows twitched. He looked down at the table and smiled.

"What?" she said, unable to stand his silence.

He raised his head and looked straight at her. "*Merda*? Sofia, even *I* know that word."

The blush started in her toes and crawled through her body to settle in her chest, her neck and of course, because where else would it go but her face? "I am sorry," she said, voice stilted.

"Sweetie." His baritone voice was a low caress. "Because you cursed? Forget it. I know you think maybe us together isn't such a good idea. You're scared."

Now the moment was here and she was going to have to ask some embarrassing questions, made more embarrassing because asking them would make her seem like a child.

"How would we do it?" she asked in a low voice.

"What do you mean? The usual way."

Her hands were clasped together. Squeezed tight, in fact. "You do not remember? I do not know the usual way. I read about the usual way—and the not so usual way—but what is your usual way?"

"What do you want to know?" He made a strange sound. "What it's like when we'd...?" He made the sound again.

"Yes, in the bed. Would we have all the clothes off? Would you remove mine? Would I remove yours? Would it be dark..." She took a deep breath, looked down, and again felt red heat burn her face, "... when you... um..."

"Let's not worry about the details." He sounded like he was strangling. "Why don't we play it by ear?"

She looked up, startled. "The ear is involved too?" What was the matter with her? *The ear is involved too?* Of course the ear wouldn't be involved. Well, perhaps for kisses and, as she thought about it, that wouldn't be so bad.

Car began to laugh; his laughter touched off hers.

"It is not funny," she said, putting the lie to her own words, when chuckles began to bubble up from inside.

What would have come next she wouldn't know, for the sound of steps behind her. She turned to look, and sighed with frustration. Lorenzo. What timing.

"Here you are," he said in a strangely nervous voice.

She began to speak, to tell him to go away, when she saw who was with him.

Antonio Lupino, the Maestro.

Her heart gave a joyous leap. "Yes, here I am," she said. "Lorenzo, you..."

But Lorenzo was looking not at her, but Car. It was toward him he held out his hand, with all the jewel-thick rings on every finger. "Here you are. Wonderful."

Car didn't move or raise a hand from the table to take Lorenzo's. Instead he stared at him flinty-eyed. Lorenzo, who didn't know she'd just told Car the story of how he'd assaulted her, knew Car wanted to do violence to him.

With a stuttering laugh, Lorenzo dropped his hand and said, "I would like to introduce you to one of New York's most illustrious personages, Antonio Lupino, the general manager and music director of the Municipal Opera House."

In an instant, Car came to his feet. His face smoothed out. It was the look Sofia saw on Car's face when he came to home plate to bat. It gave nothing away. "Nice to meet you, Antonio." He reached out a hand to take the Maestro's.

Again Lorenzo laughed, a high, screechy, nervous bray. *Like an ass.*

The Maestro frowned at Lorenzo. To Car he gave a smile that settled on his small mouth, a mouth that went with his narrow face, a smile that showed all his natural European teeth. "This is an amazing pleasure, sir." He turned to Sofia, and said, "May I have the pleasure of being introduced to your lovely companion?"

Car put a hand on Sofia's shoulder. "Of course, Antonio. Say hello to Sofia de' Medici."

Eyes growing large, the smile on the Maestro's face froze in place.

He hadn't recognized her. If she'd been wearing her usual black dress and her hair had been scraped back in the tight bun, he would have. Now she looked like a different woman.

He gave Sofia a jerky nod and shot her a curious look.

It lasted a fraction of a section. Still she saw it. Her breath caught. He must know about La Scala. The story had reached him.

The Maestro turned back to Car and pumped his hand with enthusiasm. "I am such an admirer. When I saw it was you sitting here, I told Lorenzo he must introduce us. He objected. Mightily, I must add, for some reason I fail to understand. Naturally, I insisted."

Ah. Lorenzo hadn't wanted to be near her. Car was right. He was embarrassed.

"Outstanding." Car continued shaking the Maestro's. "I didn't know they liked baseball in Italy."

"I always liked baseball, even before my association with the Mosbachers," the Maestro said, "I am most impressed with your home run output."

"You haven't enjoyed it this year." Car indicated the Maestro and Lorenzo should pull chairs into their tent.

"I'm looking forward to seeing you back in the lineup," said the Maestro, stepping aside as, with a slave-like shuffle, Lorenzo dragged two chairs toward them.

The men paid Sofia no attention. She might as well have been one of those chairs.

"I'm real pleased that you're such a fan," Car said. The three men seated themselves. "You should come to a game sometime as my guest."

The Maestro inclined his head, all graciousness. "That is very nice of you, but as you know, because of my relationship with the Mosbachers, I can attend as many games as I have time for."

"Oh yes. How could I forget?" said Car.

How could he forget? Sofia wondered how, without making a scene, she might disappear.

"You know, Antonio, I bet there's something you can do for me, something I've wanted for a long time."

The Maestro cocked his skinny head to one side. "What is that?"

Yes, what? Sofia felt herself grow smaller and smaller. She was sinking into the pink of her dress. *Just like the witch. Melting.*

"I've always wanted to see how an opera works. You know, the stage, the scenery, the costumes. How do you get it all together?"

Sofia was surprised the buttons of his sleek Italian suit didn't pop off, the Maestro's chest swelled up so. "Would you like to come to the Muni and see?" he asked.

"Now, that would be great," said Car. "I want to see if it's the same as what Sofia's told me."

The Maestro shot her an unsure look.

Sofia stopped melting.

Car placed a hand on her arm. "Sofia's described how it goes when she's singing Cherubino in *The Marriage of Figaro*." The smile on Car's face held a glint of wickedness. "She's really good, isn't she?"

The Maestro flicked a glance at her. "Yes, so I am told." He half-rose and gave a nod in her direction.

"*Grazie*," she murmured, her heart taking up a quick tattoo of trepidation.

"So Antonio, I think I can show you something the Mosbachers wouldn't think to show you." Car sat back in the little chair, a smile on his lips, his blue-green eyes fixed, unblinking, on the Maestro. "How would you like to come to batting practice, come right up to the cage?"

"Marvelous," the Maestro said. "I would love it, especially to hear what the batting coach and the batters say to each other." A question came into his eyes. "Do you truly think you can make the arrangement?"

Car snapped his fingers. "Consider it done."

"May I return the favor and invite you to a performance at the Muni?"

"I'd love that." Car dropped his hand down between their chairs and took Sofia's hand. "Wait. Didn't I hear you're having a big performance of *Carmen* on July Fourth?"

The Maestro waved a hand in the air. "Yes, we are having a special performance to celebrate the grand re-opening of the Muni, which is currently in renovation. But you don't want to go to that. It will be a PR spectacle." He glanced quickly at Sofia and away.

Car slid his hand further into Sofia's. "But I love spectacles. Like the All-Star Game. That's a spectacle."

The Maestro's eyes widened. "I have never gone to an All-Star Game."

"Would you like to go? If you do, I'm sure I can arrange it. Even though I won't make the team this year, I'll still have access to tickets."

Crossing both hands over his chest, fingers splayed, the Maestro said, "I am all gratitude. Thank you, my dear friend."

"My pleasure, Antonio."

There was a round of cretinous male laughter from all three, even Lorenzo, who eyed Sofia nervously.

Car squeezed Sofia's hand. "Ah... Wait a minute."

The laughter stopped.

"Yes?" The smile froze on the Maestro's face.

"I just remembered." Car looked straight into Sofia's eyes. "Didn't you want to audition for Antonio? Wasn't that for the Muni's grand reopening? Didn't you tell me you wanted to try out for the part of Carmen?" He turned back to the Maestro, eyebrows raised.

Dead silence. The adrenalin began to race, unrestrained, through Sofia's veins. She risked a glance at the Maestro's face. The smile was gone. To Car, she said, "Yes, I did want to sing for Maestro Lupino."

One of his eyebrows, vaulting up towards the hat line on his forehead, Car said, "What happened with that?"

"I..." She allowed her voice to fade and clasped her hands together in front of her on the table. Wringing them, she said, "I am unable to speak to him. Perhaps I do not try hard enough?"

"How can that be, Sofia? You always give it your all."

"*Grazie*, Car." She let her voice die away on a dramatic sigh.

Car turned to the Maestro. "Antonio, is it possible your assistant doesn't give you messages?"

"I cannot believe that to be true." The Maestro's nose wiggled, an elephant's trunk seeking a peanut.

"You know, I understand." Car shook his head. "The woman who helps me with tickets for the All-Star game is great. But there used to be this guy who was impossible to work with. I'd ask him to get me tickets and he'd promise and never deliver. I'd hate it if that guy came back."

He stopped for a beat and went on. "Wouldn't it be terrible if you had someone like that in your office? I don't know much about opera, but it seems to me it would be a shame if you didn't hear Sofia sing because nobody told you she was interested in trying out for *Carmen*." He leaned toward the Maestro. "By the way, it's my opinion that she'd make you one great Carmen."

That was a little too much, but Sofia could see, from the steely determination on his face, Car didn't care.

The Maestro opened his mouth to speak, but Car held up a hand. "I know you haven't heard her. Well, I understand that. There's this guy Brent's looking at who's with one of the Japanese teams. We've heard he makes Ichiro, when he first came up, look like a Little Leaguer— but hey, no one's actually seen him. Could he make it here? Who knows? Brent's got to give him a chance to try out."

Car stopped and gave the Maestro a look filled with blue steel. "I guess you'd have to do that with Sofia."

What could the Maestro say? Car had led him into a corner and he couldn't get out without jeopardizing his chance to get tickets for the All-Star Game, perhaps not even to see batting practice. Sofia studied the vase of riotous flowers on their table.

"You're making an interesting point," the Maestro said. "I'll check to see what happened."

Sofia cleared her throat. "This means I can sing for you, yes?"

The Maestro cleared his throat too. "But of course. You will call my office tomorrow and schedule a time with my assistant."

"But Maestro," Sofia said. Car had started it, but she was going to finish it. "Surely you carry your calendar in your cellphone."

Now the Maestro wasn't just backed into a corner; he was stuck.

"Of course." He reached into his jacket and extracted the phone. With studious concentration, he held it up. "I'll have a half hour for you at noon tomorrow. Can you be there?"

"I will be there," Sofia answered, triumph filling her. "Most assuredly."

"You understand I am close to making my decision about who will sing Carmen. This is the beginning of May. There are a mere two months left before the performance. Thank God Lorenzo is here this week. I want to work with him at least once or twice."

Sofia let her eyes close for a split second, her triumph dimmed. "It is Lorenzo who will sing Don José?"

The Maestro arched an eyebrow at her. "You didn't know? Is there a problem?"

"No problem." Car had said knowledge was power. She knew Lorenzo couldn't do to her what he'd done before. If she got the part—*when* she got the part—she'd be sure to let him know.

She firmed her voice. "I will be there at your office to sing for you tomorrow at noon."

"Don't be late."

Afterwards, when they were seated in the cozy amphitheater awaiting the performance, Sofia nudged Car with her shoulder and murmured, "It is quite shocking how different the Maestro's voice is when he speaks to me than when he speaks to you."

There was a pleasant buzz of voices around them. Sofia glanced once at the Maestro, seated in the front row next to Vauxhall's director.

The smile had long since gone from Car's face. He crossed one very long leg over the other, not such an easy thing in the narrow space between the rows. "The Maestro doesn't impress me much."

"But you impress me."

He twisted toward her, eyes lighting with a mischievous, little boy grin. "I was good, wasn't I?"

She had to laugh.

Car's smile faded. "I'm not altogether sure what the problem is with the Maestro."

"I know. It is what you said. Lorenzo has told the Maestro the lies about La Scala and the Maestro believes them."

"I don't think Lupino is the kind of person who listens to gossip. And I don't get, from his body language, that he has much respect for Lorenzo. Which makes me wonder why he hired him to sing Don José."

"That I can tell you. He has a big reputation."

"Oh." With one finger, Car stroked his bottom lip. "Well then, why has he resisted you so hard?"

That moment the lights came up on the stage and the audience fell into a hushed silence. Car leaned toward her. "What I think is even after your wardrobe change and the good PR you're getting, he still doesn't see you as Carmen."

"He will. When he hears me sing."

"That's for sure."

Just then Camerata Bonn and Lorenzo came onto the

stage.

Car leaned in as the applause began and pressed his mouth close to her ear. "You know what else I'm thinking?"

She felt the puffs of his breath against her cheek and shivered. "What?"

"I think by the end of tonight," he whispered, so low, she almost didn't hear, "We could have one thing squared away."

She didn't understand what it meant to be squared away, but his hand sliding across her hip, his fingers curling beneath her bottom? She understood that completely.

"You can go to the audition tomorrow, knowing you have at least one thing in common with Carmen."

As beautiful as the performance was, Sofia heard not one note in ten. Car's words kept playing back, like bars of music sung so many times, they were part of her. *You can go to the audition tomorrow, knowing you have at least one thing in common with Carmen*. This was fantastic. Only when it happened, she'd be naked.

This wasn't fantastic.

Visually, her new clothes had transformed her. On the inside, though, she was still Sofia with her back end, hips, and melons. It would be a relief if, when she was naked, she could keep Car from seeing all that.

It was Lorenzo's pianissimo during his singing of Strauss' "*Dedication* that shook her out of her anxiety. His voice held the clear, sweet timbre that had been his at the beginning of his career. It was too bad he'd allowed others to convince him to take on roles for which he wasn't ready—Manrico, Radames, Cavaradossi. Everyone knew a voice that wasn't ready was doomed to dry out. Or worse.

Not once did Car let go of her hand during Lorenzo's performance. Sometimes he held it loosely, skimming a finger across the arch between her thumb and first finger.

Sometimes he squeezed, but tenderly. And sometimes he took her hand and rubbed it back and forth across his thigh. It was then, when she felt the taut muscle of his leg beneath the smoothness of his trousers that she imagined the smoothness of his skin. Without his trousers.

The anxiety returned. But it warred with the anxiety of what would happen tomorrow at the audition. No matter where she looked, her gaze seemed always to zero in on the erect, unmoving figure of the Maestro.

At last she got sick of looking at him and turned toward Car. He bent his head to hers, his arm coming around her shoulder and brought her closer to him. "How long?" he whispered.

"One more song. Then the performance will be over."

"Good."

Lorenzo crossed both hands over his heart, and closed his eyes, seeming to enthrall himself with the sound of his own singing.

She felt the play of Car's muscles, and took in the clean scent of him. She looked into the intensity of his eyes.

Her heart gave a lurch sideways. Or was it up, then down? Whatever it was doing, it wasn't obeying her warning to stay calm. She was going to do this. She was going to make love. With him.

Chapter Fourteen

By the time Car had them back on the road, Sofia was jabbering again. For a while he listened. She talked about chest tones, and staccatos and runs, and while he listened with a little more curiosity when she said runs, he knew she meant something besides scoring them.

"I bought you something," he said, when he could get in a word.

"You did?"

It tickled him how she went from full steam to full stop in the same breath. "Yeah. I got it just before I picked you up. It's something I thought you'd like. Open the glove box."

She let the front down slowly and stared. And stared.

"It's not alive."

She gave him a quick sideways grin and pulled out the bag. The paper crackled. She reached in, and let the swath of black, silky material flow into her lap.

He heard a hitch in her breath. "Well?"

She ran her hand across its length. "It is a mantilla."

"What do you think?"

She turned toward him, her eyes filled with tears. "*Grazie di cuore.*"

"I know there's a thanks in there, but what's the rest?"

"Thank you from my heart," she whispered the translation. "It is so beautiful. It is perfect."

He relaxed muscles he hadn't realized were tight.

"How did you know Carmen wears a mantilla?"

He angled his chin in the direction of the glove box. "The mantilla isn't the only thing I bought. Look again."

This time she didn't hesitate, but reached in and came out with the square box he'd picked up right before the last game in Kansas City.

"On the cover Carmen is wearing a mantilla. That's how I knew what to buy."

She held the CD box and the mantilla clutched to her chest, which was heaving with silent sobs. Tears streamed from her eyes. Her face was contorted in what looked like pain.

"Oh my God," he muttered and pulled to the shoulder. Throwing the stick into park, he unsnapped her seat belt, and pulled her as close to him as he could with the damn console between them. "Sweetheart, what's the matter?"

"You are so good to me," she sobbed.

"You're crying because I'm good to you?" The tears were too numerous to count.

"Y-y-yes. And because nobody is good to me like you."

He cursed the console for keeping him from hauling her into his lap. "I've heard of crying when you're happy, crying when you're sad, but this is crying I can't figure out."

"I too. I am so confused." She hiccupped and dabbed at her face with a shred of tissue she'd pulled from her purse.

"I'd say you need something more to get that job done. Use the mantilla."

"Car!"

He knew that would stop the waterworks. "I was kidding." He didn't bother to keep the grin off his face.

Ignoring his suggestion, she dabbed some more with that ridiculous scrap. "You have a kind and good heart."

"Not kind or good. I bought the stuff because I wanted to," he insisted.

"You gave much thought to purchasing these things for me," she said, holding up both the mantilla and CD box.

He was, uncomfortable with her compliments. "Are we finished with the tears?"

"*Si*, I am finished." She straightened. "*Andiamo*. Let us go."

Sofia was wrong about him. He wasn't kind or good. He knew some people thought he was because he was always buying things for them. But he understood the real reason. He'd sat next to the team's shrink on a cross-continental flight once and they'd talked. Not that Car wanted to talk. The guy made him.

Buying, doing stuff for people, the shrink explained, the appearances at hospitals, the big chunks of change he gave to various charities, the money he gave to Louise at the end of the month when she was running out, the gifts he made to friends, even doing those damn endorsements for Mosbacher, it was all about him needing to make up for what was missing inside him. He could give things. He couldn't give himself.

Still that didn't explain why he'd gone to that store and bought the best mantilla—according to the store owner—or why he'd almost missed the flight from KC because he'd spent so much time making sure he bought the best version of *Carmen*. There was no guilt, just pleasure seeing Sofia happy.

They talked non-stop on the way home. But when they crossed the bridge into Manhattan, she grew silent. As he pulled into his building's garage, she stirred.

"Where are we?"

"My place."

She stared at him, her face striped with light cast from the fluorescent tubing that ran across the garage's ceiling. "Chelsea will know."

More curves. Maybe a red light. He wasn't stopping for it. He'd waited twenty-four whole hours to have her. "Call. Tell her you're with me."

"I do not have my cellphone with me."

"You don't? Why not?"

"I do not like to answer when it rings."

He had no idea where she was going with this. But he was beyond asking her to explain. "Here, use mine." He fished it out of his jacket.

"I..."

He snaked a hand around the back of her neck and yanked her toward him. She made a little sound of protest, which he ignored, because his mouth got busy devouring hers. Her whimpering sounds quickly went from protest to pleasure.

By the time he pulled back, he was breathing hard. "I'll make the call."

"That would be good, Car," she whispered, eyes hazy with passion.

He waited a beat. "Do you want to know what I'm going to tell her?"

"Perhaps I should make the call," Sofia said and reached for the phone.

After disconnecting, she handed the cellphone back to Car. "She knew."

Sofia didn't speak again until they were alone in the elevator. She took a deep breath to steady herself and smelled the perfume of the woman who must have been in it before them. She smiled and said, "It is better than *baccalà*."

He cocked his head to one side. "Huh?"

"Very smelly fish."

He wrinkled his nose and sniffed the air. "Better, but I'm not sure by how much."

It was silly to mention *baccalà*, but Sofia needed to say something. Her nerves were making her crazy, like moths banging themselves against naked light bulbs. She shuddered. She shouldn't think about naked anything.

When the doors slid open, they stepped into a quiet foyer with subdued lighting. At each end of the narrow hallway stood a black lacquered door, to the right of each, a recessed shelf with a clear vase set upon it. Each vase contained two flowers: one yellow, one white.

"*Crisantemi.*" She caught herself. "Chrysanthemums."

As he unlocked his door, Car threw her a smile. "Good job on the translation." He caught her hand as she began to slip past and put his arms around her. He leaned down and, with his nose, nudged aside the curls around her shoulders.

At the feel of his lips against the place where her shoulder and neck met, she shuddered and let her eyes fall shut. Her skin prickled. A heavy pulse beat against her temples. She eased back to look up into his eyes. "I like this."

He smoothed his hands over her pink dress. She felt every press of his fingers beneath. Against her flesh.

"Do you, now?" His eyes grew hungry, fierce.

"*O Dio,*" she whispered, and stiffened. She'd let the tiger loose.

His hands ceased moving. He gave her a wisp of a kiss on the forehead, and let her go. Stepping in front of a narrow, rectangular, black table set against the entry wall, he threw his keys in the bleached wooden bowl that rested upon it. They made a clinking sound. He walked around a corner and disappeared.

What had happened? Perhaps she had not loosed the tiger. "Car?"

"I'm in the kitchen."

She gazed around the room. There was a sofa, also black, but leather, to her right. Besides the sofa, two arm chairs, also black leather. On the far wall, long floor-to-ceiling windows overlooked the building across the street. She scanned the rest of the room. No paintings on the walls. No tables with pictures of Noah. She looked for the toys. Surely there'd be some, a box perhaps, But no. None. Only a large television mounted on the wall opposite the couch. Curious.

She looked once more at the sofa. She wouldn't watch much TV on this uncomfortable sofa. But she wasn't here to think about his television. Or the paintings he didn't have. She couldn't help but think about the lack of pictures. Or the toys.

Listening to him move around in the kitchen, she wondered if she was supposed to take her clothes off while he was in there. Before she could decide, he came back, in each hand a glass filled with a ruby-red wine. He'd taken off his jacket and rolled the sleeves of his blinding white shirt to his elbows. His kissed-by-the-sun skin glowed, the hair on his forearms glinted with gold in the reflection from the overhead lights. "I bet you're up for a glass," he said and held one out to her.

She took it and wrapped both palms around its satin smooth surface. "*Grazie*. It is an Italian wine, yes?" As if she cared if it was an Italian wine. She didn't care if it was wine. She cared only that she know what was going to happen next.

His blue-green eyes kind, a little smile on his beautiful mouth, he took her hand, his skin warm and firm, hard and rough. "Let's sit."

Car led her over to the couch. He sat her at one end and reached for the controller to turn on the TV. Naturally it was on ESPN. He switched to a PBS station.

He'd felt it: that moment, when he'd put his arms around her and she'd stiffened up. A curve ball. And then just now, when he'd handed her the glass, yup. One thing he'd discovered about Sofia; she was likely to put on a game face when she was scared to death. Right now her game face was on. "Sweetheart, I want to make love with you more than anything, but you have to want it more than anything too."

She blinked at the screen. He'd be willing to bet she didn't see much, not that there was much to see. Chattering like a pair of monkeys, two PBS hosts were doing their usual Beg-a-Thon thing.

She took a deep breath and turned her game face toward him. "I want this Car. I do."

"You've got a big day tomorrow. Maybe we should wait for another time?"

"But Car..." She put her hand on his knee.

It took all his willpower not to move. "Yes?"

"What we do tonight will be good for tomorrow."

He blinked. Hadn't he made that argument before, when they were at Vauxhall? Kind of. "How do you figure?" He wanted to make sure he knew where that twisty mind of hers was going.

"Everyone looks at Carmen and sees she is not a virgin. I do not want the Maestro to look at me and say this Sofia, she cannot be my Carmen because it is clear she is a virgin. So you see why it is important you make me not a virgin tonight."

Car almost roared with laughter. The appeal for understanding shining in her eyes told him, as usual, he needed to keep the laughter buttoned down. "Let's take a look and see if we can tell who's a virgin." He picked up the controller and turned off the TV, cutting the babble midstream. "I bought some opera DVDs when I picked up your *Carmen* CD."

"*Davvero*? Why did you do that?"

"I didn't know a thing about opera before I met you. Well, almost nothing, and I hate it when there's talk around me of something I don't know."

A little smile tickled her lips. "And so if you hear a discussion about nuclear physics, you buy the DVD?"

She made a joke. "Maybe not nuclear physics. But garden variety physics."

"The kind where plants in the garden grow up, not down."

"I think that's botany," he said, chuckling.

She laughed out loud, that musical laugh that got him in the gut.

"You have the curiosity to learn, Car. You are clever."

"Clever? No way." There it was again. That conviction of hers he had a level of intelligence he knew full well he didn't. "I'm just nosy."

She cocked her head to one side. "Why do you say such a thing?"

"Because it's true." He wanted off this subject and back on the one at hand. Her. "I can't..."

"I can see when I am watching the game on the TV," she interrupted him. "I know. Even when you play, when you are on the base, you use your brain. I see your eyes moving, always looking, having the anticipation of what will come next. You are thinking the strategy. Only people, who are clever, like you, think about the strategy."

"It's just baseball, Sofia. I know baseball." He drummed his fingers against his knee. "But you..."

"Yes it is baseball," she said, bulldozing over him. "But you tell me about your little MP3 player and the books you read—yes, I know, on discs—and always the curiosity to find out about things you do not know. Only clever and smart people do that."

"It's not..."

"Tell me please." She scooted closer to him. "Who is the one who has the plan, after the many weeks I try and have no success, to make the Maestro say yes, to the audition? Who is the one?" She poked him in the chest. "You. You are the successful one. You cannot read from the page to learn? *Pfft*! You do it another way. That is all I have to say about that."

And with a short, to the point tirade on a subject on which she was very sure she was right, and that she paired with one sound that took a fraction of a second to make, she dismissed every one of the years of his life during which he thought he was stupid.

She thought he was clever, smart. She believed in him. Nobody else had believed in him the way she did. Something swelled inside him. As if she hadn't just turned his world upside down, he said, "Uh, don't you want to look at the DVD I bought to see if we can tell about Carmen's virginity?" *Pfft!*

"I—do." That hesitation: it blew him away. She was sure of him, but not herself?

"Wait right here." He came to his feet and tried to tamp down the trembling inside, where everything had shifted. He succeeded in not stumbling, and moved across the room to the TV cabinet. He crouched and pulled out his three operas, brought them back to her, and sat. Now it was his turn to do something for her, give her herself, as she had just given him himself. Help her see she was beautiful in her body, because yes, he knew that's what she was afraid of. "I haven't watched them yet."

She leaned against him, her pretty pink dress bunching up in accordion pleats at her hips, and held out her hands to take the DVDs. Less than a body's width separated them.

"*Bene,*" she breathed, shuffling them in her hands. *The Barber of Seville,* the Rossini Barber. This one is the best, with Juan Diego Florez as the Count and Joyce Di Donato as Rosina." She looked up at him. "You must watch this one first."

The way she looked at him, he'd watch anything she told him to watch.

"You know this story, yes? This is before the Count marries his Rosina."

Once again, she got all perked up. He loved looking at her: the impish, black eyes, the rose-tinted cheeks, the lush, red lips curved in a smile, the way the dress revealed a length of leg and just a glimpse of lace-covered hips, which he wanted very much to see before another hour lapsed. "In this opera, he is sweet, a little foolish, but we like him. Later, in the Mozart opera, *The Marriage of Figaro,* when the Count is older and he wants to have the rights of the lord, and he is bored with his wife, Rosina, we don't like him so much, although it is a wonderful part to sing."

Car shifted in place, managing to get even closer to her. "So in this one it doesn't matter about the virginity part because Rosina isn't married to the Count yet."

Eyebrows knit together in one disapproving line, Sofia nodded. "She is a good Catholic girl who would never lose the virginity without the marriage vows. And it was the Eighteenth Century. Girls did not live in the apartment with the boyfriend." Putting the Rossini DVD to the back, she pulled out the second. "Ah. The best *Italian Girl in Algiers.*"

He was shoulder to shoulder with her, hip to hip, and she didn't notice. "So virginity's not an issue here either, right?"

Sofia ignored him. Placing the third DVD on his lap, she said, "And this one, the *Carmen.*" She closed her eyes and sighed. "You are a wonder, Car. You found one of the best. Yes, this one is old, older than me, but Placido Domingo is such a Don José. It would be wonderful to be his Carmen."

She waved the DVD again. "Not now, you understand. Now he is old and has the bags under his eyes and he sings Verdi's *Falstaff* and the other roles a younger man cannot sing because younger men do not have the breathing or the presence." She cocked her head at him. "You know what this means for singers—presence?"

"Yes," he said. No, not really, but he didn't want to interrupt the flow.

She started to shuffle the DVDs, until, laying one hand over hers, he stopped her. "We were going to see if we could tell by looking if this Julia Migenes, who's playing Carmen..." He pulled that DVD out of her hands and held it up... "If she's a virgin."

She hadn't realized he'd put his arm around her, or that she'd settled into the lee of his shoulder. Her hair had gotten messed up during the evening, sitting outside at the concert and coming back in the truck. Now long lengths of her hair snaked over her shoulders. Some of the curls got caught in the back of her dress. He reached in and gently pulled them out.

She went still, and turned toward him, eyes big in her head, mouth just beginning to open. It was too much to resist. He bent towards her, his mouth hovering above hers. "May I?"

With a tiny nod, she gave him permission.

The first touch was a whisper, a press of his lips to hers. He drew back, their mouths hovering close. And then he kissed her. A press of lips that lingered. Longingly. Lovingly.

She raised one hand to his face and laid her palm on his jaw. "I do not care anymore." She turned in his arms and wound an arm around his shoulder. The DVDs dropped to the floor. He felt the soft cushion of her breasts against his chest and inhaled her rose scent. She offered her mouth to him. He took it. With tongue and teeth.

He closed his eyes, and let there be nothing but the kiss, the satin-smoothness of her skin against his, and the little wanting noises she made, the kernels of sound.

His breath shortened. Heat prickled his skin. He shoved his hands into her hair and pressed his fingers against her scalp. Curls cascaded down to cover his wrists and slither across his forearms.

She gasped, and wedged her hands between their bodies. She leaned away, the back of one hand pressed to her mouth. "*O Dio*, it will be real, this lovemaking."

"Yes."

She swallowed hard. "I am still afraid."

He stroked her arm to calm himself as much as her. When finally he could speak, he said, "I meant it. We don't have to do this."

She jumped up, game face set in place and took his hand. "Come with me." Wine sloshing in her glass, she marched down the short hallway. "I have thought of a way," she said, and stepped into the coolness of his bedroom.

For a moment Sofia forgot about making love to Car. She stared at the two pieces of furniture, a side table with a lamp, and a bed, very low, very large, covered with round pillows and squares, so many she couldn't count, all white and black. The headboard was black, the bedspread white. "You do not like colors?"

He smiled and walked to the far side of the room. "Black and white works. It's easier than trying to figure out what colors go with what."

Sliding open a door, he reached in among a multitude of jackets, trousers, and shirts, all in shades of black, bone, white, with a few olive green, all organized by type, and all neatly hung.

Surveying the display, Sofia shook her head. "*Naturalmente.*"

"Naturally?" He started toward her, unbuttoning his shirt as he came. "Is that what you said?"

She opened her mouth to answer, but no words came out. Instead her eye followed his fingers down the placket of his shirt. As he slipped each button from its button hole, more and more of his skin was revealed. When he came to the last button, just above the waistband of his trousers, he pulled out the tails of the shirt and shed it from his shoulders in one movement.

Mouth suddenly dry as a desert that had not seen rain in years, she took a gulp of her wine. "You are not afraid you will tear the shirt the way you pull it from the..." And she faltered because below the waistband was his trousers—his raised-up trousers.

"Not a problem," he said, eyes lit with blue-green fire.

He stood with his shirt bunched up in one hand. Her gaze traveled his body. His shoulders were wider than when he was clothed, his arms corded with long, sleek muscles, a tracery of veins running from elbow to wrist. His skin glowed, the neat, upside-down triangle of brown hair at the center of his chest narrowed and tapered and disappeared beneath the waistband of his trousers.

She took another gulp of her wine. Glass clutched in her hand, she began to back up.

He looked up at the ceiling, sighed, dropped the shirt, and came towards her. "Sofia, there's nothing wrong with saying no. I want you. Very much. But if you don't want me, if this isn't right for you, the audition be damned, the virginity be damned. Tomorrow, you'll knock Lupino out of the batter's box and he'll know who's singing for him: the great Sofia de' Medici and you'll be the best Carmen ever. But please decide. You're making a wreck out of me."

She didn't want to make a wreck of him. Or herself. And she wanted him too. "This is how we will do it," she said, willing the tremble in her voice to go away. She pointed to her glass of wine. "I will drink this glass of wine, and you will pour me many more. I will know what is going on, but it will be like I am looking at myself from outside my body."

He put his hands on her shoulders and gave her a little shake. "I've never made love to a woman who had to get drunk to be with me, and I'm not starting with you."

"What then, can we do?"

He was silent for a moment. "What if we played a game? What if I made you laugh? What if every time you laughed I got to take off one piece of your clothing?"

Chapter Fifteen

For a moment she said nothing. Then she tilted her head and whispered, "That is very exciting, Car. I like this idea. When can we start?"

"How about we start right now?"

"All right. Yes."

From the wild look in his eyes, Sofia could tell Car was, indeed, a wreck. If he was a wreck, this made up for her fear. His words, that he wanted her, the look in his eye that told her he believed in her, this was everything. Almost everything. Still she wished she was as beautiful as he was handsome and then all would be complete.

"I must ask you." She stared at the odd-shaped lamp—naturally, it was white—on his black night table. "I am not so happy about the light."

He followed her glance. "How do I make you laugh if you can't see me?"

"Is it only when I am looking at you that you will make me laugh?" Emboldened by the logic, she stepped close to him and walked her fingers up the center of his chest, gratified to feel him take an unsteady breath.

He slid his hands up her arms, his thumbs, caressing the flesh in the crook of her elbows. "That's the idea."

She looked over her shoulder at his bed. It was bigger than some hotel rooms she had stayed in. She eased out of his arms and took the few steps toward the colossus, sat, and leaned back on her elbows, suddenly Zerlina, or how she thought Zerlina would act if Mozart had included a bedroom scene in *Don Giovanni*. She didn't spread her legs as wide as Zerlina would. "I have the idea."

"Okay." He seated himself next to her, the mattress dipping, her heart dipping with it. Sofia could hear his breathing, like hers, had sped up. "Tell me your idea."

"I agree to keep the light on for the first laugh, but after that, you must turn it off."

"Then we'll make the first laugh a good one." A wicked smile curved his lips.

It was too wicked. She swallowed hard. "O-okay. But I have another idea."

He rolled his eyes.

"Perhaps for this first time while the light remains shining, you can keep your eyes closed?"

He turned and planted both hands on the mattress, bracketing her. The heat of his skin, the scent of his body surrounded her.

Drawing his face close to hers, he kissed her nose. "Nope. I want to see that pretty mouth of yours turn up in a smile before you give me one of those great big laughs of yours."

"Then perhaps *I* could keep *my* eyes closed."

"No. Eyes stay open." With one long finger, he traced a line along her eyebrows. Her eyelids became heavy. Fine hairs stood at the back of her neck, goose bumps rose there and everywhere.

"They." That finger began to trace across her cheek. "Stay." It trailed around her ear, down the side of her neck, to the hollow at the base of her throat. "Open."

With just the least movement of her head, she nodded her agreement.

Kissing the corner of her mouth, he eased away from her and slid to his feet. "Wait right here."

As he walked over to his closet and began to root around in the back of it, Sofia sat up. After long minutes, during which she heard him mutter a time or two, he said, "Close your eyes."

"But you said...?"

"I know. Just for a couple of seconds."

Taking a deep breath, she did what he asked. She heard a rustling, a pause, and then his steps coming toward her.

"Now, open."

She did. Froze. Burst into laughter. There he stood, in trousers, bare-chested, bare-footed, with an old-fashioned black opera cape that fell from his broad shoulders to the floor, a single button at his throat holding it together.

She laughed and laughed, the laughter as much about how funny he looked, how unexpected it was to think that he had, of all things, a piece of clothing only an old *impresario* would wear, as it was about her nerves.

He flung his arms out wide. She could see, beneath the cape, the expanse of his beautiful chest, all glowing golden skin, the muscles that overlay his ribcage, his belly. The taut navel. She licked her lips.

On his face was a triumphant smile. "What do you think? Could I be one of those old-fashioned opera stars in this rig?"

This sent her off in more laughter. When at last she was able to stop, she wiped her eyes. "Where did you get this?"

"The team did a Halloween party out in New Jersey at a hospital for kids. We all dressed up. I was a pirate." He slipped the one button from its button hole and let it drop to the carpet. Eyes never leaving her face, he said, "The rest of the costume is in the closet. I thought you'd like this part the best."

He padded over to the light, turned, and looked at her. She gave him one quick nod and he turned it off, plunging the room into darkness.

The trembling began inside her and then it spread to her fingers, the flesh of her arms, her shoulders, her chin, her lips. "Do not forget, Car. Each time you must make me laugh," she whispered.

"I didn't forget. But I think *you* did. You owe me."

"Yes, I owe for the first laugh." More trembling. "What do I take off?"

He sank to his knees in front of her. "You don't get to take anything off. I do." He slid his palms, his strong fingers, up from her ankles, to her knees, and across her thighs, where they stopped. "What's this?"

If the light was on, he would see the color rise bright in her face. "I thought they would be sexy." She put a hand over her heart and swallowed. "I thought they would make me feel sexy."

"Sweet Sofia. You've got some great ideas. This garter belt..." He palmed her bare skin at the edge of the stocking...it makes *me* feel sexy."

Her heart surged. Her back arched. She spread her legs a little further apart. Perhaps as far apart as Zerlina.

His fingers continued their upward trail, over her hips to her waist, where he unsnapped the garter belt she bought with Tina in a Madison Avenue lingerie shop.

"I think the first laugh entitles me to..." He tugged the hooks open that held her stockings in place, first one leg and then the other "...The garter belt and the stockings."

Everywhere his hands touched, Sofia's skin felt on fire. "Okay," she whispered. He smoothed his hands down her legs, taking the hose over her knees to her ankles. Her breath caught. "But I think first you must take off my shoes."

He stopped. "Was that a laugh I heard? I say it was. And that means I get to take off both your shoes." He fumbled with the back of one heel and then the other. The shoes dropped to the carpeted floor with a soft clunk.

"You are the dictator, Car."

He rose to sit beside her on the bed. Running his fingers down the length of her arm, he said, "Did I tell you this dress is a knock-out? When I first saw you tonight, my eyes almost popped out of my head. I thought I was seeing a goddess."

She placed a hand across his mouth. His breath gusted hot in the center of her palm. "You do not need to say this, Car. I know what I look like."

He shifted; the bed shifted with him. "You don't know what you look like to me."

"I know what I look like to me. That is the same thing."

"It's not." He lay down. "Put your arms around my neck."

She did. It felt so good, so forever.

"I need to explain."

What could he explain? She drew in a breath. She'd never been and never would be a goddess. But he was a god, who, without Brent's scheming, she would never have known, in whose bed she would never have been. He could explain and she would listen. But she couldn't believe him. Still, she would savor each tiny sensation of being held by him and holding him—the clean smell, the solid strength of his muscles, and the warmth of his skin. She closed her eyes, and pressed her forehead to his chest.

"I look at you and I see you." His breath tickled her ear. "Only you. Even in the beginning it was like that, even when I thought, jeez, this woman is crazy."

She couldn't help chuckling. She *had* been crazy.

"Is that another laugh? Does that mean I can take off something else?" He slid one long, muscled leg between hers.

She gasped at the sensation of his knee pressed. There.

Perhaps she would have spoken. But he laid a finger across her lips. "Don't. I need to say this."

"Okay," she whispered.

"In movies, you know how the camera focuses on one actor and it looks like the rest of the people in the scene are out of focus?"

"In opera we have a special curtain, a scrim. The audience sees the singer in front, but cannot see those behind."

"That's exactly what it's like for me with you. When you're around, everyone and everything else is out of focus."

Sofia's couldn't swallow.

"What I think, it's..." He shrugged, and lay back on the bed, slipping out of her arms, leaving her to struggle for breath, like a fish taken from the sea and flung onto land.

Why had he stopped? Suddenly, she was terror-stricken. If, when he was with her, he saw no one else, did this mean she stood alone in his mind? If she stood alone in his mind, was he...? Could it mean...? Could he be in love with her? That was ridiculous. It was crazy. It wasn't love.

And so she was silent. But her heart still hoped.

After long moments, Car moved, lifted up and pulled her toward him. She felt him everywhere, the way his chest brushed against the fabric of her dress, the hardness of his thighs. He pressed his lips against the soft hollow beneath her ear. "I can't explain. I'm sorry."

Her heart sank. She was right to say nothing. How it would have crushed her if she'd asked, if she'd let him know about her wretched wish. She swallowed, her throat dry. "Does this mean we will not play the laughing game?"

He placed a light kiss on her chin. "Do you want to play?"

She squeezed her eyes shut against her tears. "Yes."

"Well then. Let's do it." He moved away from her again.

She scrubbed the wet from her face. She was done with sadness. She'd take pleasure from whatever he offered her this night, and not think about what would not be. She rose up on her elbows to see what he was doing, not that she could see more than shadows in the dark of the room.

There was a snick of a sound and instantly a bright white light. Squinting, Sofia saw, in one hand, Car held a miniature book light, in the other, a piece of paper. For a moment he was quiet and then said, "*La see dar-em la manoh, la see dar-em dee see.*" His voice rose and fell on the syllables.

She could not help the giggle that escaped. "What is that?"

He began to sing.

With one part of her mind, Sofia noted Car could sing a proper melody. With the other part of her mind, she realized he was singing Don Giovanni's tempting words to Zerlina: "*La ci darem la mano.*" *Here, take my hand.* "You are singing, yes, and the singing is fine, but the words are..." Hers failed her. In spurts of laughter, she fell back on the bed.

He knelt on the bed next to her and placed his hand on her belly. "Does this count as two laughs or one?"

She lifted her head, her breath catching. "I do not know."

"Then I'll make the decision." Which he did, slipping off the two gold bangles she'd worn, the ones she'd bought to go with the pink dress.

They made a clinking sound when he placed them on the bedside table.

"Your Italian is very bad," she said.

"It made you laugh. It can't be that bad." He came off

his knees and lay down next to her. He pulled her over to lie with him face to face. "How do you feel about another kiss?" She could tell he was working hard to regulate his breathing.

"I would like a kiss, a real kiss."

"Okay." His hands were gentle as, barely pressing, they skimmed over the bodice of her pink dress, lingering on her breasts, and then linking at her nape, to press against the back of her head beneath the curls that had fallen down long ago.

She gasped. She wanted his hands back on her breasts, the breasts covered by the beautiful lacy bra. This achy feeling, to be touched—she hadn't known a fraction of what it would feel like that day in the dressing room when she touched herself. Now she knew; it was better when he touched her. Much better.

Insinuating a hand between their bodies, she reached up and, with one finger, stroked across his face to a tiny beauty mark just beneath his left eye. "This is a gift from the gods."

"Not like Lorenzo's, I hope."

She gave him a playful slap. "You bring Lorenzo into this bed?"

"No." His lips touched hers. "It's just us." Which is when the real kisses began. On her lips, at the corners of her eyes, nose, chin, ear—oh God, the ear *was* involved— and again her lips. His hot breath branded her skin. His hands stroked her, shoulder to elbow, again and again, caressing her breasts in ways that made her shiver. His hands moved to her waist, her hips, to her bottom, his fingers pressing into her flesh. But always, always there were his lips and his tongue, on her body, on her face, in her mouth, licking, sucking, doing things she hadn't known could be done with mouths.

When at last he laid back, panting, eyes closed she said, her voice a wisp of itself, "That was very nice."

"Nice, was it?" He ran a finger down the side of her nose. "If nice is the only thing you can say about that kiss, I better take some lessons."

He didn't need lessons. "*Forse*—perhaps it was more than nice."

"Thanks for saving my pride."

"I think I would like another laugh now."

On a deep exhale, he said, "This has to be the last one."

He reached across her, a giant shadow in the pitch dark of the room. She laid a hand flat on his chest, smoothing and lingering on one nipple and then the other. She had wanted to do that the moment he took off his shirt.

"Stop that," he growled, fumbling with something on the side-table.

She smiled. "You like that?"

"Yes, you witch. Now, pay attention."

Again there was a rustle of paper. Was he going to sing her another song in his terrible Italian? In the next moment he was lying beside her, sliding an arm under her shoulders. She thought of how she could grow accustomed to him holding her like this. Just once a day in the morning would be enough. Although at night too, before she went to sleep, that would be splendid.

She ran the tips of her fingers across the bristles on his cheeks, grown since he shaved this morning. After tonight, no matter what came after, she wanted to store the tactile memory of him in the place where she kept the special parts of her life. "What do you have now to make me laugh?"

"Take a look." Once more he snapped on the little light. In his hand, a picture with many people in it. In the background, the ocean. Each person held a glass or bottle. Each was laughing at the figure that stood squarely in the center: Lorenzo Latte. A Lorenzo Sofia had never seen.

Lorenzo was stripped to the waist, his hairy belly hanging over the tiny Speedo all that stood between him and being arrested for scaring the world to death. But that was not all. His arms were flung out wide, and his mouth open in a wide O; he was singing. And there on the top of his head was a sombrero, a child's sombrero. She blinked. Then, like the people in the photo, she went off in whoops. She kept on laughing. And laughing. And laughing.

"Breathe, Sofia, breathe." Car pressed his hand against her diaphragm.

"Where did you find this? She gasped.

"It's amazing what you can find on the Internet."

"Surely, Lorenzo hates this picture." She patted the skin under her eyes. "I will never be able to think of him the same way again."

"That's why I showed it to you. After this, whenever he tries to say anything to make you feel small, make you think you're not beautiful, make you think you're not special, think of him in this picture."

He took her breath away. In the middle of seducing her, he had shown her how to drive the demon who had plagued her so long from her life. At last, with this appalling picture, she believed him; she was beautiful, inside and out. In his eyes—and now in hers—she was special.

He dropped the picture to the floor. "But you're right. Lorenzo doesn't belong in this bed with us. Not when I'm about to take off the next piece of your clothing. Only it won't be a bracelet or a pair of earrings."

"No jewelry," she breathed, and forgot Lorenzo. For her, now, there was nothing but Car's lemon-lime scent, the heat radiating from his body, her back on his sheets, and him hovering above her, where she had always wanted him to be. "What do you think? My belt?"

"Nope. The belt is jewelry."

"But there is only my dress after the belt."

"I don't think so, sweetheart. There's this." He slipped his hands under her dress and hooked his hands into her lacy panties, his fingers teasing the soft flesh between her thighs. She shuddered.

Slowly, so slowly, he eased the panties down. His hot hands slid them over her hips. Down, slowly down they came. Until he urged her legs together to pull them off her body.

She licked her lips. "What will you do with them?"

"Your panties?"

"Yes."

He pressed them against his face. "I'm keeping them forever."

Her breath caught. "Car." Her voice was a wisp of itself. "I am naked. Underneath." Yes, she was. If she got off this bed, and slipped into her shoes, she could walk out into the street and no one would know that underneath her dress, she was naked. Naked and aching and wet.

This time his kiss didn't stray. He descended upon Sofia's mouth and attacked. He kissed her with hunger, he kissed her with intensity.

Her head spun. Her heart thudded in her throat. "No more laughing." She drew away from his greedy mouth. "I am ready to not be a virgin anymore."

"Be sure," he said, his nimble fingers slipping the clasp on the gold linked belt. In a sweet cadenza, it slithered to the floor.

"I am sure. Please, Car."

"Well, then," he whispered and pushed the dress up, across her belly, across her breasts, to her shoulders. "Let's play ball." He slid her arms out of the dress' armholes, one by one, and tugged it over her head. He got rid of the bra almost as fast.

At last she was truly naked.

"I've wanted to touch you here from the beginning." He bent to take her nipples in his mouth, first one and then the other. His fingers slid around each breast to squeeze gently. "Outstanding," he whispered against her skin.

Before she knew what was happening, his hand skimmed across her belly, between her legs to *that* place. She jumped. "*O Dio... che succede*?" she stuttered.

"Jesus, Sofia," the sound he made, a pained chuckle. "We said no more laughing."

She would have pointed out it was not she doing the laughing, if she could. But his hand between her legs, palming her, rubbing her, his fingers inside her, left her mute. Her head buzzed, her breath came fast, and she knew. What his fingers were doing to her, these were the surges. "Please. The virginity," she gasped, her head spinning as if she were on a dizzying Ride of the Valkyries. "Take it away."

Which, after he put on what he called 'the protection,' he did.

Chapter Sixteen

Afterwards, they lay side by side, sweaty skin to sweaty skin. She was sore, achy. She should have minded, but she didn't. Losing her virginity was painful, but it was so far outside anything she'd imagined, Sofia spent more time being amazed at how it worked, than worried about how it hurt.

The second time was much better.

"You waited for me to..."

"To come," he supplied, tucking her close. "Yes, I did."

She pressed her face into the hollow at the base of his throat and breathed him in. His lemon-lime cologne was an after-thought to the scent of his body and of the sex between them. She let it swirl around her head. Now that she had lost herself in the surges and the soaring to the heavens that existed only in her mind, she understood why women read so many romances. "This was so nice of you to wait."

"You're saying I'm nice? Again?" He chuckled, running his fingers over her nipples, palming the roundness of her breasts.

She arched into his hands, not understanding why the surges were back so soon.

"Waiting for you doesn't make me nice. Greedy maybe, because your enjoyment increases mine."

But he *was* nice. He was always doing wonderful things, holding the door for her, kissing her hand without wet lips, and giving her one spectacular orgasm after another. Orgasm. She mouthed the word against his skin.

Lying so close together was like being man and wife.

She, of course, wouldn't know anything about it, but Car would. "When you were married to your wife, did you enjoy being together in the bed afterward?"

He was running his hand up and down her spine. He stopped. "If we didn't want Lorenzo in bed with us, why would we want Louise?"

Yes, why, she wondered. Why had her mouth taken over from her brain at such a sublime moment? "It is not important," she said, with haste.

He shifted onto his back, took his arm from beneath her shoulder. "There wasn't any afterward."

"I do not need to know." She rolled toward him, pressed against his side, seeking to recapture his warmth.

"It's not a big deal. I'll tell you."

They were touching still, but he had withdrawn. "You do not have to tell me such a thing. I am sorry I asked."

"I married Louise because I got her pregnant." He sat up and moved away from her. "We knew we were going to get a divorce once she had the kid. But first I made sure there'd be no question about responsibility."

She sat up too. "You do not believe in having a child when you are not married?"

"If other people want to? I don't care. For me? That would never work."

"Noah, he lives with his mama from the beginning?"

"Yes."

She had been interested in the boy from that time in Brent's suite. She had loved his solemn eyes and his sweet smile. "Does he stay with you sometimes?"

"He has. But it's always hard." Car stood and picked up the sheet that had fallen to the floor during their love-making. He shook it out and replaced it on the bed. "Eight or nine months out of the year, I'm playing baseball, mostly at night, when kids are supposed to be at home. But that's going to change soon. When I get custody. And then he'll live with me." He slipped in next to her and pulled the sheet over them.

"That is wonderful. You love him, yes?"

"I...yes." He turned onto his back and threw an arm over his forehead. "Of course I love him. It's complicated."

This was a strange response. How could love be

complicated? "I am hungry," she announced, eager to change the subject that had become too odd.

He reached out to lay a hand on her back when she sat up, and stroked his fingers down her spine. "Isn't it a lucky thing I've got a kitchen?"

She laughed in spite of her uneasiness. She wouldn't ask him about his son again. Not right away. "Then let us go there." She felt around on the bed. "Once I find my clothing."

"Forget your clothing." He padded on bare feet over to his closet. She admired his tight posterior, and how his skin gleamed in the half-light from the windows.

He came back and tossed something soft in her lap. "Here. Put this on."

It was a plain, white tee-shirt. She slipped it over her head. Its hem slithered down her body. "How do I look?" She got up and turned for him.

"Tempting." He stuck out a hand and grabbed hers. "Let's go before I change my mind."

Laughing, she went with him.

The appliances in his kitchen were either black or white. "*Ridicolo*," she muttered. The colors were, most assuredly, ridiculous. The appliances were not. "You have a Sub-Zero refrigerator." She stared, awestruck, at its burnished black surface. Opening it, she peered in at the shelves, which had very little on them: a gallon of milk, a loaf of bread, two cans of beer, and some small bottles. "Where is the food?"

"I eat out a lot, or bring in."

Turning around, she studied the Viking stove. "It is terrible. You have five burners on this stove. Why? So you can cook the food you do not have in your refrigerator?"

"Everything in here came with the apartment. If I'd had a choice, I would have told them to keep the stove. All I need is a sink, the refrigerator. Oh, and my microwave."

"*Poverino*," she muttered.

"Oh, now you're calling me names?" he said, tickling her.

She slapped his hand away, opened one of the cabinets, and smiled in delight. "*Bene*! Pasta. Where are the pots?"

163

She stooped and swung open a cabinet next to the stove. The shirt, which had reached almost to her knees, shaped her rounded bottom as she bent. Before she could think, he lifted her to her feet. She dropped the pot, which fell to the floor with a loud clang. "*Che succede?*" she shrieked.

"I have to do this," he muttered and lifted her onto the counter. First he kissed her mouth, then thumbed her nipples and caressed her breasts through the shirt. He pressed his face against her, and crowded her body with his. He ran his hand down the center of her body, over her belly to touch her.

"So wet," he muttered, sliding his fingers inside and began to move them. In. Out. Again. And Again.

She leaned back against his white cabinets, clutched the edge of the black granite counter top, and screamed.

"It's a good thing this apartment's sound-proofed, because you've got a pair of major league lungs," he said, when she slid off her perch of pleasure. She would have fallen if he hadn't caught her.

Voice weak, she said, "I will scream if you do this thing to me again." She sagged in his arms. "Can we do other things also?"

He chuckled. "We can experiment."

She held her hands up. "This moment, I cannot take more experiments."

She staggered against him. He held her, caressed her, gentled her, took her to the bathroom where they showered in his black-tiled shower with its multiple shower heads, set in the walls, and they experimented. Afterwards, she returned to the kitchen to cook the pasta.

When it was on the table, he sat and admired his steaming bowl. "How did you get this done?"

"I put it in the pot." She sat down and whisked a napkin onto her lap.

"I meant how did you cook it so fast?" He reached for a knife and fork and began to cut the spaghetti.

She shrieked.

The utensils clattered to the table. "What's wrong?" he demanded, looking around for danger.

She pointed at his bowl. "You cut the spaghetti."

He frowned. "How else am I going to eat it? I can't shove it in my mouth with both hands, or slurp it like a kid."

"*Barbaro*! You do not cut the pasta with the knife and the fork." She reached for his fork and slapped it into his hand. "You do like this."

She proceeded to guide him in how to take three or four strands of spaghetti onto his fork, plant the tines against the side of the bowl and twirl. "That is how it is done."

He stared at the example of perfectly twirled spaghetti that she held up to him.

"Car, you must eat now," she said, the fork inches from his mouth.

He grinned, opened, and she fed him. He chewed. His eyes drifted shut. "The flavors—they just exploded in my mouth."

"It is only pasta with butter and cheese, some salt and pepper, and parsley flakes from a bottle I found in the cabinet."

"It tastes amazing." He made his first attempt at twirling. Sofia laughed, but he managed to get the spaghetti into his mouth. "How do you know how to cook so well?"

She waved a dismissive hand in the air. "It is nothing special."

"It tastes special to me."

"*Grazie*, Car. I love to cook. It is one of my favorite things in all the world."

"Do you love it better than singing?"

"Ah." She bit her lip. "I should say no; singing is what I love more, yes?"

"Only if it's true."

"To sing is my natural state. The cooking exists deep inside me. It is what I do when I show love."

He shifted in his chair and looked down. He stuck his fork into some strands of spaghetti.

She did the same.

The silence was broken only by the sound of forks scraping against bowls.

It was he who broke it. "I thought you wouldn't consider yourself a success until you sang Carmen. It's why you came to New York."

"I did, I did," Sofia said, rushing. "You know, my English, still is not so good. What I mean to say about the cooking is I love to cook. That is clear, yes?" She laughed, relieved to have explained herself better, or at least so her heart was not as exposed as her body.

"Yeah, loving to cook. That makes sense." He looked at his watch. "It's late. Are you..." He hesitated. "Are you staying? Or, I could take you home. Whichever."

"I must get a good sleep so I can sing my best for the Maestro, so I will return to the hotel."

"Okay. Don't forget to take your mantilla with you. It'll help you be more like Carmen."

"This is my plan."

Car rose, taking their plates with him. "Go get dressed. I'll clean." He pushed her out of the kitchen, toward his bedroom, where she picked up her clothes and put them on. When she cooked for the housekeepers and cleaners, the doormen, the receptionists, yes, even the cooks, she did so because she liked them. And she wanted company. Yes, she loved to cook for them. But show love? Bah!

She loved to sing. Yes, she did. She loved seeing the faces of the people, who were overwhelmed with joy when she sang her best. Tomorrow she would hope the Maestro was taken with joy when she sang her heart out for the role of her lifetime. What she said to Car about cooking and love? She had misspoken.

She didn't sleep well. She couldn't close her eyes without remembering every moment of being with Car in his bed, with him being inside her body, where it felt like he belonged. She tried hard to forget. But she couldn't, even while she dressed for the audition with the Maestro.

"I will wear the black skirt with the white, scoop-necked blouse," she announced, standing with Chelsea in front of the dresser.

"I approve." Chelsea picked through the box where she kept her bracelets. "Take these."

They were the bangles Car removed from her body during their game. Sofia ducked her head so Chelsea wouldn't see her red face and ask why.

Once she slipped the bangles on, she gave herself a critical look in the mirror. "Well? Do I look like a cigarette girl who makes the slave of every man?"

"Exactly like a cigarette girl." Chelsea leaned back. "I like the way you slicked back your hair and flattened those curls in front of your ears."

Sofia clapped a hand to her head. "I should have bought castanets."

"You'll do fine without castanets."

"*Accidenti*, I almost forget the most important thing." She pulled open a drawer. "My mantilla." She held it aloft; it was a thing of amazing beauty, black and gauzy, with long fringes. "Car gave this to me."

"You two have become very cozy, very quickly. You've gone from not wanting to be anywhere near each other to...?" Chelsea raised an eyebrow. "Coming in at almost three in the morning?"

A flush started in Sofia's neck. "We..."

Chelsea waved away her discomfort. "Don't tell me. I'm happy for you. He's a decent guy, besides being an amazing hottie. With that look of you-know-what on your face, if Antonio Lupino doesn't see you as Carmen, then I don't know about that man."

Great. If Chelsea saw she was no longer a virgin, perhaps the Maestro would too. "*Grazie*, Chelsea. Still, my singing will get me the role."

Sofia would have added more, but for the knock at the door. "Did we ask the front desk to send something to us this morning?"

"I didn't," said Chelsea, crossing the living room.

Sofia followed, but stopped the moment the door swung open to reveal Car standing in the doorway. He was wearing a tee-shirt, this one black, over jeans frayed at the pockets. His blue-green eyes searched her face. "We're playing an evening game, so I'm free until about 3 o'clock. I thought I'd drive you over to the opera house."

Sofia's heartbeat began to leap like wavelets in the lake in the first scene of *Russalka*. "It would be nice to ride with you to the Muni, Car," she said, voice breathless.

"I figured you'd like a little fan support on your big day."

Never had she gone to an audition with fan support. Her father sent her with warnings. Her heart swelled with emotion.

"On your way now, Sofia," said Chelsea.

"You are coming, yes?" Sofia protested, but weakly.

"Nope. I'll be a third wheel."

"What is this third wheel?"

Sofia caught the quick glance Chelsea gave Car and the little grin that followed. "I think Car will explain. Now, shoo." Chelsea gave Sofia a nudge in the direction of the door.

"I do not agree, but I accept this is what you want."

"You're right. It's what I want. Go."

"What is a third wheel?"

Car closed his door and started up the motor. "One person too many."

She bit her lip. "Chelsea knows what we did."

Car raised one eyebrow. "You didn't tell her?"

"For me it was the most private thing."

He took her hand and squeezed her fingers.

Chelsea was not the person she wanted to talk to about last night. It was him. It was to him she wanted to tell of her feelings. But she reminded herself this was dangerous, when she didn't know how he felt.

The ride to the Municipal Opera House took mere minutes. "Here we are." Car pulled into the circle in front of the Muni's white stone facade and its long, glass windows. Before she could fumble the seatbelt open, he was coming around to her side, opening her door, holding out a hand, a soft smile on his face.

She let him lift her down. She slid down his body, firm in the grip of his strong hands, feeling the outline of his ribs, the muscles of his thighs. The bulge.

"I like the blouse." He wasn't looking at the blouse. He was looking at what the blouse covered. "You have it pulled down far enough. Let Lupino imagine the rest."

"I will leave it where it is." To tease him, she ran her fingers along the edge of the blouse, tugging it a drop.

He smoothed her hair back. "Knock the guy dead, sweetheart. Knock him on his ass."

"I do not know about all the knocking but what you must tell me is *in bocca al lupo*."

"Which means?"

"It means in the mouth of the wolf."

He cupped a cheek. "Whatever I'm supposed to say, you know what I wish for you." He pulled her to him, hard, held her tight for a moment. Then, letting her go, he said, "I'll wait."

"I hope it will not take a long time."

"Take whatever time you need."

She stepped away from the Hummer and blew him a kiss. "I will come back when I am finished."

"Okay, Carmen."

She blew him a kiss, turned, and made her way across the wide plaza to the opera house's broad glass doors.

They were still working on the lobby. There was a smell of new wood and paint in the air. Whole sections of walls were covered in plastic, and sawdust coated the floor. She got directions to the Maestro's office, up a winding staircase giving her a view of the entire plaza.

At the top of the steps, she paused, and looked back to where Car stood, leaning against his parked vehicle, arms folded across his chest, legs crossed at the ankles. She smiled. She was still smiling when she opened the door to the Maestro's office.

A woman with bulging eyes, sitting behind a desk against the far wall, looked up as Sofia entered. "May I help you?"

"I am Sofia de' Medici, here to sing for Maestro Lupino."

"Have a seat."

For what seemed hours, but surely was no longer than a half hour, Sofia waited. She spent her time looking at the pictures lining the walls. They all featured the Maestro. There he was with Domingo and Pavarotti, with Fleming and Netrebko. She studied the picture of him at the podium, arms raised, head flung back, the passion of the music illuminating his face.

Sofia wondered if, when she sang, her face was lit with such ecstasy. Or if it looked like that when she and Car made love. Thinking about how it felt when they were joined, his flesh in hers, she shivered. Wiggling, she shifted her gaze to the next picture, this one, an older picture of Dame Joan Sutherland and her husband, the great conductor, Sir Richard Bonynge.

With the Maestro. Naturally.

Soon, she grew tired of staring at the pictures. "It will be much longer?" she asked the receptionist.

The receptionist raised one eyebrow, as if to indicate this was a ridiculous question. "I really don't know."

"Ah." Perhaps the woman didn't know about the Maestro's busy schedule and Sofia's appointment at twelve o'clock, to which she wasn't supposed to be late. Giving her a sarcastic answer would be pointless. She was the Maestro's guardian, and Sofia was nothing to her.

Sofia felt temper begin to build inside. She looked down at her hands, where they creased her black Carmen skirt. "*Disgraziato*," she muttered. "*Cretino*." How much longer would the Maestro make her wait? But she knew. Forever. He had never had any intention of letting her sing for him. Last night had been a ploy. Just to put her off.

She narrowed her eyes at the Maestro's closed door. What would Carmen do, faced with that closed door? What if she was waiting at Lillas Pastia's inn and the Toreador said he wouldn't sing his famous song for her? Sofia knew what Carmen would *not* do. She would *not* smile and say I'm okay with that, even though you're saving that great basso voice of yours for some other woman. She would *not* say it's okay for you to move right on to Seville and the bullring and not let me fall in lust with you. She would *not* let him get away with any of that.

She jumped to her feet. The receptionist made a

squeaky sound. She half-rose from her chair.

"Do not get up." Sofia marched past her. Without knocking, she pushed open the door to the Maestro's office.

There he sat, feet up on a desk covered with piles of scores over every inch, and talking on his cellphone. He scrambled to his feet. "What are you doing?" Shock lit his eyes.

She stamped her foot. "You keep me waiting? Me? You do not keep Carmen waiting." She tossed her head back, put a hand on one hip, and thrust her breasts forward. She threw her handbag on his desk. The papers scattered and flew; some fell to the floor. He looked first at his papers and then at her. His mouth pursed.

She pulled her blouse down, almost to the nipples. "Sit down," she ordered.

He sat.

Reaching into her handbag, she pulled out the mantilla. Wrapping it around her shoulders, she closed her eyes, but only for a second.

She began to hum. And sway. She leaned across the Maestro's desk, making sure he got a good look at her breasts.

Then she turned away and began, softly, to sing the *Seguidilla*.

"*Près des remparts de Séville... Near the walls of the city of Seville, near my friend Lillas Pastia's inn...*"

The receptionist was standing in the doorway. Perhaps she thought about kicking Sofia out? Sofia gave her Carmen's haughty stare. The receptionist left.

"*I'll dance the seguidilla and drink some manzanilla...*" Sofia cocked one shoulder upward and swayed. She could feel the mantilla's fringes brush against her hips.

"*Yes, but it's so boring when you're alone, and true pleasure comes when we're together...*" She looked at the Maestro over her shoulder and, between phrases, pantomimed a kiss.

He stared at her mouth.

"*So to keep me company, I'll take my lover with me...*" She whirled, and slunk toward the desk. Her eyes fixed on the Maestro, she shoved her handbag to the floor. It landed with a thud.

She crawled onto the desk. "*Who wants my soul? It's here for the taking...*" Her breasts were falling out of her blouse. She bent forward to help them along.

The Maestro's gaze flickered between her lips and her breasts, back and forth.

"*You came at the right moment. I cannot wait much longer... Près des remparts de Séville.*"

She hopped off the back of the desk, ambled around to the front, sat, and placed her foot on the front of his chair. The pointy toe of her shoe fit snugly between his thighs and nudged up against his bulge.

He stared at her foot.

It looked good there, she thought—the toe of that sexy, black shoe with its rhinestone curlicues on the front.

When at last he looked up, she tossed her head back, pulled the mantilla from her shoulders, and ran the fringes across his face. "Well?"

Visibly, he gathered himself. "You surprise me, *Signorina*."

She sat back, and held herself still. "Yes?"

He put his hands on the arms of his chair, looked at her foot, still lodged between his thighs, looked at her, and slid his chair back a few inches, enough that her foot fell from the spot where she had wedged it. "I may have been wrong," he said.

A surge of triumph rose inside her.

He gazed up at her, eyes narrowed with consideration. "The voice I did not doubt. The rest?" He tapped his chin, kept unblinking eyes on her. "This may be a mistake. In fact it may be one I regret in the end."

What mistake? What regret? Sofia stopped breathing.

"But it is clear to me," the Maestro said. "You are my Carmen."

She began to breathe again. She jumped off the desk, grabbed her handbag and swayed toward the door. "You will call me later today with the schedule for rehearsals."

"I..."

"Call me."

Chapter Seventeen

Her legs trembled so badly, Sofia feared she would fall down the marble steps to the lobby. Only by clutching the railing did she prevent it from happening. Once at the bottom, she tottered to the nearest canvassed-over work area. The floor within was covered with a layer of sawdust, littered with pieces of wood, a couple of cans of paint and, in the middle, a hammer. Thank God, there were no workmen.

She put one shaking hand to her chest, where her heart threatened to burst through her ribs. Anger had carried her into the Maestro's office. Anger had pushed her to sing. But what anger? Anger to mask the fear she'd fail and have to admit she could do nothing without her father guiding her way? But it wasn't her father she thought of. It was Car. And it wasn't anger. It was fear she'd disappoint him.

She clapped a hand across her mouth. From the start she'd been infatuated with his stardom, his body, and of course his beautiful eyes. It was infatuation when he kissed her at the Pitti Palace. It was infatuation when he kissed her at the hotel.

But last night when they made love, it wasn't infatuation.

She loved him. *Loved him*. Not merely his physical self, which she had always loved. But his gentle sense of humor, the way he cared for her, the way he made her feel happy in her body. It was the conversation and the smiles they shared. It was everything. She loved it all.

Perhaps not his Hummer.

Unexpected tears, both bitter and sweet, pricked her eyelids. She dashed them away. What foolishness was this? She could love him forever. But he? What could she expect of him, he who could have any woman he wanted? Could she expect him to love her? No. She couldn't. And she wouldn't. She'd take what she could get.

Sofia took a deep breath, looked down at her black skirt to make sure she hadn't gotten sawdust or grime on it. She pulled the heavy canvas aside and picked her way across the lobby. The sunlight almost blinded her when she stepped out into the plaza and saw Car straighten away from the Hummer. She quickened her steps. He did too. She held out her arms and began to laugh. She laughed all the way across the plaza and into his arms.

The damn audition had taken forever—one hour and twenty minutes, during which time Car had gone over every possible outcome, good and bad. He'd told her to take as long as she needed, but the longer it took, the more he worried. The moment he saw her in the Muni's doorway, her body practically glowing, the smile on her face so big, he could see it clear across the plaza, he knew. She'd gotten the role.

She jumped him, crying and laughing and sprinkling kisses on his neck. They bumped noses when he shifted her in his arms to kiss her laughing mouth. "Tell me what happened," he demanded, shaking her a little, and letting her slide down his body.

The grin that lit her face was bigger than her little self. She did a dance in front of him; although how she could in those killer heels, he had no idea. She stopped, grabbed both his hands and squeezed. "I sat for a long time."

Car stopped smiling.

Looking up at him, her eyes snapped with excitement. "He wanted me to go away, to give up the waiting. Perhaps it was what we thought. He heard Lorenzo's story that I would destroy the production."

Car began to smile again. "But you changed his mind."

"Yes, I changed it." She stepped back and swayed in a circle, hands raised, snapping her fingers as if she were wielding a pair of castanets. "I danced and I sang for him. Like Don José, he thought he could make me the prisoner of him, but I showed him he is the prisoner of me."

"You could make anyone a prisoner." Car slid his hands around her waist and pulled her close.

Her eyes were lit with pleasure, her red lips wide in a radiant smile. "It is only because you gave me such excellent help that I was able to sing for the Maestro, Car. I give you a thousand thank-yous."

"I didn't sing for him. You did." He needed to kiss her, this sweet, giving woman, just coming from her big triumph and still, she gave *him* the credit for her success. He lowered his head and took her mouth with his. She stilled in his arms, made a little sound of capitulation.

Somewhere behind them, the sound of a horn.

Car put a hand around Sofia's waist. "Let's go before we have more audience than we need." He threw the door open on her side of the Hummer, and lifted her.

She was fussing with the fringes of the mantilla when he got in and started the motor. Which was when he noticed the neckline of her blouse. It was pulled way, far down. "What's with the blouse?"

"The Maestro is like any man. He loves a woman's bosoms. I would never, never show him all my breasts. But I tease him with what he might see."

"You are evil." He reached into the blouse, all the time watching her face for her reaction. The feel of her nipple hardening against his palm shot straight to Car's groin.

Sofia's eyes widened. She relaxed into his hand, sighed, and closed her eyes. Her breath quickened, and she arched into the heat of his hand. "The Maestro, he wants to do to me what you do to me," she whispered, her head falling back against the seat. "He can want, but he will not get. Only you can see me this way. Only you can touch me this way."

"This is crazy. We're in public." Reluctantly, he slid his hand out of her blouse.

"We can go back to your apartment, yes?"

"No. I have to get to the stadium. Remember, I told you I need to be there at three o'clock? It's almost two. I'll drop you off and go."

"I want to see you play."

"I thought you didn't like baseball."

"That was before you explained it to me. Now I want to make the cheer for you."

"You'll probably want to change from this get-up you have on to something more..."

"More like for a baseball game and less like for the bullring?" She flashed an impudent smile at him from under her black-as-night eyelashes. "*Si, señor.*"

"I'm sorry." He ran a finger down her cheek. "Much as I'd like you to come with me to the stadium, I can't wait."

She pouted her disappointment. But then she brightened. "I will come to you on the subway train."

He chuckled. "I'd like to see that."

"You think I cannot?"

Angling his head toward her, he considered the look on her face that said this was about to become a challenge and, that instant, decided to go along with it. "I'd give anything to see you do it, because truth is, I don't think you can."

She threw her head back and gave him one of her big belly laughs. Damn, but he loved that laugh of hers.

"You will give me anything? Does that mean I can ask for anything?"

He pulled away from the curb. "That's what it means, sweetheart."

She reached across the console and tapped him on the shoulder. "This is a bet, yes?"

"Yes."

"I am taking your bet."

Later, at batting practice, he could hardly find his

rhythm. All he could think of was Sofia, hoping she would figure out the subway, or get a limo and come to the game. He made sure there was room for her in the wives' box.

He'd about finished when Dawg came up to take his turn.

"So what's this with you and Sofia?" Dawg knocked his bat against a cleat.

"What do you mean?" Car took a last swing.

"You still hanging out with her?"

Car stepped out of the batting cage. "Yeah. Why do you ask?"

Dawg smiled sheepishly and stepped into the cage Car had vacated. He took a swing at the first pitch and the ball landed in the back of the stands in dead centerfield. He turned to Car and cocked his head to one side. "So are you?"

Car's senses went on alert. "I'll repeat. Why?"

"Oh, man. Can't you just answer?" The awkward smile remained on Dawg's face.

"Since when is this what you and I need to discuss?"

Dawg shook his head vigorously. "Not me. Tina. She's the one who wants to know what's between you and Sofia."

"Tell Tina we're just fine."

"That's good." Dawg sighed, and began to make like a demolition derby, smashing one ball after another, every single one of them ending up somewhere in the second tier.

Car stood in awe of this powerful man who was such a pussy for his wife, he was willing to ask a friend about his social life. He began to laugh. "Dawg, you are so whipped."

"Oh, yeah." Dawg grinned and kept on hitting. "And I plan to stay that way."

All during the game, Car kept playing Tina's question over in his mind; what *was* between them? If his brain could have clamped on the answer, he'd have been grateful.

Skip put him in for Michaels. Two times he was up at bat; he, with his great eye, struck out both times. The guys looked past him when he came back to the dugout. He knew why. They wanted him back, the Car Bradford from before last fall's surgery.

Game over, another one in the lost column. He walked down the hallway toward the wives' door, thinking how frustrating it was he couldn't contribute. Until he saw Sofia, waiting for him, a warm glow surrounding her, and he forgot about the game. "I see you made it," he said, and broke into a grin.

"I am so sorry you lose the game," she said, hands clasped under her chin.

"It's okay."

She'd changed into a pair of trousers, a brown as deep as dark chocolate, a white high-collared sweater, and a long lighter brown sweater with big sleeves. "The voyage here was wonderful. I tell the taxi cab driver to take me to the subway..." She punched him on the arm. "Why you do not tell me it is a subway and not a subway train? The driver laughed at my words."

"Wait, wait." He pressed a hand to his head. "Isn't there a subway station around the corner from the hotel?"

"Yes, but I do not know this when I am always taking the taxis. And excuse me, but who is telling the story?"

He took a breath, dizzy. "Sorry." But he wasn't. He'd gotten so he loved dizzy.

What was between them?

"*Allora, w*hen I am in the subway, I ask how do I get to the stadium for the Federals? A nice gentleman helps me buy the Metro Card and shows me how to slide it in the entry place."

"The turnstile."

"Yes, that. He shows me where to stand on the platform, and tells me where to get off the train." She threw her arms wide. "And here I am. This means I am the winner of the bet."

Snaking an arm around her neck, he pulled her into him. He bent at the knees, put his forehead against hers. "Yup."

"And now I choose what I have won?"

He squeezed his eyes shut, wanting to imprint the essence of her against his skin. "Yup."

"Then I say we go back to your apartment and I cook dinner for you."

He remembered what she'd said about cooking. Refused to think about it. "But then I win too, because I get to eat what you make."

"I do not mind if you win, if I win first."

They stopped at one of those expensive grocers. "We must buy food for your house." She set off down the produce aisle.

He followed, having been assigned cart duty. She started with tomatoes. While she smelled them, squeezed them, hefted them in her hands, and talked to them, he thought about her in his bed last night. He'd wanted her to sleep with him, right through until the morning. He never did that. He always got up and went home if he was at the woman's house. If she was at his, he made sure she knew she wasn't spending the night.

What was between them?

Sofia dropped a couple of the tomatoes and some other vegetables she'd been eyeing into the cart, and marched on to the meat counter. She looked at everything until a butcher appeared and asked if she needed any help.

Her head came up at the sound of his voice. "*Lei è italiano?*"

The man got excited and began to blab away in Italian. She blabbed right back.

When he held up a finger—which Car took to mean wait—and disappeared again, Car said, "What was that about?"

"I ask him if he is Italian and *certamente*, he is. From Naples, but I forgive him, since he gets me what I want."

Just then the man came back, holding up a slab of meat. No, he didn't hold it; he cradled it. He began to speak in a low voice, to which Sofia responded with a bunch of oohs and ahs. On occasion, as the butcher caressed the damn slab, Sofia let out a burst of Italian, to which they both nodded in agreement. It was a love fest over a piece of protein. Then finally, from Sofia, a *grazie,* and the man disappeared.

Sofia sighed. "*Allora*, he will slice it very thin and I

will make you scaloppini for dinner."

"Sca..." he began, working hard to keep the smile from his face.

"*Ska-low-pee-nee*," she enunciated. "It is when you pound the meat to make it so thin you can almost see through it. I already know you like meat prepared just so."

He ran a finger down her nose. "I know what scallopini is. I was teasing you."

"*Disgraziato*." She wagged a finger at him. "We come back in a few minutes after I get the wine, some butter, more pasta—you have none, believe me, I have looked—and the radicchio and the endive." And she was off in yet another direction. "*Dove*... where... Ah!" She pounced on a fancy bottle of olive oil. Then it was back to the produce.

He followed her up and down the aisles. As she stopped here, then there, his mind wandered. He remembered how the second time they made love, he almost forgot a condom. How had that happened? Was it the passion of the moment? He'd had passionate moments with other women and he'd never almost forgotten to use a condom.

What was between them?

She threw something in the cart.

He shook himself. "What are we having besides the scaloppini?"

"We are having a nice salad and vermicelli—that is the very thin pasta—with a simple sauce I will make to complement the scallopini. Also strawberries in a zabaglione sauce for dessert. I remember from Vittorio's. You love this dessert."

His mouth watered.

Out of the corner of his eye he caught movement back at the meat counter. "I think your friend is looking for you."

"My scaloppini is ready!" And she was off.

While Car waited for them to say the final benediction over the veal, he signed an autograph for a man who thought it was pretty funny that Car Bradford wheeled his own cart around a grocery store.

Later, at home, after they unpacked everything, Car sat on his couch, television on, the sound muted, because he was listening to a woman in his kitchen singing a melody so sweet and beautiful that his throat tightened. The smell of the veal cooking in a wine sauce filled his head. He turned toward his dining area, where the table was all fancied up with plates and cutlery and glasses. Lighted candles sat in the middle, casting a warm-as-honey light on his bare white walls.

What was between them?

When had he begun to like the idea of having a meal on his table instead of eating take-out in front of the TV? When had he begun to like the idea of having a woman singing in the kitchen? He stared, empty-eyed at the screen. He scrubbed his cheeks, jumped up and made for the kitchen, because all at once he felt a compulsion to be with her.

She'd taken one of his towels, a white one—he had white towels and black towels—and wrapped it around her waist. Her hair, which she'd put up, was falling down around her shoulders. Her cheeks were rosy from the heat. A glass of wine sat to one side of the stove, which she stood in front of, a spatula in hand, turning the pieces of meat her butcher friend had pounded exactly to her liking. On the back burners were two pots: on one burner, his biggest pot, with steam billowing out of it. The other burner held one pot inside the other. That, she'd explained, is how you make a double boiler when you don't have one.

She'd hulled the strawberries, washed them, and patted each one dry. They sat, glistening, in a bowl in his refrigerator, waiting for the sauce she told him she would make in the double boiler.

He slid his arms around her slender waist, and fitted himself against her warm, gorgeous, womanly body.

"*O Dio!*" She shrieked with one startled glance over her shoulder, and dropped the spatula with a clatter. "*Mi hai spaventato a morte!*"

"Are you cursing me again, Sofia?"

"I said you scared me to death, idiotic man." She wriggled, trying to escape from his arms, pretending to be irritated, but failing.

"Sorry. I couldn't help it. You look too good." Gently he bit the tender skin on the back of her neck. "Good enough to eat."

"Do not lose the appetite with this biting. I am making a dinner so delicious, even you, with your terrible eating habits, will be transported to heaven."

He already was, but only a little because of the food.

What was between them?

"How long before food is on the table?"

She brought up her wrist. "Twenty minutes. Go and sit. Let me finish without the distraction."

He backed away. "Okay. I guess I can wait twenty minutes."

It was twenty minutes. True to her word, he was transported to heaven. The scaloppini melted in his mouth; the taste was so fine, his jaws ached. The pasta, which he very carefully wound around his fork, was flecked with fresh basil, a little fresh pepper, a sprinkle of cheese, and a glaze of butter and wine. Even the salad was outstanding, which for him, was saying a lot. He hated most everything green.

"What do you think," she asked when he had scraped the bottom of the bowl she'd given him with the strawberries and the zabaglione, which, because he was interested, she explained was some eggs, sugar, and champagne.

"I've never had such a fantastic meal." He picked up the bowl and ran his tongue along the bottom, which sent her off into peals of laughter.

"I will make you more. Perhaps even for breakfast." Her eyes were sparkling.

"Oh ho, so you think you're staying for breakfast?"

The smile dimmed.

"I'm just kidding," he said, reaching for her hand, running his thumb across the back of her fingers. "You better be staying for breakfast."

The smile came back, this time with a crafty little slant. "Then I will wash the dishes before it gets too late."

He pushed his chair back. "No way. Either you let me wash them with you, or I wash them by myself, and you put your feet up and relax." He came up behind her chair and leaned over, breathing against her ear, kissing her on the shoulder. "Your choice."

"I am not tired. I do not need to put up the feet. I

choose together."

He washed, she dried. It was all done in a flash. He didn't think he could have waited much longer than that to get her into bed. He needed her there, his skin to her skin, with no separation between them.

Still the whisper wouldn't go away: *what was between them?*

Chapter Eighteen

Sometime during the early morning hours, after they had tried out some of the positions into which Sofia had not thought they could twist themselves, Car lay on his back with her curled up into his side. She'd thrown one possessive leg over his; a beautiful, plump breast pressed into his rib cage, her cheek rested against his chest, her head nestled into the crook of his neck, and her hair lay loose on her shoulders. He tunneled his fingers into her curls, winding and unwinding. For some reason, he had no idea how, they began to talk about the game and why he'd struck out twice.

"Perhaps you cannot make the hits now because you are nervous."

"How could I be nervous doing something I've done my entire adult life?"

She reached up and cupped his face in her hands. "Before, have you ever had an operation?"

"Never."

"*Allora*, you have never played baseball after such a big injury and then an operation. Of course you are nervous. You do not know what you can expect. Can I hit the ball as far? Can I catch the ball as nicely? This is what you say to yourself, as would any person who plays baseball the entire adult life." She clicked her tongue against her teeth and patted his face. "You must cut yourself the slack."

And so she spoke. As if that was that. And somehow that was that. The anxiety he'd been carrying around for months slid off him like warm zabaglione off a strawberry.

"*Aspetta*." She eased out of bed and padding over to

where her clothing lay in a pile on the floor.

More Italian. "Translate," he said. But he wasn't focused on the translation. He was focused on the miracle Sofia had given to him, the thing he'd never had, and it wasn't whatever she was rooting around for. Once more, she set him straight: first about not being a dumb jock, and now about his injury. Each time she'd reminded him that he was okay.

There was a whole bunch of muttering. For the first time in forever, he felt at peace with himself. Really, clearly, undeniably at peace. His insides humming with contentment, he turned on his side, curled his arm under his head, and gave himself up to studying the view. He loved a plump ass. Especially hers.

At last she scurried back into bed. "Let me in," she said, pushing him so she could crawl under the covers. "It is cold in your apartment. Do you not have the heat?"

"I have the heat," he imitated. "Now tell me what *aspetta* means."

She laid something cold on his chest. "It means wait. I wanted you to wait for me to bring this to you."

He picked up the thing, squinting to see it in the dark. It was a coin, about the size of an old American silver dollar. "Is this Italian?"

"*Si*, Italian and old. A five hundred lire piece. We do not use lire anymore in Italy because we are part of the European Union. The most terrible thing is now we have one money, the Euro, and no more lire. The Euro is boring."

"But useful if you're traveling from Germany to Spain and you don't want to constantly be changing money." He turned her coin over in his hand and ran his thumb across the raised portions. "What's this one worth?"

"I do not know what it is worth in Euros. But it is worth much to me. It is my lucky piece. I have it with me when I go on the stage to sing."

He picked up his head to look at her. "Okay, so why are we talking about it now?"

"We are not talking. I am giving it to you."

"Oh no, you're not." He tried to give it back.

She wagged a finger in his face. "Oh yes, I am."

"You're not giving me the charm you use when you go on stage. I won't let you."

"You do not have the choice. I want you to have it. Even though I know you will be better now when you are at home plate and in the field, this will help you a little more."

Everyone he knew had a talisman. Maybe a cord tied around a wrist, or some other thing that protected them against things going wrong. He had one. It hadn't been working.

Now Sofia was giving him hers.

"How will you go onstage if you don't have it with you?"

"Perhaps when I sing *Carmen* you will lend it to me?"

He tried to answer her, but failed. She had taken his breath away. He leaned over and put the coin on his night table. Then he turned her on her side and took her in his arms. "Of course I'll lend it to you. Thank you so much for giving it to me." He pulled her close, kissed her softly, as she settled against him.

And there: the question that wouldn't leave him alone: *what was between them?*

The phone didn't wake her, but it did him.

Picking up his head, he stared at the bedside clock. 7:03 a.m. He fumbled for the handset, and grabbed it before he dropped it on the floor. Sofia still slept. He smiled down at her, curled on her side, facing him, and snoring softly. He'd have to tease her about the snoring. He turned away and, as softly as he could, said, "Hello."

"You are such a bastard!"

He closed his eyes. Louise. "You called to tell me that?"

"No, I called to tell you it's your fault."

He sighed. "What's my fault?"

"There's a picture of you on the Internet. With that Italian bitch." She started to sob. "How could you?"

He sat up, pulled the covers aside, bent to pick up his trousers, and slipped out of the bedroom. Bracing the phone between chin and shoulder, he buttoned and zipped his pants as he walked. "What?"

"How could you embarrass me with... with..."

"With what?"

There was lots of sniffing and then she whined, "With her. With your hand down her blouse."

He froze.

She sobbed some more. "I wanted people to think it was a friendly divorce. That we really still loved each other, just couldn't live together."

"Dammit, Louise," Car ground out. "That whole acting thing was your idea, not mine. We're not friends, the divorce wasn't friendly, neither was the marriage. And will you please get it through your head? It wasn't love. It was sex."

"We made love," she sobbed.

He clapped a hand to his head and threw himself down on the couch. Everyone else he knew who was divorced had nothing to do with the ex. How did he get so lucky his wouldn't leave him alone? "Louise..."

"There was love when we made Noah."

She was working herself into a frenzy. As usual. "Love? You were talking about having an abortion."

"I wouldn't have done it." More sobs.

Car held the handset away from his ear, After listening to her sobs as long as he could, he sighed, and said, "Louise, are you drunk?"

More sobbing. "You just want to make my life miserable."

No, he didn't. What he wanted was to turn back time to before that night at the Mosbachers', the team Christmas party, the night he met Louise, and the first time he heard the sobs. Now he was accustomed to them, but then he made the mistake of feeling sorry for her, because her mother was treating her like a child. Ass that he was, he decided to comfort her. Yeah, comfort. And what did it get him?

Well, it got him Noah.

"Where are we going with this?"

"If I give you custody, it makes me look selfish, like I don't want him."

This had been an issue from the get-go. Car thought they'd gotten past it. "It doesn't. It makes you look like you're smart enough to know you're not able to care for him the way I can right now. That's smart. Not selfish."

"I can take care of him. I can." More sobs, these deeper.

"But your life is changing, isn't it? You need space." Yeah, space. To be with Jensen.

She was hiccupping now, in addition to keeping up with the gut-wrenching sobs. If Car didn't understand Louise's need for everyone to pity her, his heart might have softened. But he did understand. "What do you want from me, Louise?"

"You have to do something for me."

"What's that?" He was tired of the conversation. Tired of her.

The sobbing stopped. "Make sure I never see any more pictures of you with the fat girl."

He sat up straight. "Dammit, Louise. Her name is Sofia. And she's not..."

"Yes, she is fat."

Car ground his teeth together. He was at the end of his patience. He needed off this call. "Okay. No more pictures with her."

"No more pictures and no more embarrassing me because then I'll walk away from the negotiations."

Something snapped. "How's this? I'll stop seeing her," he said, his voice heavy with sarcasm. "I'll do it."

"Just make the promise." She sniffed.

"Okay." He exhaled in disgust. "I promise, I really promise I'll stop seeing her. But you need to..."

"I know what I need to do. You'll have your agreement," she interrupted him, all business now, "by the last week in June."

"That long?"

"Pete and I are going to be out of the country, and then to a film festival in Colorado. I'll be too busy to sign the papers until then. Take it or leave it, Car." And she clicked off.

Car dropped the phone next to him on the couch. The woman was exhausting. After any conversation with her, he needed a rest. Right now he knew exactly what kind of rest he needed. In bed. With Sofia. He smiled and stood.

And there she was in the doorway, eyes wide, lips pressed tightly together, a blanket thrown around her shoulders.

"Sofia, I..."

She turned back toward the bedroom.

His heart began to thrum. She'd heard. He raced after her. "Sofia, wait a minute."

She'd placed the blanket back on his bed and began to put on her panties and bra.

"Sweetheart, it's not what you think."

She slipped her sweater over her head and reached for her trousers.

"That conversation with Louise, I know it sounded bad. But I've told you. She can be difficult."

Sofia stooped to pick up her shoes.

He held out his hands toward her. "She threatened me with Noah. About getting custody. "

"For Noah you must do what you must do."

He tried to take her hand. She shrugged away from him. "I was trying to get Louise off the phone."

"It is okay. You do not need to say this. The child must come first." Inflexibility sat squarely on her pale face.

He grabbed her arms. "Yes, the child comes first. But for me you come first, too."

She extricated herself from his grip. "Two cannot come first."

"Dammit, Sofia! Yes, they can."

She sat to put on her shoes.

He stood in front of her, thoughts racing around in helpless circles, his heart keeping pace with them.

What was between them... what was between them...

"Look," he said, and crouched in front of her. "If you had two children, would you say one came before the other?"

"Of course not. But I am not your child."

"No, you're not." He crouched and pulled her onto the floor into his lap. "You're a woman. A beautiful woman."

"Please, Car." She pushed against his shoulders. "You must let me up."

He shook his head. "I can't."

"Why not?" Tears stood big in her eyes.

"Because if I let you up, you'll leave. I can't let you leave."

"Why not?"

"Because... because I..." He stopped dead into silence.

She pulled her head back to stare at him.

He stared back, heart racing like he'd run three home runs worth of bases. He cupped her face and pressed a hard kiss on her lips. "You're special to me. I want you in my life."

She studied his face and said, "You said..." Her voice faltered. "You would not see me anymore. "

He shoved his hands into the heft of her hair. "Sweetheart..." It was his turn to falter. "It's our history, mine and Louise's." He plunged on. "Sometimes I give in to her so I can get her out of my hair." He cleared his throat and stared straight into Sofia's tear-sheened eyes. "Sometimes I say stupid things. What I said was a stupid thing. It wasn't true. You know that, don't you?"

She stared into the distance. After a beat, she said, "Yes."

He all but collapsed in relief. "Thank you," he muttered and closed his eyes.

She tried to slide off of his lap. He wouldn't let her. Breathing hard, he stroked her cheek and nuzzled into the velvety soft place behind her ear. "We'll be together. Carefully. But together," he said, hoping and hoping she believed him.

"I want you to have your son, Car." She smoothed a hand over his jaw, her touch feather-light. "Now let me up, please."

He did. And walked her to the door. He gave her an almost chaste kiss and closed the door behind her. Then he climbed back into bed. Arms folded beneath his head, he stared at the beams of sunlight spearing through the slats in the blinds that covered his east-facing windows and thought about the words he hadn't said. He could have said them. Should have. But hadn't. Never had.

"Goddamn Louise," he whispered. But it wasn't Louise's fault. It was his. He sat up and threw off the blankets, shot to his feet, and began to pace. It was there, all the reasons why he'd be in love with Sofia. She was good for him, the best thing that ever happened to him, his best friend. In love?

What the fuck was love anyway? He thought about the song. Until he'd heard it, he thought maybe he was the only one who didn't know.

He'd wanted to get her a cab or take her back to the hotel himself. Sofia told him she would take the subway. She loved the subway. And she wanted to be alone.

She should be happy now. She'd gotten her dream role. She'd have the career she always wanted. But happiness wasn't what she felt. She felt emptiness. She found a seat among the crush of people heading to their jobs, squeezed her eyes shut, and closed out the talk around her.

How stupid she'd been to think Car couldn't love her because she'd been a fat virgin pygmy, rather than a beautiful, thin model. It didn't matter what she looked like. Tina had shown her that could be fixed: with primary colors, and soft materials.

She opened her eyes as the train came swaying to a halt. She squinted at the sign; not her station.

Sofia believed Car when he said he wanted her. Just now, when he wouldn't let her go, she saw it in his desperate eyes. But he couldn't say the words she longed to hear. *I love you.* Her heart jumped into her throat. Even for his little boy, Noah. He even said that his feelings for his own child were complicated. Could it be he didn't have true love in him?

She knew the sound of grief she made was audible, for the woman sitting next to her glanced her way and shifted as far from her as she could on the crowded bench.

Sofia knew she loved Car. And she would love what would come from being in bed with him: beautiful, strong children. She longed for them. With him. But how could she be with a man who wouldn't have love in him for his own children?

The train came to a shrieking halt at her station. She stepped off and trudged up the steps to the street. She knew she had to separate herself from him emotionally because there would be no love. And there would be no children. But poor beggar that she was, she'd take whatever crumbs he gave her. Even if the crumbs stopped at a scrim—no, not a scrim, but an impenetrable barrier, one that she couldn't cross.

He was tired of hashing over what he didn't know how to change. But there were things he could. He'd made Louise that promise? He couldn't be near Sofia in public? Nobody said anything about not being near Lorenzo.

Two hours later, he was outside the Muni, waiting for Latte to show up for the first rehearsal. When the man exited his taxi, Car hopped out of the Hummer. "Hey, Lorenzo."

Latte turned, a smile on his full face that faded when he saw who called him.

"My man." Car clapped a hand on his shoulder. "What's up?"

"What a pleasure to see you." Lorenzo tried to ease out of Car's grip.

Car gripped him harder. "So, Sofia's going to be Carmen. And you're going to be Don José. That's something, huh?"

"Yes, it will be fantastic to perform again with Sofia," said Lorenzo, looking everywhere except at Car.

"But not like when you played Almaviva and she played Rosina. You know, in Florence?"

Latte's skin blanched white. His mouth dropped open.

"That's okay. You don't have to say anything." Car let go of Lorenzo, who stumbled before catching himself.

"This time it's different," continued Car. "Once you're off stage." He gripped Lorenzo's shoulder again with more force. Latte squealed like a mouse. "If you get my meaning."

Lorenzo ducked his head, and said something under his breath Car took to be agreement.

As Lorenzo ran up the Muni's steps, yanking the door open, the smile of satisfaction on Car's face faded, leaving him as edgy as before. He wished he could make everything right, like he had this. Later, on the field, he made sure to bring the five-hundred-lire piece with him, and he got a couple of hits.

That night, Car reported his success to Sofia. She gave him a congratulatory kiss, but her real attention was on the picture Louise had been up in his face about. She let out a scream when she saw it, taken of them in the Hummer, when Car had picked her up after her audition.

"Where was the *paparazzo*?" she raged. "And how did I let you feel my bosom when we were in public? *Che stupida!*"

"You are not stupid. I shouldn't have done it." They were sitting in bed, his laptop between them, looking at the picture of them inside the vehicle. It was kind of blurry, but not so blurry they couldn't see where his hand was. He flipped the lid closed. "But it sure felt good."

She threw herself on him and began to pound him around the head. "*Che cretino!*"

He cracked up. The laptop banged against his knee. "Ow! Stop! I have to run with that knee." He put his hands around it and then around his head. He kept laughing, let her go at him, until with a quick move of his wrists, he flipped her over. It had the expected effect. At least this part of what was between them was right.

Over the next few weeks, whenever they were together, he considered telling her about his discussion with Lorenzo and about the phone call he made to her father. Letting Lorenzo know Sofia had someone looking out for her, backing Sofia's father off, telling him he better not be running his mouth and hurting her chances of success, this was right too. But he didn't tell her. The mood between them continued to feel breakable as a raw egg. He hungered for things to be back where they'd been before Louise's phone call.

"When will you get the room ready for Noah?" she asked him one night when they were sitting in bed.

He'd volunteered to take Noah the following weekend, the weekend before Sofia's big performance at the Muni.

"I've got time to think about it," he said, laying back.

"It is too bad Helena will be in Chicago."

"How can I ask her to stay when what she really wants to do is say goodbye to her aunt before she has to go back to Poland next month?"

"Noah knows this and already he is missing her." Sofia pulled the covers up around her shoulders and ran her fingers through the thatch of hair in the center of his chest. He loved when she did that.

"It's crazy what they're making her go through all because she filled out her visa wrong." He put his hand over hers.

Sofia's mouth turned down a little. "This is why always now Noah is doing the acting out. He wonders what will happen to him. First he leaves his mama's house. Then he leaves his grandpapa's house, and goes back to his mama's. You have told him he will come to live with you. He does not know if this is true. He knows Helena, but she leaves him. He is frightened. *Poverino.*"

Car had hired the best immigration lawyers. But as one snotty INS guy said, "even when you think you've bought the best, we still have the last word."

Car shifted and turned toward Sofia. "I know he's frightened. But I have time to figure it out."

She sat up, pulled the sheet up to cover her breasts, and stared down at him. "You cannot figure it out. You must plan."

"What's there to plan?" His stomach clenched. "He'll come with his clothes, his toys, anything else that's important to him. All I have to do is supply the bed and the dresser."

She withdrew a little "You must make him feel welcome."

He looked away. He already knew he needed to make him feel welcome. It was the other part that was freaking him out. "Yeah, how do I do that?"

"You must paint his room a nice yellow or a little boy blue. You must take him to a store and buy... how do you say...? The pictures of the baseball players he likes."

"Posters."

"Yes, posters. You must get posters with autographs from your friends. He will love them."

"Anything else, boss?"

She stilled. "Do not make fun of me."

He didn't mean to make fun, but the conversation had veered too close to something he didn't want to talk about. "What should I do?"

She lay down and, cupping his face, looked directly into his eyes. "You must ask him what he likes." She ran a finger across his eyebrows. "He loves and admires his papa, the famous baseball player. You must listen to him, and look into his face so you can tell if he is feeling alone or perhaps frightened again. And you must hold him."

"I'm willing to hold him."

Frowning, she said, "You must be more than willing."

He rolled her over, and began to kiss that mouth of hers. He eased the hem of the sheet down and cupped one breast. "I'm not a touchy-feely guy."

Sofia narrowed her eyes at him and the dynamic in the room changed. She planted a hand on his chest and pushed him over onto his back. She pulled the sheet across her shoulders and straddled him. "This is nonsense. You do the touching and the feeling with me." She arched her back and took him in. "I see I must remind you."

Later she brought the subject up again.

"Tell me about Noah," she said. She'd taken her shower and put on a very revealing white nightgown. He could see the sway of her gorgeous, full breasts beneath the bodice.

"I told you before," he said, looking.

"You want him, yes?"

"Yes, I want him. Why else would I be asking for custody?"

"I do not know. Why?"

She was probing. As usual. "I told you. My life's complicated, Sofia. Can we change the subject?" Although now it was too late. He was already thinking about the time in the hospital and how it had changed everything.

"You want to tell me about today's rehearsal?" He could hear how loud he'd said it. As if loud would drive the vision out of his head.

Her black as night eyebrows came down together. "I will tell you about how Lorenzo behaves himself like a perfect gentleman always now, but this will not mean I do not know you make a change to the subject. We will return to it. Later."

Chapter Nineteen

He thought he got off easy. He didn't. She kept up with Noah references, mornings before games, evenings when she was finished with rehearsals and they both returned to his apartment. Right after the phone call with Louise, she'd insisted on going to some games. There'd be no danger of pictures being taken of them together since they wouldn't be together, she argued.

Wrong, he argued back. If some camera caught her in the stands cheering him on, Louise might take exception.

"I do not agree with you, Car, but I will do what you ask." She'd held up a finger. "But you must promise me you will always carry the five-hundred-lire piece when you play."

He had. And began to hit in earnest. He stole a couple bases, knee and all. When the Federals' outfielder, Sam Logan, went down for the season with a torn ACL, Skip slotted Car in the starting lineup. He kept hitting. Suddenly Bob and Rob went from busting him, as some kind of useless has-been, to some hype a twenty-something writer on 'roids came up with: the Resurrection of a Star. Car wanted to heave.

The day he hit for the cycle, the duo went into raptures. Not that Car cared what they had to say. He did care that Sofia wasn't there to share the triumph with him. How special it would have been for them to be together when, for the first time in the fifteen years he'd played in the majors, he hit a single, double, triple, and a home run in the same game.

Afterwards, the guys teased him without let-up, the

press gathered around, looking for face-time with him. When the Mosbachers walked into the clubhouse, there was a momentary hush before the noise picked up again.

The Mosbachers came over, congratulated him, and crossed back to spend time with Skip. After a while, Victoria separated herself from Brent and started back Car's way. He fingered the five-hundred-lire piece in his pocket. The guys stepped away; the reporters didn't. The guy from WTVB-AM stuck his mic in Victoria's face and said, "There's a rumor floating that management's been thinking of trading Car. The way he's been playing, and after tonight, is a trade still a possibility?"

Victoria gave the guy a blank look. "I don't know about any rumor."

The reporters began talking over each other. She held up a hand. "I'm sorry, but really, you shouldn't ask me." She pointed toward where Brent stood with Skip. "Perhaps my husband can answer your question."

Car watched them lope over to where the two men stood, deep in conversation. The rumor about a trade to the White Sox was back again. He needed to think about why. But first, he had Victoria to contend with.

"What's going on with you and Sofia de' Medici?" Victoria's voice was soft as baby's breath, her face hard and brittle as fossilized stone.

He shrugged, not willing to answer until he knew where she was going with the question.

One side of Victoria's mouth turned up in a derisive smile. "You do know Brent's been fucking her for years?"

Car flinched. That crude language didn't belong anywhere near Sofia's name. "You're mistaken."

She made a disgusted sound. "No, I'm not. I've known almost since she arrived from Italy, when I saw them together in a restaurant my dear husband arranged. I saw it clearly the way he looked at her. Can you imagine? He puts his wife and his whore together at the same table?"

"Victoria—" he said, scrambling to remain impassive.

"Are you fucking her?"

"I'm sorry." His temper unraveled at last. "Is any of this your business?"

Victoria pressed her lips together so hard a white line

rimmed them and her face went all over a pale gray-green. "Perhaps you remember I am part of your personal life, through my daughter."

Car gripped the coin. She was right. Point to her. Dammit.

"The other day when Louise picked up Noah, she cried. You're so busy with that Italian bitch, you don't see she can't handle it? I don't like that, Car."

He set his jaw, teeth gritted. "I can remember a time when you didn't care how you treated Louise. Are you feeling differently about your daughter now?"

Victoria's eyes went misty. "I have never been the best mother." But then she angled her face up so her lips were inches from his ear and said, "Whatever I did, Louise is my daughter. I will make you pay if you hurt her. Just as I'll make my husband pay."

And she was gone, striding from the clubhouse.

Before Car could process what had happened, Mo gave him a shove. "Car, you fake you. Pretending you been put out to the farm. What bullshit. You looking to shame us?"

Car took a deep breath and focused on Mo's beaming face. "Oh yeah; that's exactly what I was thinking of: ways to shame the team."

That brought the reporters back. He tried to get away. He listened to the softball questions they lobbed at him. He answered by rote. "No, I wasn't worried about coming back... You go into slumps sometimes... The knee is fine..."

Finally, he let them know he was done.

Later, on his way to pick up Noah, he thought about Victoria and their more than strange history. He understood her threatening him because of it, but Mosbacher? If she thought Sofia was her husband's lover, and it seemed she had for a while, why was she intent on making Mosbacher pay now? Maybe it was a package deal, two for the price of one in the vengeance category.

Louise was down in the lobby with Noah in hand, as Car pulled up in front. He stepped out of the Hummer. "You all right?"

She tossed her head and laughed. Her laugh had a brittle edge to it. "What could be wrong?"

Car studied her flushed face. Maybe Victoria was

yanking his chain. Louise didn't look upset. She looked like someone on the way to getting trashed. Good that he had Noah this weekend.

Bending down to Noah, who hadn't yet made eye contact with him, she said, "Now you mind your dad, sweetums. Don't be a bad boy or ask him for things he can't give you. And don't make him angry."

"Don't scare the boy," Car said under his breath. The kid had picked up his head at last and was looking at him like he was Freddy Krueger.

Holding onto something Car couldn't see, Noah climbed into the car-seat in the back and buckled himself in. He was silent as they drove off. The Noah he saw in the park, the Noah he saw at his grandparents' apartment all those weeks ago was not the Noah who sat in the back seat of the Hummer. "Hey man, we're going to have a good time this weekend," he said, not sure at the moment if that was true.

"I'll be good," the boy said, voice quiet.

Car checked the rear view mirror. *What was going on*? "I know you'll be good."

Silence. Maybe Louise followed through on her threat? If she did, he needed to work harder at putting Noah at ease. It would've been easier if Sofia had come with him, she was so good with kids. But Louise had fixed that one too.

"Hey, do you like macaroni and cheese?" Sofia had made a big pot of the stuff and called to tell him it was in the refrigerator ready to be baked.

"Is it good macaroni and cheese?"

"My friend made it. It's really good."

"Is your friend a good cook?"

"She's the best cook in the world."

"Can she make cookies?"

Yeah, Sofia could make cookies. Last night when what he wanted more than her filling his apartment with the smell of sugar and cinnamon was to get her into bed, she'd spent hours shaping cookies in half-moons and stars, and something that had a sound he couldn't make—it began with *sf*—that she said were typical Italian cookies and were for him alone.

He kept sneaking them from the paper towel she had put them on to drain. Until she got tired of telling him to leave them alone and smacked his hand with a wooden spoon.

"She makes the best cookies."

"Okay." Noah began to play with the thing he'd been holding behind his back: Larry the Alligator. Car smiled.

Maybe things weren't going to be so bad after all.

By the time they got back to Car's apartment, Noah had warmed up a little. "Do you have a bed for me in your house?"

Car led Noah toward the elevator. "Of course I have a bed for you."

"Does it have a nice pillow? I like nice pillows."

Car thought of the black pillow case and sheets he had on the single bed in the second bedroom. He'd meant to buy some sheets a little boy might like, maybe Spiderman or Toy Story or something, like Sofia suggested. He'd never gotten around to hitting the store.

The cookie smell lingered from last night, greeting them when they opened the door.

"Is your friend here?"

"No, she had to go to work."

"Oh." Noah looked around the living room. Of course he'd look. He'd never been in this apartment. Car had nothing for the kid to play with, another thing he should have thought about, maybe gotten some Lego or Transformers. Looking at the little suitcase the kid carried in, Car pretty much knew he hadn't brought any toys.

The message light on his phone was blinking. Dropping the suitcase, he went to check it out, hoping it was Sofia. It wasn't. It was his agent, Jed, telling him how the search was going for a nanny to replace Helena. Not so good. He eyed Noah, turned away, mumbled, "Shit," and pressed delete.

Car stepped into the kitchen. He opened the refrigerator, already knowing it was chockfull with cartons of milk and juice and bags of carrots and spinach and apples and grapes. He turned back to survey the counters. There were notes from Sofia everywhere, with instructions about what temperature he should set to heat up the mac and cheese, how long he should leave it in, where the pot-holders were, how to put the vegetables on the plate next to the mac and cheese.

After Sofia got the cookies in the oven, she'd cooked up some spinach and beaten it with eggs to make it fluffy and then baked it into star shapes.

"He will eat the green vegetables," Sofia had said. In Car's experience, little boys didn't eat green vegetables. Even some big boys didn't.

She'd left him a note taped to the whisk she'd bought for him, instructing him how to beat body into the whipped cream, which he was to put on the ice cream he was to serve with the cookies.

Noah had disappeared down the hallway to the bedrooms. He came back, trailing Larry.

"C'mon Noah. Let's wash and eat."

Car was not looking forward to the meal. What would he do if the kid pitched a fit about the spinach? What would he do if the mac and cheese was not the way he liked it, which, according to what the wives said, was probably the crappy boxed kind?

He shouldn't have worried. Noah loved Sofia's mac and cheese. His eyes opened wide at the spinach. Sofia had prepared the plates Car was to put the stars on when he took the spinach out of the oven. On each plate she had painted little rainbows with cake icing. "Just for the decoration. Even if he wants to eat the rainbows, it will not be so bad."

Car voiced the opinion that boys didn't take to rainbows. Rainbows were more for girls.

"He is not yet five years old," she had answered him, one black eyebrow raised. "He does not yet drink the beer or make the adjustments to his main part in public. He will like the rainbows."

"Cool," Noah declared, as he took a spoon, dug into the spinach star, and ate everything, including the rainbow.

After dinner, Car washed up, and Noah began to unbend. They sat down to watch the Yankees play the Red Sox. As the game progressed, Noah told Car about a funny man he'd seen on the street when he'd gone out with Helena, about a new friend at school, and how his new friend didn't think his daddy was Car Bradford. Car promised to go with him one day as show and tell.

Toward the end of the game, Noah grew quiet. Then stroking the stuffed animal, he asked, "Do you like the Yankees?"

"Better than the Red Sox," Car answered easily. "I like all the New York teams. Even the Stars."

"Me too." Noah kicked his legs a couple of times for emphasis.

Car was startled when he inched closer.

"Pete doesn't like baseball." Noah buried his face in the belly of the alligator.

Just the mention of Jensen's name gave Car heartburn. "Not everyone likes baseball," he said, careful not to signal his feelings.

Noah kicked his feet again. Once. "He should."

Car wanted to ask what this last bit meant, but knew better. He looked at his watch. "Oh boy, look at that. It's time for bed. Let's get to it, buddy."

"Can I ask you a question?"

"Shoot."

"Do you have another bed?"

"Sure. I have my bed."

"But do you have another boy bed?"

"I'm afraid not."

"Mine has black covers and black sheets. I don't like black."

Sofia had told him, hadn't she? "When the light's out you can't see what color the sheets are."

"Yes I can, 'cause I have my Buzz Lightyear nightlight."

"How about tomorrow we go out and get yellow or blue sheets? Which do you like better?"

"Why can't we go out tonight?"

"The stores are closed."

"Can we find some other sheets in your closet?"

There were white sheets. For *his* bed. He supposed he'd put the bigger sheets on Noah's bed.

But that didn't work.

"They don't fit," Noah wailed, when Car finished tucking in as much of the sheet as he could.

Frazzled, he said, "I know they don't. Until tomorrow, we'll have to make do with what we've got."

"I don't want to make do." A tear tracked down one of Noah's flushed cheeks.

Now what? "Noah." Car hesitated. "What can I do to make it better?"

Noah looked up at him with big, little-boy eyes and said, "I want the friend who made the stars to come over."

Played. Car wanted to laugh. "Remember I told you she's busy tonight?"

"No!" Noah stamped his foot, hurled Larry across the room, and ran into the living room, where he threw himself on the couch, folded his arms across his chest, and said, "I don't want to sleep in the black bed."

Car blinked. When had this wild man replaced the scared little boy he'd picked up earlier, the one who vowed he'd be good?

They needed a distraction. "What do you think... want to go out and get some candy?"

Noah frowned at him ferociously. "If the candy store is open, why isn't the sheet store open?"

Logical question. "I have no idea. All I know is Dylan's is open and the sheet store isn't. Do you want to go?"

"Okay." And just like that, the storm passed. Noah hopped off the couch and ran into the bedroom with the bed and its hated black sheets. He came running out a moment later. "I put Larry on my suitcase so he knows I'm coming back."

They went to Dylan's. Lots of kids, lots of parents, lots of strollers clogging up the narrow aisles, canyons of candy, lined with every kind ever produced in every size and color. Some of the parents recognized Car and he was obliged to give autographs. Noah, once he felt sure Car would follow right behind him wherever he went, began to dart in every direction, stopping at every display, taking samples when they were offered to him by too helpful store employees.

They chose a bagful of candy to take home. When they got into the taxi, Car sneaked a quick look inside the bag, not believing what he'd been blackmailed into buying.

Noah was bouncing on the seat like he had a spring attached to his little rear end, his face smeared with something red. By the time the cab let them out in front of the apartment house, he was screeching.

"Remind me never to take you to a candy store again," Car muttered, as Noah ran in circles around him while they waited for the elevator.

It didn't get better when they got upstairs. If the white sheet had been bad before, it was worse now. In addition to dealing with the sheets, now there was a new issue: no bedside lamp. "How will you read me a story?" Noah asked, a worried look on his face.

"I've got a flashlight," Car said, remembering the book light he'd used that first night with Sofia. "How will that do?"

"No!" Noah was back to foot stamping. "That's a bad idea. I don't like it. I want a lamp! And I want a story."

"I'll read a story to you." The sweat trickled down Car's spine. "Let's pick something out of your suitcase. I know your mom sent over a few books."

"Not my mom. She didn't send the books. Helena did."

"I'm sorry," he said, helplessly. What had he let himself in for? He'd faced bad-ass pitchers who threw one hundred miles per hour at his head and none of them were as scary as this three-and-a-half-foot terror. He hoped by the time the papers got signed, Jed had a nanny lined up. Again he asked, "What can I do?"

Noah gave him one quick, crafty look out of eyes filmed over with tears. Wily tears. Triumphant tears.

"I want your friend to come and read me a story. And I want her to bring good sheets and a blanket and a lamp."

Played again. Not caring he was. "Will you go to sleep then?"

"Yes, but she has to come over now."

Chapter Twenty

Sofia could not believe her eyes when she opened the door with the key Car had given her. The apartment she left just hours before, neat, clean, and cool, looked as if a windstorm from the African coast had come through and left disaster behind. A little suitcase, a stuffed animal, and many pieces of candy were strewn across the floor.

"What has happened here?"

At once Car appeared in the doorway that led to the bedrooms, a look of relief on his face. He opened his mouth to speak, when the windstorm rushed out from behind him. He was a small windstorm, but Sofia could see how powerful he was. He came to a sudden halt, mere steps in front of her, looked up, and said, "I remember you from my grandpa's stadium."

"I remember you too. You are Noah Bradford."

"Noah Cody Bradford," he answered promptly. "I'm almost five years old."

"It is a pleasure to meet you, Noah Cody Bradford. I am Sofia de' Medici." Sofia smoothed sweaty hair from his forehead.

"I know that." He put a hand on his hip and frowned. "Are you my daddy's friend?"

"I am."

Hotel housekeeping had given her linens that would fit a single bed, and a blanket; she'd taken a bedside lamp from her room. Sofia set the bag down.

He scooted around her and looked into the bag on the floor. "Is the lamp in here?" He pulled out a book. "How did you know this is my favorite?"

"I went to the bookstore and I see it and know it must be your favorite."

Car came over and looked. "Good title."

Sofia made sure not to smile. "Yes. *Where the Wild Things Are.*"

"Will you read it to me?" asked Noah.

"That is why I came over."

"And to bring the good sheets and the blanket and the lamp."

"Yes, to do that." She took Noah in one hand and the bag in the other. "Let us fix everything."

She looked over her shoulder as she led the little boy into the bedroom. On Car's face she saw relief and shock. Well, what could be expected? He had an almost five-year-old boy in his charge. Even if the boy was his son, even as much as she had been trying to encourage him to learn to love him, he still didn't know. She wondered if he ever would.

But she didn't have time to think about that now. She had a little boy on her hands who acted like a storm from Africa because he was frightened of this strange place. And he was afraid he wasn't wanted. She understood. Growing up with her father, she knew he didn't love her, even then. She knew he only loved her voice. Tonight she wouldn't let Noah be afraid, or feel unwanted. She would have a discussion about love with his father. Perhaps she could, at last, help Car see he could love his son. That discussion would be tricky.

"You talk funny," Noah said.

"You are right. Perhaps you will help me so I do not talk funny?"

"I don't talk funny. I'll help you. But only if you make the bed."

"That is without question."

After they made the bed, they plugged in the lamp. At last, with the lamp and the white sheets and white blanket, Noah was ready to take a bath, put on his pajamas, and brush his teeth.

"Am I glad you're here," Car whispered to Sofia, as Noah ran ahead of her into the bathroom.

A feeling of warmth filled her. This was a thing he

needed from her, even if it was only one of the crumbs. "I am glad too." She reached up and caressed his cheek, the stubble rough against her palm.

He pulled her close, and rested his chin upon her head. "Thank you."

She patted his cheek, and stepped away. Knocking on the bathroom door, she called out, "Noah, it is okay I come in?"

He didn't object.

Afterwards, with a clean little boy in tow, Sofia led the way to the bedroom. "And now, Noah Cody Bradford, we will read this story."

He threw himself on the bed, clutched his alligator, and made room for her.

She kicked off her shoes. Lying down, she opened the book and began. *"The night Max wore his wolf suit..."*

They read the story more than once; there were five, two more than she had guessed, but Noah did not give up, even with his eyes closing. Finally as Max sailed home for the last time, Noah sailed off into his own dreamland, but not before he forced his eyelids open one last time. "Will you make more green stars?"

She placed a gentle kiss on his forehead. "Most assuredly."

One second he sighed, the next he was asleep.

Car was lying down on his own bed with his headset on when she stepped into his bedroom. He unplugged and came toward her on bare feet, the button of his jeans open at the waist. She could see his belly button. It was a mouth-watering sight.

"I thought you'd never finish."

"He was very resistant." She kissed what she could reach: the very warm skin of his chest and the lovely patch of hair in the center.

"I tried everything," he said, smoothing a hand up and down her back. "Nothing worked."

"He was frightened, Car." She took him by the hand and drew him over to the bed. When they were sitting, she squeezed his fingers, and stared straight into his beautiful blue-gray eyes.

His eyebrows came down to meet in the middle.

"What?"

All the way over from the hotel, Sofia asked herself if she should be so bold to ask the question she knew she must ask. Not for her, but for him, this man she loved, this man who was confused, perhaps hurt on the inside. She thought she knew why. Most assuredly, she knew she must start the conversation, because he wouldn't. She would have to be almost as brave as she had been getting on the airplane in Milan. Almost as brave as she had been marching into the Maestro's office and making him listen to her sing the *Seguidilla*. She gave Car's fingers one more squeeze and said, "You remember when I say we will return to the subject of complication? We are now doing that."

He turned his head away.

She almost lost her courage. But no, she couldn't afford that. "What does this mean: it is complicated with Noah?"

He eased his hand from hers and stood up. He paced around the bed to the other side, pulled the blinds aside and looked out the window. He looked without moving. At last he let the edge of the blinds go. They made a snicking sound as they met the glass.

"It's not easy for me to talk about," he began, his words low and hesitating.

She took his hand again as he sat down next to her. She ran a thumb across his knuckles. "You may tell me anything. I will understand."

"Will you? I'm not sure *I* understand. "He was silent only for a moment. "It wasn't complicated to begin with. I..."

"Sofia."

They both jumped.

Standing in the doorway, Noah, one little fist to an eye, rubbing. "I can't sleep," he said, his voice scratchy. "You have to come back and read some more."

"Noah," began Car.

But Sofia put a hand on his arm to stop him. She stood on tiptoes and kissed his chin. "I will go. But I will be back soon, and we will talk."

She wasn't back soon. In fact when Car looked in fifteen minutes later, they were both sound asleep, Sofia's arms around Noah, Noah's head on her breast. Poor Sofia. He had to figure the rehearsals were exhausting. He picked up the book, where it lay between them, and put it on the night table. He turned off the light.

For some stupid reason, tears rose in his eyes. He backed away and retreated on soft feet to his room. He looked around. At the rumpled black sheets on his bed where he'd been waiting for her to come back to him. At the white lamp that shone on the rumpled sheets.

He'd told the decorator keep it simple in this new apartment. Stay with black and white, no colors. Keep it plain. Uncomplicated. She'd done a great job. The result? This room, the whole apartment, was what he'd wanted. And it was a reflection of his life. Yes, uncomplicated. But also bare. Barren. Lonely.

If Sofia lived with him, there would be nothing bare about the apartment. There would be color everywhere. Red pillows thrown on his black couch. Paintings of landscapes in nature's riotous colors on all the walls. Pictures of Noah on the tables. And toys everywhere.

He spun around and padded back into Noah's room. He eased up to the side of the bed. They were wound together, Sofia and Noah, their breathing synchronized. How was it she knew, as instinctively as breathing, how to be with *his* child and he had to work at it? He'd had a bitch of a mother, who had given him nothing good. But Sofia, she had the same thing in her father. What did she know he didn't?

He reached out a hand to touch one of curls that now covered her shoulders. And he knew.

She shifted a little. He backed out of the room. He wouldn't wake her. He'd wait until she came back to him later to tell her he'd figured it out. What she knew and he didn't. Until now.

What was between them?
Simple: love.

It seemed only minutes later that Noah woke him.

"Daddy, I'm hungry."

Car lifted his head to see Noah in the doorway, dragging Larry in one hand. He turned his head. There, on his night table, a note. He held it up. Sofia had come back to the bedroom and found him asleep. She decided to go back to the hotel. This was the best thing for the night, she said, so everyone could rest. She left a big lipstick kiss at the bottom of the paper. He grinned. In a rusty voice, he said, "Okay, sport. Let's see what there is to eat."

He slipped into his jeans, which he'd left on the floor last night and started toward the kitchen.

Noah followed. "Did Sofia make my breakfast?"

"She did. Let's get it out of the refrigerator."

"Sofia promised she would make me more green stars."

"If she promised, she will. I don't think that's what she made for breakfast, though."

"My mom makes promises all the time. But she doesn't keep them."

What to say to that? He imagined what Sofia would say. "Well, your mom's a busy lady." *Yup. That sounded exactly like what Sofia would say.* "Sometimes a mom thinks she can do something she can't."

"Then she shouldn't say she will."

No kid, not yet five, should be that observant. He pulled a bowl of pancake mix out of the refrigerator. "Will you look at what's here?"

"She keeps all her promises to Pete."

That caught Car. "What kind of promises?"

"She promises to give him money."

Car put the bowl down on the counter, being careful not to slam it. Each of the last few months Louise had asked for extra money from him. Unexpected expenses she'd said. Maybe it wasn't? Maybe the money was for the bastard she'd brought into her life? "She does, huh?"

"Want to know why I don't like Pete?"

"If you want to tell me." He knew he wasn't going to like what came next.

"Because he's not nice to me when Helena goes out."

The skin on the back of Car's neck prickled. "What's does he do?"

Noah didn't answer, but drew circles on the floor with one foot.

Car's heartbeat ratcheted up. "Noah, what does Pete do?" he asked, careful not to let the child hear the dread in his voice. His imagination was already spinning in alarming directions. When he couldn't stand the silence any longer, he raised Noah's chin with one finger. "You know you can tell me, right?"

"I don't like to tell anybody, 'cause I was bad."

"It's okay." He kept his voice even. "You weren't bad."

"But Pete says I'm bad because I don't listen to him." Noah looked up at Car at last, eyes pleading for understanding. "When I'm bad he locks me in my closet. It scares me when he locks me in my closet."

An icy-cold shiver rippled through Car's body. "He locks…" His voice failed him.

"And he says not to tell Helena 'cause then he'll put her on fire."

Car swallowed. "Fire her."

"And I don't want him to fire Helena. She loves me."

Car took Noah by the hand and led him over to the table. He lifted the kid, placed him carefully in a chair. He sat in another. "Is that all Pete does to make you so sad?"

"Sometimes he hits me."

Car braced one palm on the table's smooth surface. "Where does he hit you, son?"

Noah began to kick his feet. He looked down. "On my butt." He kicked some more. "And a lot on my face."

Oh God. The piece of shit bastard. Hit his son. In the face. Car closed his eyes. His mother used to hit him in the face. Sometimes in front of others. It shamed him. And it hurt. This was what fucking Jensen was doing to Noah. His son. Gently, he lifted Noah off the chair and sat him on his lap, knowing he needed to ask this next hard question. "Does he do anything else?"

Noah didn't answer, just shook his head slowly from side to side.

Car was filled with both relief and a rock-hard, killing rage. He wanted to punch Jensen. Not punch. Kill.

He managed to keep a steady voice. "You know you're coming to live with me, right?"

Noah looked up and then down again. "My mom says you don't want me to come live with you."

Car closed his eyes, remembering yesterday. So Louise had followed through. She'd lied. To hurt him. But she'd hurt Noah instead. What kind of a mother was she? In her way, no different than his. All that was changing. As of this moment.

"I do want you, Noah. I'll always want you. And I make you a promise. I will never do what Pete does to you. Lock you in your closet. Hit you."

"Okay." He laid his head trustingly against Car's chest. Car prayed Noah wouldn't understand what that frantic beating of his heart was all about.

After a moment, Noah lifted his head. "Will you go away and leave me with my mom again?"

He wound his arms around his child. "You know I have to go away to play baseball, but I always come back, right? But don't you worry. I'm going to work something out." Car would have to discuss temporary living arrangements for Noah with Mosbacher. No way was he letting Noah go back to Louise. Plus there was the discussion Car would have first thing Monday morning. With his lawyers. And the cops.

"Will Sofia come to live with us?"

Car made himself dial it back. Concentrate. "We'll have to ask the next time we see her."

"Okay." Noah's tiny face cleared, his eyes lost their dullness and he jumped off Car's lap and pushed one of the chairs up to the island. "Can I see what's in the bowl?"

Car took a deep breath. "It's pancakes. Want some?"

Car brought Noah with him to the game and sat him with Tina and the two eldest Huggins kids, Josh and Brianna, in the wives' box. Nothing about the change in location made Car feel less murderous toward Jensen. Or Louise. Even so, Car was focused enough to hit a grand slam.

On the way home Noah was wild. "Did you see that, Daddy?" he yelled from the back seat where he gyrated in his car seat. "Did you see the ball go way, way, way up in the air? The outfielder, he ran and ran and ran, but he couldn't catch the ball because it went up into the...the..."

"Stands."

"... the stands and there was a man who catched it there and held it up so everybody saw it." Noah gyrated some more and waved his hands in the air. "My Daddy hit a grand slam! My Daddy hit a grand slam!"

"That was fun, sport, wasn't it?"

"It wasn't *fun*. It was very, very, very *good* because it made the Federals win the game," Noah said, chastising Car for his misrepresentation of what that home run signified.

"You're right."

Noah was still jabbering away when they drove into the building's underground garage, and when they waited for the elevator, which took forever, because only one of the two was working. He kept at it all the way up to Car's floor. Until the instant the elevator door opened and he saw Louise standing there.

It took Car's brain a moment to process, which was why his first thought was, "who let her up?"

The shock of the fist to the side of his head killed the second thought in formation.

He stumbled out of the elevator, careening into the wall opposite. He tried to clear his vision, reaching out a hand to grab Noah, but it was too late. Louise already had him.

"I need him," she cried.

Noah began to scream. "No, Daddy, no! I don't want to go, don't make me go." He kicked madly, his arms thrust straight up. But Louise had hers wrapped around his chest.

Woozy from Jensen's shot, Car staggered toward them, but fell to his knees when Jensen tripped him and then jumped past the elevator door Louise was holding open.

Before Car could get to his feet, it closed.

Car could hear Noah's scream fade as the elevator descended. With an inarticulate howl, he launched himself at the door and pounded. "Bitch! Goddamn bitch!" He slammed his fist once more against the door and then turned, pounded down the hallway to the stairwell, threw the door open, and hurtled down the stairs. In the time it took him to reach the lobby, they were gone.

"Oscar!" He erupted out of the stairwell and bolted across the lobby's marble floor. "That woman. And my kid. Where'd they go?"

Oscar pointed to the street. "They left."

"Why didn't you stop them?" he yelled, not caring he sounded irrational.

Oscar looked at him blank-eyed.

Car clamped both hands to his temples. Think! He needed to think. Louise had always been sane in her craziness. Maybe this charade was about her trying to milk more money out of him before the agreement was finalized. With fingers he did his best to keep steady, he took out his cell to call her. He didn't think it would go through. But on the sixth ring, she answered. He could hear Noah wailing. "Louise, I'll give..."

"You don't understand. I have to."

He began to pace around the lobby. "What? Whatever, we can work it out."

"No, no!"

That was Noah.

"Shut the fuck up!" Jensen. There was the sound of flesh on flesh and then silence.

"Louise!" Car thought his heart would beat itself out of his body.

Louise spoke unintelligible words and hung up.

218

Cursing steadily, Car tried again and again to get her back, but each call went to voice mail.

He knew people were staring: other tenants, the building concierge, Oscar. He didn't care. Turning, he stalked to the elevators and slammed his hand against the call button.

When he was safely in his apartment he threw back his head and bellowed his anguish. He began to laugh. What a joke, what a bad, cosmic joke. Finally, he got it. Finally, he knew. He wanted him. His son. Had always wanted him. Why did it have to take something like this for him to see?

Chapter Twenty-One

He called Dan Foreman, his attorney. For the next few minutes, he listened to an explanation of his rights as the non-custodial parent. Foreman talked about material changes of circumstances and clear and convincing evidence and lesser burden and all the rest of the bullshit. But the bottom line was it being the weekend, there was not much they could do until Monday. Besides, they didn't know where Louise had gone.

After, he thought about calling Sofia. But she might have been sleeping. He thought about calling Dan back. But hell, he'd already been told there was nothing to do right now. He paced some more, hating the feeling of helplessness. Finally he went into the kitchen and grabbed the bowl he'd washed and left on the counter to put away after they returned from the game. *They. Noah and him.* His heart lurched. There was no 'they' right now. Only him. He squatted down to stow the bowl in a cabinet under the counter.

Looking in, he frowned at the neatly stacked bowls. When had he stacked them?

He hadn't. Sofia had. As if the cabinet was hers.

What if they were living together and the cabinet was hers? What if Sofia had been with him tonight? Would she have let Louise take Noah? She would not. About children, she was very clear.

"How do you know so much about children?" he'd asked her.

"I love children," she'd said. "They are precious to me."

Bending onto his knees, he closed his eyes and pressed his forehead against the cabinet's cool surface. Sofia would have fought right by his side to keep Louise from taking Noah. She would have screamed her head off, thrown herself on Jensen when the bastard cold-cocked him. Car couldn't let go the image of Sofia fighting for Noah. And for him. Could he have had Sofia with him just now? Yes. Too bad the light bulb came on after the power was off.

But the power wasn't entirely off. He came to his feet, cursing that he hadn't thought of Victoria. Maybe she knew where Louise had gone. He had to hope she did and she'd help, despite their history. He looked at his watch. 11 o'clock. He didn't mind calling at this late hour to find out.

He found Victoria at home in her ten-room condo on Fifth Avenue, overlooking Central Park. She was alone. She opened the door and regarded him silently. Stepping aside for him, she said, "Really? Almost midnight?"

"I need your help."

. Victoria ambled into the living room and sat herself on a plush, forest green sofa. "You must be desperate to come here." Dressed in a rainbow-colored dressing gown, she crossed one leg over the other, and waited.

"It's not about me. It's about Noah."

A wrinkle that passed for a frown, rippled across her forehead. "Let's just get to it, Car. It's late and I want to go to bed."

So he told her.

By the time he came to what happened at the elevator, she'd folded her arms across her chest and gave him a pitying look. "I told you, didn't I? She's a sensitive girl. All this talk of custody has taken its toll."

Like he cared. "Do you know where she's gone?"

Victoria scooted to one side of the couch. "Don't tower over me. Sit down."

Unwillingly, he sat.

"Louise was here today. She wanted to borrow my diamond and sapphire earrings."

"They were going to a party." Car took up a ceaseless tap of his fingers against his knee. "That's why I have Noah for the weekend."

"Not a party. A festival. In the Islands."

"Islands?" He stopped tapping.

"The Bahamas."

"Jesus." He jumped up. "She can't take Noah out of the country unless she has my permission. And she doesn't."

Victoria had risen too. "I don't know anything about your legal issues."

Car flashed back to the sound of Jensen hitting Noah. "Victoria," he said, raising his voice. "Forget the legal issues. I have to get Noah back. Now."

She tilted her head to the side. "Why the rush?"

"Isn't Jensen enough of a reason?" he said, each word knife-sharp.

She waved his words away.

Stunned, he stared at her. Who was this woman who dismissed the safety of her grandson with a wave of a hand? His brain cycled through the why, coming up with one insane thought. "Are you using Noah to get back at me?"

She said nothing, only smiled.

Car jumped up and strode to the other side of the room, suddenly unwilling to be anywhere near the woman who had once been his mother-in-law, and who, long before, had come onto him when he was a fresh-faced nineteen, new in the Federals system. "Play this game another time. Not now."

Lips pressed together, she raised her chin in childish defiance. "Louise has it in her mind that people think she's not a good mother. There's going to be media at the festival. If she's got Noah with her, she's convinced it will put paid to that problem."

"I need you to find it within yourself to care that no one's around to protect Noah against that bastard. We know for sure that Louise isn't capable of doing it, don't we?"

What passed for shame marked Victoria's face. "I can probably get Noah back."

He stared hard at her. "Couldn't you have said that from the beginning?"

Victoria narrowed her eyes at him. "You don't want to irritate me, Car."

He ignored her. "Will Louise listen?"

"Yes, she will." Victoria rose from the couch and slipped into another room. She closed the door behind her, keeping Car from hearing any part of the conversation except murmurings.

He hadn't thought about it forever, that business with Victoria. He'd been so young, he hadn't recognized what she was doing, when she and Brent would visit the team during spring training. She'd sidle up to him, press her body up against his, and run a hand up and down his back. When he finally got it, he felt miserably uncomfortable not knowing how to make her stop.

Besides, what would he say? She was the boss' wife and how did you tell the boss' wife to leave you alone? When he realized all he had to do was walk away—one of the older guys had to clue him in—he made sure he was nowhere near her when she and Brent visited. After that, she was always cold, almost hostile, especially after his fake marriage with Louise.

Was this escapade of Louise's Victoria's way of finally getting back at him? He had a feeling he was about to find out.

A minute later she returned. "I've convinced her, at least for the most part."

"For the most part?" He sat. "What else is it going to take?"

"Other than what I've already promised her?" She tapped her bottom lip, the secret smile back. "There is one thing. For me."

Of course.

Folding her arms across her chest, her smile broadened. "I'm very impressed with how you've come back from your injury."

Car wasn't interested in Victoria's pseudo-compliments.

"I thought your career was over. That would have been too bad. But now? I think you have quite a number of years left before you have to start thinking about retiring."

He made a fist and held it against his thigh. "Get to the point."

"You do know Brent has been talking to the White Sox."

The trade rumor. "I don't listen in on Brent's conversations." Which was true, as far as it went.

"You should."

"C'mon, Victoria."

"I'm surprised you haven't figured it out. If I can't get what I want..." Her lips turned up in a smile he didn't like. "Well then..."

"Enough!" He stalked across the room to stand over her.

She held a staying hand up in his face. "If you want Noah back, you're going to let yourself be traded to the White Sox."

"It doesn't work like that."

"Yes, it does. You tell Brent. He trades you."

"The White Sox don't need me, Victoria. I'm thirty-four, a short-term solution. They need young blood."

"They have a chance to go to the World Series this year. You can help them. Next year they'll trade you away, but that will be nothing to me." Once more she folded her arms across her chest. The multi-colored robe lapels gapped showing more of Victoria's chest than Car cared to see. "And at last I will have gotten what I want."

Which was a fifteen-year-old vendetta satisfied. He sighed. "Okay. What's next?"

"You tell Brent you'll waive your no-trade clause."

Car had always wanted to retire as a Federal. He didn't want to go to Chicago, even for a few months. Yeah, Noah was young enough that he could take him to Chicago. But he had enough upset in his life, he'd be scared in a new place with no Helena, and a dad who was absent for long stretches. Did he want to do this to his boy? What choice did he have? If this was the only way Victoria would help, the decision was a no-brainer.

"I'll see Brent tomorrow. In the meantime, you make

sure Louise agrees to let Noah go. If you don't, there's no deal."

It was three in the morning by the time he got back to his apartment. All he had to do was wait for tomorrow. But he wasn't good at waiting. And he didn't want to be alone. He shouldn't have called, but the need to be with her was overwhelming. She answered the phone, sounding wide awake.

"Sofia..."

"*Che succede?*"

"Louise took Noah."

"I am coming to you now."

By the time he opened the door to her knock, he was so ready for her. She stood there, looking up at him, apprehension and anger warring for control on her face. Whatever she saw on his—he was sure what was there came of the emotional roller coaster he'd been riding for the last hours—melted the anger away. Her gaze traveled across his face, touching him everywhere with its warmth, and yeah, love.

He picked her up, and buried his face against her neck. She wound her arms around his shoulders and murmured words to him in Italian. The words meant nothing to Car, but their sound curled around his heart, gave him the scrap of solace he needed to keep himself together to tell the story.

He carried her to the couch and sat close. By the time he finished, her face had colored and whitened, and colored again. She rose and filled their glasses with hefty shots of the brandy he kept in one of kitchen cabinets. "We must take Noah from the reach of his foolish mama and that terrible man."

Setting the glass on the floor, he rose in one lithe movement. "Maybe—just maybe—Victoria's jerking me around. But here's what's eating at me: will Noah be safe until we get him?"

Since she didn't have to be at dress rehearsal until eleven, Sofia was still awake, getting ready for bed when Car called. Yes, she needed a good night's sleep, but not to go to Car because of that? This wouldn't happen. And now she'd stay, be strong for her *Signore* Beautiful Eyes, whose grief and fear was clear to see, so worried was he for his child. She, too, was frightened. She didn't think she could be more filled with terror if Noah were the child of her own body.

"We must wait until the morning. You will see; the *Signora* will call to say Noah is safe."

He walked to the windows and stared at the darkened building opposite, a window here and there lit with feeble light. "The thing about Noah—I should have told you when you asked why it was complicated for me."

She came up behind him and placed a comforting hand on his back.

Shoulders slumping, he turned to face her and placed one hand over his mouth. His shirt was wrinkled, as if he had worn it for many days, the hem on one leg of his jeans folded back carelessly. There were black marks beneath both eyes, and a scruff of beard on his face. She wanted to reach for him, and comfort him, but that would be the wrong thing now. He needed to tell her and she needed to listen.

"When Noah was born, as bad as it was between Louise and me, I was excited." He smiled, took her hand, led her over to the sofa, and sat. "They put him in my arms.

I'd never held a newborn before." It amazed him how warm his body was. He'd studied each feature: the tiny pursing lips; flickering eyelids; skin, mottled from the ordeal of birth. His smile faded. "Well, I did hold Stevie when he was about a week old."

In Car's exhausted eyes, Sofia saw the memory of the past. But she didn't know if it was about Stevie or Noah.

He turned a little to her. "I'd bought a duplex for us, with an upstairs and a downstairs. I let Louise have the master bedroom upstairs; the nurse had a smaller adjacent room she shared with the baby. I took the room downstairs next to the kitchen." He let go of her hand and began rubbing his palms across his thighs. "The baby was on formula. Louise wouldn't breast-feed."

Sofia felt a stab of pain in her breasts. She could almost feel a small being in her arms, her own child, with a small, ravenous mouth fastened upon her nipple, tugging at her, drinking in her milk. Her love.

"I'd lie in that bed downstairs every night and hear the nurse running into Noah's room. It seemed like it happened every hour. He cried a lot. And threw up. He threw up every time the nurse fed him."

"It was perhaps the formula?" Sofia asked.

"Yeah, that's what we thought. We tried different ones, but whatever we used, he threw up."

Sofia shivered. "You worried, yes?"

He sighed and nodded. "The nurse said some babies throw up. But I didn't know how he could be getting any nourishment. To me he looked like he was getting smaller. And he never seemed to sleep. It went on like that for three weeks until..." He stopped.

"Until?"

"Until he threw up blood."

Sofia put a hand over her heart. "*O Dio.*"

"I wasn't waiting for the nurse to tell me not to worry. I picked him up, got a taxi, and took him to the nearest hospital."

"And Louise." Sofia hesitated. "She went with you?"

"Yes. Screaming and crying. I think she cried louder than the baby."

"You will tell me what was wrong, please," Sofia said,

her voice raised. "I have the fear to listen without knowing, even though I know the ending."

A quick smile appeared and disappeared on Car's face. "It was a blockage to the upper intestine. Something called hypertrophic pyloric stenosis, which I never heard of. Common, the doctor said. Noah just needed an operation."

"*O Dio.*"

"Yeah, oh God. That was what I thought. How could anyone operate on that small body? Wouldn't the surgeon's hands be bigger than the kid? But they do it laparoscopically, so the surgeon's hands weren't an issue. "

"*Poverino,*" she whispered. "And poor Car too."

He stood and put a hand to the back of his head. "They let me carry him down as far as the door to the operating room. That feeling, handing the baby over to the nurse..." He caught his breath. "When she took him from me, and when the door closed behind her, I thought if he's going to die, let him die now before I get to love him the way I loved Stevie."

Sofia jumped up and rushed up behind Car. She wound her arms around him, and pressed her face against the tense muscles of his back. "This is the reason for the complication," she whispered, clutching him to her.

He put his hand over hers where they were linked across his stomach. "When they let us know the surgery was successful and Noah was okay, I thought to myself, what would I do if he wasn't okay? What would I do if I had to go through that again?" He stepped out of her arms, and turned toward her. "I knew I couldn't."

Sofia almost gasped out loud. Pain had etched age into his face. His beautiful blue-green eyes were filmed with tears, the lines across his forehead furrowed deep, his jaw hard in desolation.

He drew her to him and, stooping, laid his head on her shoulder. "You probably think I'm a monster," he said, voice muffled, his face pressed into the hollow between her shoulder and neck. "A father who gives up custodial rights to a mother he wasn't sure, even then, was the right parent to have them."

"No, no." She laid a hand on the crown of his head, stroking him with what comfort she could. "I do not think that. Your love was deep, but your fear was deeper."

He tore himself away. "Fear," he said, his voice the crack of a whip. "That's fucking great. I'm supposed to be an adult. I understood what I was doing, letting Louise have him. And I didn't need any psychologist to tell me why I was afraid. I knew." He clutched both hands, hard, to his head. "I was supposed to take Stevie home from school that day, but practice was late and he started home without me."

He began to breathe rapidly. "I got there at the same time as the ambulance. He was already dead. And my mother..." He kept his hands clutched to his head and began to walk around the room with stiff strides. "She never let me forget. It was my fault because I wasn't there."

"Oh, Car." Sofia's heart broke. "It was an accident. And it was not your fault." It wasn't the mother's either. But to blame the accident on Car... for this, Sofia would never forgive that woman.

"I know it wasn't my fault. I didn't drive the car that hit him. Killed him. But inside? I can't forgive myself because I wasn't there. And who knows? I might make another mistake, not show up when I'm supposed to, and my kid will get hurt or worse because I..." He gave a pained laugh.

Tears began to track down her face. "Car, you must not."

"Must not what? Acknowledge what I know is true? That I'm not a fit parent? That I'm a monster?"

"Car." She reached for him and dragged one hand down. It wasn't easy. After an insistent pull, she succeeded. "You must stop this beating up. You must put the past away." She urged him to come with her into the bedroom, to the bed. Easing him down, sitting beside him, she turned and took him in her arms. "We cannot know what will happen in the future. But we have love. And I have the confidence you will do everything you know to take care of your little boy."

He fell back, taking her with him. "But what will I do if it's like Stevie all over again, if I lose..." His voice caught and he huffed a laugh that was more a sob. "I can't even say the words."

"This is your fear, my darling." She smoothed a hand over his short, silky hair. Heat seeped through from his scalp. "It is a fear that every mama, every papa has. It is normal."

"But..." He curled his tall body into hers. She surrounded him.

"Shh. Shh." She wrapped her arms around his shoulders. "Do not spend the time thinking of the thing that might happen. That does nothing. You must love him. Love your son. That is all that matters."

He was silent then, his body stiff, until he rolled onto his back and pulled her with him. He smoothed his hands down her arms. She didn't think he was aware of what he was doing. She looked up. His eyes, those beautiful green-blue eyes, swam with tears. "Oh, Sofia," he whispered.

Sofia wanted to cry, too. For the prison he'd made of his life. For the way he closed himself off from love because he was afraid he couldn't withstand its loss. For the fear his heart would break again as it had when he lost his little brother.

Now, just as he'd been strong for her, she'd be strong for him. She would never tell him of that time when on the subway, she'd thought him incapable of love, either for Noah or for herself. She shifted to lie next to him. And took a deep breath. What she said next would make her naked, not in body, but in her heart. "I must tell you something. I have the feelings for you. They are deep. Very, very deep. I..."

He began to smile, his eyes, still shining with tears, but with humor too. He ran a finger across her lips. "Are you talking about the feelings you had for me when we had sex?"

She swallowed once, although it was difficult, because all the saliva in her mouth had dried up. "Yes, then, but..."

He stroked her with more purpose now. His hand lingered first on her shoulder and then swept down her arm, to her bottom, where he stroked firmly—and remained. "It was more than sex; that's what you want to say, right?"

"Yes, this is what I want to say. It is more love. And I must tell you..." She took another deep breath. "I have fallen in love with you."

It was frightening to listen to the silence in the room. She heard a shudder of wind against the window, his breath even, hers not so even. Which was why when she spoke again, so rushed. "I know the women, they fall in love with you because you are so handsome, and you have the beautiful body and you do not..."

He pressed his fingers against her mouth. "*Ssh*. You're worrying about saying the words? I should have said them, a long time ago." He bent and touched his lips to hers. "Before I said you were a job." He kissed her. "You were never a job. If only I'd been smart enough to see it, I would have told you then how much I love you, Sofia because now I know. Somehow, I've loved you forever. And how I'm going to love you forever."

He leaned down and kissed her. It was not a gentle kiss. He devoured her with his mouth, his lips everywhere, on her mouth, in the hollow at the base of her throat, across each breast and in between. There was not a part of her body that he did not touch with his lips or with his hands. And she touched in return.

They were rough with each other. And gentle. Their clothes came off slowly and then all at once when they couldn't wait any longer. He brought her quickly to completion and followed right after.

When Sofia could breathe again, when she could speak, she held him close and whispered all the words she'd been afraid to whisper before. And he, in return, whispered them back.

"You're going to have to figure out what to do with Chelsea, sweetheart, decide if she stays in that big suite all by herself, or you get her another hotel room, because from now on, you're staying with me."

Chapter Twenty-Two

Brent could see him at one o'clock. With nothing to do until then, Car drove over to the Muni and sneaked into the dress rehearsal. Everyone was in costume, the scenery in place. It was what the opening night audience would see the next night. Lorenzo, at whom he glanced when he could take his eyes off Sofia, seemed as much like Don José—the jealous, obsessed boy-man—as a ballerina in one of those short, puffy pink dresses dancers wore.

Sofia, on the other hand, looked exactly like Carmen: sexy and haughty. A queen. She sang the *Habanera*. She swayed and looked at the soldiers, gathered around her, with bold, suggestive eyes. She taunted them with promises she wouldn't keep because she was Carmen and she did what she liked.

This woman, this Sofia-Carmen. He wanted to keep her. He wanted a life with her. Wanted her to have his children. To love them. And to love him.

He stayed for a few minutes more and left. Nobody had seen him enter the balcony. Nobody saw him leave.

At Federals Stadium, he took the elevator up to the Mosbacher box. It was an off day, one of the few the team had in July, except for the upcoming All-Star Break.

It was muggy, and so cloudy all the lights in the team's

luxury box were switched on. In the middle of the room stood three round tables covered with white cloths, the tails reaching the floor. Water glasses stood, military straight, next to white plates and silver-plated flatware. Car figured there was a party on tap.

Mosbacher sat at a table at the back of the room, this one covered not by a cloth but by piles of paper. His cell was flat against his ear, and he was yelling into it. His assistant stood off to the side. She glanced once at Car and then away.

Car crossed the room as Mosbacher laid the phone down on the table. A cup of coffee, black, half drunk, sat at his elbow.

"Thanks for seeing me, Brent."

"No problem." Brent sported a wide smile. "I always want to see the star of the Federals. Damn, but you've been on a tear, hitting like the old Car Bradford. That home run last night... man, you gave it a ride. Where did it land? The second tier?"

The home run Noah had been yakking about. Before the nightmare. "Yeah, the second tier."

"What's gotten into you?"

He knew the answer to that. The five-hundred-lire piece. And the woman who'd given it to him. "I guess I got my mojo back."

Mosbacher took up the coffee and sipped. Over the rim, he gazed at Car with expectant scrutiny. "Can I get you something to drink?"

"No, thanks."

"So what's up?"

"Did Victoria tell you I was at your place last night?"

Brent frowned. "No, she didn't."

"You remember that discussion we had way back when about you trading me to the White Sox?"

"That was talk, Car." He cocked his head to the side. "But it's not why you were at my place last night."

"It was. In a way. Are the White Sox still interested?"

Brent stood. The coffee in his cup shivered. "What's going on here?"

"I want you to trade me."

"What?" Brent's face whitened. The assistant took a

step sideways. "Stop joking around."

"I'm not joking."

Brent snapped his fingers at the assistant. "Leave us alone, will you, Kim?" As the door closed behind her, Brent folded his arms and said, "Okay, put it together for me: the reason you were with Victoria last night, the business about trading you."

"Louise and Jensen have taken Noah. If that isn't bad enough, I think Jensen is abusing him."

Brent's eyes went wide.

"Victoria will help get Noah back, if I agree to be traded to the White Sox.

Brent got paler still, and began to pace.

"And not that this has anything to do with it, but I'm in love with Sofia."

"What?" Brent stopped pacing. He waved a hand and sat heavily. He leaned an elbow on the table and dropped his head into his hand. "I don't know what you know about me. Maybe it's time I told you." He gave Car a fleeting smile. "I never did when I was your father-in-law."

The situation being what it was between him and Louise, it was understandable.

"I grew up in a mill town in Ohio. No father, a mother who worked all the time. I won't bore you with the details. And I won't tell you how I got a baseball scholarship to Western Ohio State." He smiled then. "Betcha you didn't know I played."

"Good for you."

Brent made a dismissive sound. "Anyway, all four years I played, studied, and not much else. Until my senior year. By then I knew I wasn't major league material. I'd met someone. A nice girl, kind of tall, plain, a little shy. Victoria." He stroked his chin. "I knew she had issues." He grimaced. "We didn't call them issues back then."

There was a pause. "Then I found out who her father was."

Car raised an eyebrow.

"Everything changed. I convinced myself she was more than nice. I convinced myself I could fall in love with her." Brent's smile disappeared. "Right after we got married, I stopped lying to myself and owned up to the truth. I'd married Victoria because of her father."

Car took the chair Brent had offered.

"I knew Victoria didn't want children; I didn't either. She had her opera. I would have baseball. Old man Kirk brought me into the organization, told me if I did good, I'd be general partner some day." He extended a beseeching hand. "Tell me that's not exciting for a kid who came up from nothing and was obsessed with baseball?"

As much as he'd never been able to warm up to him, Car had always thought Mosbacher was the decent one in the marriage. Now he wasn't so sure.

"Victoria didn't know about any of this. But then something happened. On our honeymoon. In Florence."

A chill ran up Car's spine.

"One night she wanted to go to the opera for a performance of *Il Matrimonio Segreto*, which is funny. Translated into English, that's the secret marriage. I was about to discover we had a secret in *our* marriage: Victoria's temper."

Car crossed one leg over the other. "And...?"

"I wanted to travel up to Turin to see Juventus play. But Victoria didn't like soccer. She said she wasn't traveling for hours to sit on a cement bench with a bunch of sweaty, low-class Italians to watch a game she had no interest in. She wanted what she wanted. Soccer wasn't it. End of story."

"Sounds like you weren't surprised."

"I'd forgotten, or maybe didn't remember. She grew up an only child with parents who never put her first."

"Poor little rich girl, huh?"

"Yeah, her stepmother had her charities, her father, baseball. Victoria was dead last on their list of priorities. When I wanted to go see that soccer game, that said she wasn't first with me, the way it was supposed to be. She pitched a fit, threw things. That's when I realized it was going to cost a whole lot more than I'd bargained for to be close to my obsession."

"That's why you stayed with Victoria all these years." Contempt he could barely hide slipped into Car's voice. "But why did Victoria stay with you?"

"In the beginning it was my looks. And no, I don't

think I'm vain saying it. Back then I was a big man on campus, with my varsity jacket and all." He reached into a cabinet behind him and brought out a framed photograph of the two of them. Victoria looked much the same as now: plain, pale, just younger. But Brent? He was a handsome son of a bitch.

"I heard Victoria bragging to her stepmother one night. She'd caught me: the best-looking guy at school, better looking than most every guy there. I was a trophy. She'd won. Everyone else lost."

"That's crazy."

"Isn't it? But Victoria always needs to come in first, to win. To make up for when she was a kid. And if she doesn't win, she gets even."

Car knew that, didn't he?

"Anyway, there I was, finally understanding what I'd done. I high-tailed it out of the hotel and walked for hours." He smiled again. "Ever been to Florence?"

"No."

"It's no hardship to walk in Florence. After a few hours I found myself in a restaurant on the Piazza della Signoria. It was close to midnight. I sat, got myself a bottle of wine, and was on my way to getting drunk, when a woman sat down at the table next to mine."

Brent got a lost look on his face. "My God, she was beautiful. She had the most sensational, black hair. It was loose, fell below her shoulders, wavy all over. Her head was bent, but I could see her eyelashes. Did you ever fall in love with eyelashes?" A half-smile curled his lips.

"They were thick and black, like brushes, but brushes that fluttered. When she raised her head, I fell in love all over again with her soft, black eyes."

He shifted and sighed. "She was crying. I don't know what made me do it, but I grabbed my bottle, and went over to her table."

"She didn't throw something at you?"

"I thought she might, but she didn't." He laughed again. "I wanted to make it all better for her. Can you imagine feeling like that for someone you don't know?"

Remembering the night Sofia sang the anthem, when she almost fell because she was wearing those god-awful shoes, hadn't he wanted to jump onto the field and rescue her? "Yeah, I can."

"Here's the sad part. I knew, right then, I'd met the love of my life on my honeymoon with another woman. Tell me that doesn't suck."

Car didn't bother to answer.

Brent took a deep breath. "Her name was Caterina de' Medici."

For the smallest moment, Car thought he hadn't heard right.

"She joked she was no relation to the Catherine who was Queen of France," Brent went on, while Car suffered tsunami-like turmoil.

"It was her husband's name, she said, and yes, he was descended from the famous family. That part didn't impress her. What did was he was much older, and she thought that meant he'd treat her with respect, unlike a younger man, who'd give her a couple of kids and then find someone else to get into bed with."

Brent lifted the cup and took a healthy swig of coffee, and continued. "What she got was a tyrant: demanding, jealous, possessive. She couldn't have her own friends. He expected dinner on the table every night whenever he came home, if he came home. She had to wear the clothes he picked out for her. A relationship with her family was out. She couldn't even visit her sister in Lucca, which is near Florence. The only place she could go alone was to grocery shop or to church. She was one unhappy woman."

Like Federico de' Medici was to his wife, he was to his daughter, Car thought.

"They'd had an argument. Federico had left the house and told her not to expect him home that night. She suspected he'd gone to an opera out of town."

"So here you were, unhappy in your marriage, hooking up with a woman who was unhappy in hers."

Mosbacher sighed. "We drank. Too much. You know what happens when you drink too much? You don't think much beyond wanting to make it all go away, which is when we did what we shouldn't have done."

"You found a hotel room."

"After that, I managed to sneak out every night. Not

that it was a problem. Victoria went to sleep early. You couldn't have awakened her with a bomb. Federico was at his beloved opera."

Car grew uncomfortable, hearing about Brent's private memories. He wondered if Sofia's father had had any idea Brent was screwing his wife.

"I found out Victoria was pregnant. That was the reason she was sleeping so deeply." He rubbed his mouth. "This is the hard part. You won't like what you're about to hear."

Car hadn't liked what he'd already heard.

"I decided we'd head back to the States, I'd tell Old Man Kirk, damn the training he was going to give me; I wanted a divorce and a few hundred thousand dollars to go away. I wouldn't tell the world what a bitch his daughter was. That was a good argument, I thought, with the Kirks being so big on privacy."

"You bastard. You were going to blackmail Mr. Kirk?"

"I told you this part of the story would be ugly."

"But not how ugly."

"I was willing to sacrifice my need to be part of baseball for the woman I loved."

"And for this you gave yourself a pat on the back?"

Brent took a deep breath and slowly shook his head.

"It didn't work out?"

"Christ, no. As I got ready to tell my plans to Victoria, we got a phone call from Inez, Victoria's stepmother. The old man had had a stroke. He was in a coma. They weren't sure he was going to make it. Inez begged us to come home. We caught the first flight out."

"That afternoon, before we were scheduled to leave, I slipped out to meet Caterina. She cried. It killed me to see her cry. I begged her to leave Federico, but she wouldn't do it. I told her Victoria was pregnant; she wondered if the pregnancy would keep me from leaving Victoria. I didn't pick up on the importance of that question. I told her it wouldn't be long and we'd be together."

"Then you flew home."

"I was prepared to go forward with my plan, and leave after the old man was back on his feet. I'd already set up a bank account for Caterina with her sister, Barbara, in

Lucca. Caterina could get whatever money she needed if she did finally decide to leave Federico. If she needed anything, she was to write to me at a PO Box I set up in New York. But then the old man recovered enough to tell me what for me changed everything. He needed someone to take control of the team. Right away. It had to be someone in the family. Since Victoria hated baseball, that left me. Damn, but hearing those words—I was overwhelmed. I accepted the offer."

Car sat straight. "It wasn't enough you were lying to your wife and your father-in-law, who happens to be one of the most decent men in the world, but now you threw Caterina, the woman you say you loved, under the bus? How could you stand yourself?"

"I didn't think I was doing that." Mosbacher sat and stared at the table, color high in his cheeks. "It was my obsession. Remember? Here I was running a major league team. I was going to fly to Italy, and explain the situation to Caterina. I was going to insist she leave Federico I was going to set her up away from Florence, someplace where I could visit her every month."

This story didn't sound real. Yet it sounded too real. "So what did you do?"

"I accepted my father-in-law's proposition, which had a formal component to it, one he made me sign. If I left Victoria, or embarrassed her or the family in any way— remember the Kirk fixation with privacy—he'd get rid of me. Fast."

Car made a sound of disgust. "The old man knew you, didn't he?"

"Yeah, he knew. He must have had a dossier on me, known about my ambition."

"So that clipped your wings."

"It shouldn't have. Caterina and I could have been together on the sly. But then Victoria almost miscarried. She spent the next five months in and out of bed and I stayed close to her. I was concerned about the health of the baby. Not that Victoria was. She drank. A lot. I'm not sure, even given what we knew today about drinking and pregnancy, whether she would have stopped."

Car didn't give a damn about Victoria. "What

happened to Caterina?"

"She wrote to me every week. I wrote to her. As time went on, I wrote less and less, busy as I was rebuilding the team. I kept sending money."

"Can I assume you were generous?"

"In those few months, I sent over a million dollars."

Now Car knew how Sofia had gotten away from Federico and was able to live in style at that expensive hotel where she was staying midtown. "Props to you. At least you did one good thing."

"Props to me? No." Brent's face contorted with grief.

It was so sudden, so unexpected. Car's anger faded away. "What happened, Brent?" he said softly.

Mosbacher put a hand across his mouth. "She stopped writing. I thought she'd given up on me." His breath hitched. "Her sister Barbara wrote to me, letting me know Caterina had died in childbirth. But the child lived. A little girl. Sofia." He slammed the table with an open palm. "I couldn't even show I was grieving because no one was supposed to know."

More silence.

Eventually Brent sighed and said, "You asked me why I was telling you this story."

"Yes."

His throat sounded suspiciously thick. "It's because you love my daughter."

Only for one split second, maybe less, did Car think he was speaking of Louise. "How do you know Sofia's your daughter?" Car heard himself ask, his brain making sure he said the words in the right order.

"When we were seeing each other, Caterina told me she wasn't sleeping with Federico." He barked a laugh. "Like she was loyal to me. Somehow I forgot about that."

Car laid a hand on the table, amazed it wasn't shaking. "In all those letters she wrote, why didn't she mention her pregnancy?"

"I don't know!" It was a cry of agony. "Wouldn't I have found a way to...?" He pressed both hands to his temples. "Who am I fooling? I have no idea why she didn't tell me, and even if she had, I don't know what I would have done. Something more than I did, I would hope."

"But you have no way of being sure."

"A lot of years passed before Barbara contacted me. Told me she didn't like me much, said I'd broken Caterina's heart.

"What made her contact you?"

"By the time Sofia turned eleven, Barbara found out Federico was locking her in her room for days on end to control her."

"I heard about that," Car said, and wasn't it a joke, history repeating itself with Jensen locking Noah in a closet. "So Barbara held her nose and contacted you because she thought you would ride to the rescue?"

"It's when she told me Sofia was mine. But how could I be sure?"

"What about DNA?"

"It wasn't perfected. Plus I needed it all to be hush-hush. I didn't want to lose control of the Federals."

"Oh we're back to the deal you made with the devil."

"Right back there. I figured Barbara was lying just to get some more money out of me, when Sofia already had enough, and at the same time I knew she wasn't. So to get to the truth, I hired an investigator to take pictures of Sofia. But they proved inconclusive. She's the image of her mother."

"That long black hair and those big, black eyes, right?"

"The first time I saw her in person, it was like looking at a miniature Caterina."

"What was the occasion?"

"One of the Federals' major ticket holders owns a villa near Florence. His wife was big into music. They were holding an in-home concert for people to hear this amazing, child singer."

"Sofia."

"I thought maybe I'd see something that proved she wasn't mine. Only thing, when she walked into the room I knew instantly she was my daughter."

"But she looked exactly like her mother."

Brent exhaled sharply. "And has the same body shape as my mother's. Walks like she walked. Even had her mannerisms. Looking at her, I thought my mother had been reborn in the body of this little girl. I made up my mind I would do everything in my power to keep Federico from doing his worst with Sofia, to support her in every way I could."

"You sent her more money."

"Yes, and swore Barbara to secrecy. I didn't want Sofia to know about me."

"Why? The team and Mr. Kirk's secrecy agreement?"

Mosbacher shook his head. "I want to say that wasn't it, but I've been a selfish bastard my whole life. Maybe it's what I was thinking."

Car waited for him to continue.

At last, Mosbacher said, "Every performance in whatever opera house she's sung, I've recorded."

"Does Sofia know?"

"Of course not. And she won't. She's my daughter and I would acknowledge her now, if I wasn't so scared she'd hate me after all these years."

"What about the team and your position?"

Brent rubbed his face. "After this? I'm not sure I care anymore."

There was a change in the air, the sound of the door to the luxury box slamming back against the wall.

Car turned and there she was, as pale as ever, with fury blazing in her eyes.

"That's good, Brent," Victoria hissed. "Because I'm going to make sure you don't have a chance to care. Ever again."

FOR THE LOVE OF THE DAME

Chapter Twenty-Three

Victoria took deliberate steps into the room. "Don't bother to ask me if I heard, Brent."

Brent held out a hand. Victoria..."

She stalked up to the table. "You've known about that girl for how long and never told me?"

Brent's eyes flashed anger. "It wasn't any of your business."

"Any of my business?" Her voice traveled upwards. "Everything in your life is my business." She clutched her arms around her waist and took a turn around the box. "Well, at least she's not your floozy. I should be grateful for small favors, I suppose."

"I..."

"Shut up, Brent," she screamed. And then she turned on Car. "All bets are off. I won't raise a finger to help you. You'll rot before I tell you where Louise is."

"But Noah is in danger, Victoria," Brent said, skirting around the table to put a hand on her shoulder. "Don't take your anger out on our grandson. Take it out on me."

Violently, she shoved his hand away. "Oh, I am going to take it out on you. That agreement my father made you sign, the one where you promised not to embarrass the family? I'm going to invoke it, which means you'll no longer be managing partner of the Federals."

"Do your worst. I don't care."

"You will care." Victoria's laughter rang hollowly against the slate-gray walls of the box. "When I destroy the team."

Brent stared at her, astonished. "You think your father

will let you do that?"

"My father is 89 years-old and sick. He won't know. Once I sell all the top dollar players for a whole lot of losers, I'll have the money I need to make my opera house better than the Metropolitan Opera." She stared him down, said, "I *hate* baseball," and left.

After long seconds, Car said, "I'm sorry to tell you this, Brent, but I don't care what Victoria does. My first and only concern is Noah and getting him back."

Brent sat down and stared at the floor. After a minute, he said, "What a mess. I don't know what to do first. Any suggestions?"

Car sat too. "You want suggestions from me? You're the guy who made this mess."

Brent rubbed his face. "I know. And people I love are paying for it. Noah." He paused, and then shook his head. "Even Louise. I should've never let Victoria send Louise away to school. When your daughter's away all school year and then summer too, you can't teach her right from wrong." He gave Car a sideways glance. "I should have been a better father to her."

Car could sympathize, now that he'd begun to understand parents didn't always make the best decisions. "You want a suggestion? Start today and be a better father to your other daughter."

Brent took a step back. "No way."

"Why?"

"Bad timing."

"No, it's not. It's the exact right time."

"She'll freak when I tell her she's been living with my lie her whole life."

"Wrong. She'll be relieved to hear Federico's not her father."

"After she kills me," Brent said morosely.

"True, she'll have a lot to say about how you betrayed her mother."

Hope warred with anxiety on Brent's face. "But you still think it'll be okay?"

"I think it will be. She already loves you for yourself."

Brent got a distant look on his face. "The first time I met Sofia, she was sweet and loving and..." He massaged his forehead. "It was strange. I had never seen her, but it felt like we'd always been connected. Does that make sense?"

It made every kind of sense to Car.

"I've been as proud of Sofia as any father could be," said Brent, musingly. "And I've never been able to tell her."

"Tell her now."

On the way to Sofia's hotel, it came to Car how he could get Noah back. "I should have thought of this before."

Brent looked up from a silent study of his hands. The man hadn't said ten words since they'd entered the limo and left the stadium. "What?"

"She won't pick up if I call her." Car was already texting Louise. "But she'll read this. I give her ten minutes before she calls me."

"What did you say?"

"With Louise, it's a constant case of more month than money. When she asks, I send more. Just now I told her if she doesn't bring Noah back today, she'll have to live with what she's got until she does."

It wasn't ten minutes; it was five.

After a hysterical tirade, during which Car did no more than listen, he said, "Okay," and hung up. "She caved." No way could he keep the grin from his face. Or the jubilation from his voice. "She's going to have somebody from the airline fly Noah back to Newark."

Relief flooded Brent's face. "Who ever thought it would be so simple?"

"Like I said, you don't know your daughter very well."

Brent made a face. "Either daughter."

By the time Brent's driver had dropped then and rolled away from the curb, a doorman Car had never seen was holding the hotel's door for them. "Where's Edward?"

"You know that Italian opera singer who's staying with us? He's up there in her suite."

Brent raised his eyebrows as they crossed the lobby. "What's that about?"

"Wait." Car was looking forward to Brent's reaction.

When the elevator door slid open on Sofia's floor, they were assailed by the sharp scent of garlic, onions, and tomatoes.

Brent took a deep breath. "Whatever that is, it smells damn good."

Car's appetite for food, which had always been an easily controlled thing, had sprung to zesty life since Sofia. He barely suppressed a groan of anticipation as he led Brent toward the half-opened door to Sofia's suite, behind which a whole lot of laughter came.

What they saw was a Sofia party. Everywhere were her friends, a dozen of them.

"Car!" He turned his head slightly as Edward, still in his service uniform, but with tie off, waved him over. Car wondered how he could have ever been jealous of Edward.

Before he could start in Edward's direction, she was there.

"Car!" Sofia hurried towards him with a towel tied around her middle. Her hair was piled on top of her head, curls tumbling down around her ears. Her face was flushed, probably from the heat of the suite's kitchen, a poor excuse for a kitchen, she'd said, but one she made work. "Tell me about Noah," she said, voice urgent, eyes glimmering with concern.

He hiked up one thumb. "It's going to be fine."

She smiled broadly. The smile slipped a fraction when she noticed Brent. Her face registered a range of emotions in quick succession: surprise, acceptance, and at last, pleasure.

She wiped her hands on the towel and held both out toward Brent. "At last you come to have the dinner with me. "*Benvenuto*... welcome."

Brent slipped Car an inquiring look. Car said nothing.

He wanted Brent to experience hospitality *à la* Sofia for himself.

As everyone realized someone new had arrived, the noise level had abated, but with the kiss Sofia gave Brent, it picked up again. It increased even more when Sofia took Brent by the hand and introduced him around.

They were in the midst of introductions, when, as if she were once more Cristina Alvarez, queen of the runway, Tina Huggins sailed out of the kitchen. Held high in her hands was a plate from which steam rose in curlicues. Right behind her came Dawg, with an even bigger plate.

"Who's ready to eat?" sang Tina.

A chorus of "Me!"s rose. Everyone made their way toward the mammoth table, the one that a lifetime ago Car thought strange. Now he knew its purpose.

Sofia patted Brent on the arm and hurried toward the table. She steered this one and that toward a chair, only stopping when everyone was seated. She turned an inquiring eye toward Car. He knew what she wanted to know.

"Yes, we're staying. Is there room?"

She made a face. "You ask me this question?" She began to shift place settings, making room for two more. She motioned for Car and Brent to come forward.

"You going to tell me what gives here?" Brent murmured as they sat.

"This is your daughter's way of making people happy," Car answered, being careful that no one but Brent heard him.

Brent's eyes softened.

It was a raucous meal. The conversation veered from who was staying in the hotel, to the city's 311 service, to the latest political scandal, to what the Federals' chances were to go all the way this year, and finally to Car's comeback.

"Our Car, he is a hero," hollered Ermano from housekeeping, sitting clear at the other end of the table and obviously afraid Car wouldn't hear him. "If Sofia lets him come to her dinners, then he is our hero too."

Everyone shouted their approval. Someone, Car thought it was Boris from accounting, pounding on the table hard enough to make the silverware jump. "A toast.

We make a toast."

Everyone raised their glasses.

"Here's to Sofia singing the best Carmen ever. Here's to her success tomorrow night."

There was a chorus of cheers in English, Spanish, and other languages Car didn't recognize. But he recognized the look on each face. It was love. For Sofia.

Eventually, everyone left. The last to go were Tina and Dawg.

"Thanks for letting Chelsea stay with the kids," Tina said, bending from her great height to give Sofia a kiss on the cheek.

"If you do the remembering, she volunteered," Sofia said, kissing Tina back. She handed Tina a shopping bag. "I pack enough food for Joshua and Brianna. Even Tiffany and Zachary will eat what I send."

Tina turned to Car, and big smile on her knock-your-eyes-out face, gave him a pat on the back. Dawg looked on, all serious. Until he said, "You did good." He walked backwards, smiling and nodding, then grabbing the door, closed it behind them. Car knew he'd just gotten affirmation from Tina's knight in shining armor.

Chuckling, he turned toward Sofia. She had a spot of something—food, no doubt—on the left breast of her rose-colored sweater. Car wanted to touch it. Only to discover what it was, of course.

"Now you must tell me about Noah," she announced and sat on the couch.

Growing serious, Car sat at the other end, Brent on the chair opposite. "I've been giving Louise extra money for the last few months. I told her if she wanted me to deposit the latest check, I needed Noah back."

With a squeal of pleasure, Sofia clapped her hands. "Bravo. You found the key to unlocking her stupidity." She slapped a hand across her mouth. "I am sorry to say this about your daughter, Brent. But most assuredly, she has done a stupid thing."

Brent waved away her apology.

She turned back to Car. "But I am surprised when you come to the door and Brent is with you. Why you do not call me to say he is coming?"

Car leaned down and cupped his hands around her beautiful, flushed face. "And if I called you? What would you have done? Made more food?"

Sofia wouldn't have made more food. But she would have been able to compose herself better. Before, by the way Car looked at her and then at Brent, she knew something was up. It wasn't about Noah.

Now Brent was sweating. What the thing was to make him sweat, she hadn't the first idea.

While she thought about what it could be, Car stood. "I need to make a phone call." He looked at Brent and nodded. He started toward the bedroom, slipping his phone from his pocket. "Preparations for Noah. I'll be right back."

This was strange.

"Sofia," Brent began. And stopped. He jumped up, stepped to the back of the chair and gripped the top. "We have known each other a long time."

"Yes, since I am eleven years old." She folded her hands in her lap, unsettled. "What is the matter, Brent?"

He gave his head one shake. "And we have spent many evenings together. I have enjoyed every single one."

"I too." This conversation—no, it wasn't a conversation, but something else.

"I have seen every one of your performances, even the ones I wasn't able to attend. I found someone to tape those and send the videos to me." He clapped a hand to his head. "I wasn't going to tell you that."

She gripped her hands tight, now alarmed. "Why?"

"Because I am hoping you will understand." He paused, shook his head. His dear face was set in concrete, like the face of the Commendatore in the last act of *Don Giovanni*, except sweat trickled down his face, and statues didn't sweat. "I hope you'll understand what I did." His breath was coming fast.

He was scaring her.

"Sofia." He came around the chair and sat down. Leaning toward her, he looked at her with a plea for the understanding he had asked for. "You know I love you." He took a deep, deep breath. "Just as I loved your mother."

She put her hand to her chest. The pulse of blood that rushed through her palm met the frantic beat of her heart. "My mother? You knew my mother?"

"I knew her well. Very well."

"You did?" she asked, like a stupid puppet. Suddenly she remembered that time, when she sang the national anthem and she said those words to him. *I wish, sometimes, that you were my papa instead of my papa.* And he had looked at her with strange, sad eyes and said, *I wish it too, my dear.*

And she knew.

By the look of fear in his eyes, he knew that she knew.

Her brain stood still. She put her hands over her eyes. Her ears filled with the rush of her blood. "When I sang for you that time when I was eleven years old, you knew. Why did you not take me to live with you?"

This was a stupid thing to ask when there was so much else to ask. But it was the only thing that came into her jumbled mind. Which is when she felt rage and when she did something she'd never done.

She threw herself at him and hit him as hard as she could. She hit him over and over again. "Why? Why did you not come and get my mama?" she screamed. "Why did you let her die? Why did you let me grow up with that terrible man who hates me? Why?"

She began to sob, deep, harsh sounds that shook her body. She hit him until her hands began to sting. He did nothing to stop her. And then he began to cry too, great big gulps that must have hurt his chest.

She couldn't keep hitting him, not when his tears matched hers. She put her arms around his neck, laid her head against his shoulder, and cried for the pain and the years and the love that was lost.

At last, the sobs, his and hers, quieted. She eased out of his arms. "I am sorry I hit you." Her voice was thick and syrupy. "I am sorry I speak to you with the full sinuses, and a voice like the frog, which I cannot help."

Brent wiped his eyes. "I don't care about your sinuses, my darling. To me you will never sound like a frog. Your voice will always be sweet as honey."

More tears then, when she didn't think she had any more. She put a hand to her throat. "I must do the... *come si dice... gargarismi?*"

"Gargling."

"Yes, the gargling. It is an ugly word in English, but also in Italian, *si?*" She put a hand to her mouth. "We must think if I am to call you *papa.*"

He took her hands and squeezed them. "I think right now it's enough that you know I'm your papa."

"*Disgraziato!*" She popped up and glided over to the bedroom door. "Car, I know you do not make the phone call. I know you give me the time to do my damage to Br... to my papa. You must come out now."

He opened the door, a question in his eyes, but she didn't let him wait. "You do not need to do the worrying, Car. It will be all right. But now I must take the shower. You will forgive me leaving you. I need relaxation from what has just happened."

When she left the room, Car motioned for Brent to sit. "So it went okay?"

Eyes glistening, Brent gave him a half-grin. "I think so."

Car leaned back and crossed his legs. "Let's talk. Victoria. Can she truly destroy the team?"

Brent sighed. "You know she can. She can trade away our good players for second- and third-rate players the other teams want to get rid of. That'll seal the lid on the Federals for who knows how long."

"What can stop her?"

Rubbing the back of his neck, Brent shook his head. "I don't think anything can stop her."

Car sat forward. "What happens if I retire?"

Sofia chose that moment to come back into the room. "*Accidenti*! What is this?"

He jumped up. "I thought you were taking a shower."

"I forgot something. What is this retiring?"

Car looked at Brent. The man shrugged. *Big help there.* He sighed. "We're trying to figure out how to stop Victoria from doing something that's going be a huge life changer for a lot of people."

"What is it?" She sat on the end of the couch.

"Victoria found out about you."

Her eyes opened wide. "Oh. She does not like to find out I am your daughter, Brent?"

"No," answered Car for Mosbacher. "She doesn't like it any better now than when she thought you were his lover."

"My own papa's lover?" Bracing her hands on the seat cushion, an expression of nausea crossed Sofia's face. "I would like to do the hurling."

"Me too. Almost as much as when I think about how she wants to break up the Federals, trade all the good players away to get back at me and at Brent... your father."

Confusion knotted her eyebrows. "Trade?" She looked at Brent.

Brent said, "It means send our players away to other teams."

She swiped at a curl that had fallen onto her forehead. "What will happen to the Federals? We will have no players?"

"No, we'll have other players, not as good as the ones we have now."

She took a breath. "You will send Dawg away?"

"Yes," said Brent. "Probably to Seattle. They need a catcher bad."

"But what about his family, the children?"

The men shrugged.

She looked at Car. "And JJ?"

Car said, "Probably Toronto."

"What about Mo?"

Brent shifted. "The Astros will want him."

Her eyes still on Car, she said, "And you?"

"The White Sox."

In a quiet voice, Sofia said, "You must not let this happen." She turned toward Brent.

Brent leaned forward. "I can't do anything."

She rose from the couch, stood very straight. "I can do something, believe me. If you make the trade of Dawg and JJ and Car, I will phone Maestro Lupino and tell him he must find another Carmen, because I will not sing tomorrow. The *Signora*, she will not like that."

Brent frowned. "All he'll do is replace you with Jenny. Victoria will be happy if your understudy goes on in your place."

"Oh." Sofia tapped her upper lip. "I must think of something else." She skirted around the table to give Brent a kiss on his cheek. "Now I must take the shower. You and Car may stay and talk. You must turn out the lights when you leave."

She took Car by the hand and brought it to her lips. After she kissed each knuckle, she said, "Please bring Noah to me tomorrow. I want to give him big kisses and hugs."

Chapter Twenty-Four

With Sofia behind the closed door, Car kept company with Brent and a bottle of wine. "We need to think about what we can do to keep Sofia from—" He made air quotes, "—thinking of something else."

"I don't want her to do anything to jeopardize her career."

"I don't either." Car couldn't help looking toward the bedroom door, wondering if he could join her without Brent—Sofia's father—objecting.

They were silent.

Until Car chortled. "You do know she just benched both of us, right?"

They grinned at each other in companionable silence.

Car spoke to Louise the following morning just before he left for Newark to get Noah.

"Peter wants me to give up Noah. He says Noah is getting in the way of our lifestyle. That's why I'm sending him back, Car." Her voice was filled with scorn. "Your little blackmail meant nothing."

Right. "Does this mean we're done arguing over custody?"

"Well I wish those stupid columnists would stop writing bad things about me."

"So that's a yes, right?"

"All right," she said, grudgingly. "Peter and I have a big concert in Thailand. It's one thing to take Noah to the Bahamas, but Thailand? The ocean there is huge."

Car didn't try to figure out that one. "You're right." He looked at his watch. "Look, I need to get started for the airport. I want to be there when Noah gets off the plane."

But he was late. A truck carrying chickens overturned on the Jersey Turnpike. There were feathers flying everywhere and chickens running for their lives. The cops kept the road closed until all the birds could be gathered up.

When the road opened, Car floored it. He wanted to hold his son in his arms.

Chelsea was biting her nails. "I'm so nervous."

Sofia grabbed Chelsea's hand away from her mouth. "You must stop. The nails, they begin to look good. When you bite them, they become like little daggers and you will stab yourself with them and bleed." She cocked her head to the side, just keeping the smile from her face. "I can tell you, Chelsea. Red is not your color."

Chelsea didn't laugh, which gave Sofia the clue Chelsea was more scared about what was about to happen than she, herself. "You do not need to have the nerves, Chels."

Pushing her hands through her dirty-blond curls, Chelsea began to pace the small dressing room. "How can you say that? You've worked for this moment forever. Now, because that woman has a grudge against the world, you could lose it all."

Sofia rose from the bench where she was sitting. She had just fastened the buttons on the full-flowing skirt that Carmen would wear to the cigarette factory where she worked. "I will not lose."

Chelsea pointed at her white peasant blouse with the

draw string that separated the ring of ruffles. When untied, the blouse would sag. "Are you sure?"

Just then there was a knock at the door. Chelsea gave a little squeak. "He's early," she whispered.

Sofia opened the door. There he stood, Maestro Lupino. Sofia gave Chelsea a little push and urged her out of the dressing room. "Go, *cara*. It is okay."

Closing the door, Sofia said, *"Allora, parliamo, Maestro."* Naturally her words were in Italian. Why should two Italians speak English? Besides, when she told her lie, it would sound more convincing in Italian.

Maestro Lupino nodded his head, and came into the dressing room. Sofia closed the door behind him. The Maestro must allow her this one small thing if the rest was to work. She couldn't let herself think she would fail. She had to succeed. She was doing it for her friends—Dawg and JJ, Mo, and all the Federals. She was especially doing this for Car. She *couldn't* fail.

She stood at the edge of the stage as the men and women of the orchestra moved into their places in the pit. In a moment, she'd be given the signal to stroll onto the stage, Carmen, at last.

She'd stare, in her bold Carmen way, at the soldiers gathered in the square, ignore Don José, while watching him secretly, sing the *Habanera*, and sneak a quick peek at the box at the center of the horseshoe of boxes that rimmed the floor of the newly-renovated Municipal Opera House.

She knew she'd see him. The Maestro had confirmed Wellington Sotheby Kirk would attend, even in his wheelchair. Sofia crossed her fingers he would come backstage at the end of Act I. If her plan was to succeed, he must.

The concert master, violin tucked under his arm, gave her a quick kiss on her hand as he breezed by on his way to his seat next to the conductor's podium. She blew him a kiss in return and he pretended to catch it with his free hand. He was a lovely man. She didn't mind his kiss. It was sincere and he didn't have wet lips.

"Sofia."

She turned. Lorenzo. In his green uniform of the Spanish Army.

"*Sì?*"

Lorenzo shifted the shako he held under an arm. A self-satisfied smile curled his made-up red lips. "At last, you're here, ready to take your chances singing *Carmen*. Let's hope you won't struggle."

Oh, he was such a snake. "Do not worry, Lorenzo." She flicked her fingers in his face. "I know what I can sing."

Lorenzo had kept away from her during rehearsals. She didn't know why, but she was grateful. Now his gaze traveled to her chest, where it lingered for long, insulting seconds.

"*Allora*, Lorenzo. How is the corset?" She batted her Carmen eyelashes at him. "I hope it is not too tight."

Just then the best boy gave her a tap on the shoulder, indicating she should climb the stairs to the back of the cigarette factory and prepare for the beginning of the opera. She gave Lorenzo a little wave and turned toward the steps.

"It's not a corset," Lorenzo whispered to her back.

Sofia kept herself from laughing. The best boy didn't. A second later, she felt a tap on her shoulder.

Prepared to tell Lorenzo not to breathe too deeply, she turned and saw not Lorenzo, but her father—*not* her father—Federico de' Medici. For a moment she though he was a mirage. How had he gotten here? But then she realized. He never missed any of her performances. Even this one, which he had never been a part of.

He hadn't changed. Perhaps he was thinner, but his posture was still correct. Around his otherwise bald head were wisps of white hair. He held a crutch under one arm. The left leg of his trousers was wrapped, mid-thigh to ankle, in a black cloth brace.

"I see you're walking now," she said in Italian.

"Yes, at last. I would have been here, long ago, to rein you in if I could." His pale blue eyes glittered behind rimless eyeglasses. "So you are going to do it after all."

A world of responses tumbled through her brain. She said nothing.

He hitched in place; the tip of the crutch tapped once on the dusty floor. "I tried to call you. I left messages at the hotel desk and with your assistant. Were you afraid to speak to me?"

She knew he kept leaving messages, until, for some reason, just recently, he stopped. "Simple. I didn't want to speak to you."

His eyes widened. Jaw working against the anger he'd always been quick to display, he said, "You were always a disagreeable girl."

Yes, he'd think so, and he was here to remind her of that.

The sound of applause filtered through from the front of the house and rose in a crescendo, which meant Maestro Lupino was making his way toward the podium.

"You're wrong," she said, her voice composed.

He worked his chin. "Do not contradict me."

Sofia stared at the man she'd always called papa, for whom she had never, at least as long as she could remember, felt anything but fear and anger, and yes, even hate. "I will."

"What you will do is fail."

He was beginning to scare her. She motioned to the best boy to bring her some water.

"You know I'm right." her father said, self-satisfaction fixed upon his face.

He wasn't right, and he wasn't her father. He didn't create her when on the most basic of levels—the biological—he had nothing to do with her creation. She held onto that thought so she wouldn't let him frighten her and slip back into the person she'd been the last time he'd told her she would fail... as she made her way down the jet way to the plane that would take her from Milan to New York. She wouldn't. And she wouldn't tell him that he would never again have the right to tell her she would succeed or fail. Not tonight. Not yet. Later was soon enough.

The applause continued. The Maestro would be

bowing to the audience, turning to the orchestra, and urging them to stand so they, too, could be part of the up swell of welcome and anticipation for this special performance.

This gave Sofia heart. "You aren't right. I won't fail."

His mouth opened. Now it was his turn to have nothing to say. But he was resourceful. "You're nothing without me. I've tried to tell you many times. *Carmen* isn't a role you can sing at this time in your career. Now you're about to step onto a stage where you'll make a fool of yourself."

"Yet I will. Go out on the stage, that is. In minutes."

"I am shocked Maestro Lupino agreed to give you the role."

"Perhaps he heard something in my voice you can't hear."

He drew himself up to his inconsequential height. "You criticize my ability to understand what makes a great mezzo?"

"I do. Because I know what I should have known before."

"What is that? Some nonsense some stupid person planted in your head?"

"No, papa." She took in a quick breath. The word had come out without thought. But after this moment, she vowed, never again would she call Federico de' Medici papa. "This is what I should've known. I can sing any role my voice is ready for. My voice is ready for *Carmen*. It has been ready for *Carmen*. This is what I've learned."

"No. First you must sing the roles I've told you to sing. You must allow me to guide your career. I know what you need better than you."

She still felt a scrap of feeling for this man, who would soon understand she was lost to him as was his personal connection to opera. She put a hand on his arm. "You don't. From now on, and for the rest of my career, no matter where it takes me, no matter what roles I'll sing or not sing, I'll make the decision about what they'll be."

Desperation shone in his eyes. "You'll fail," he said once again.

Before she got on that plane from Milan and flew to

New York, those words would have made her collapse. Not now. She smiled. "No. I'll succeed. You can enjoy my success. Or not."

At last the best boy brought her a bottle of water. She sipped and gave it back. The orchestra had begun to play the overture. She needed to be in place. "George, please find *Signore* de' Medici a seat. I would like him to enjoy the performance if he is able." She gave her used-to-be father a little nudge. "You need to decide. I don't care if you see me as Carmen or not. But now you need to go."

After he left, Sofia hurried up the steps to the back of the staged cigarette factory. The women of the chorus, who were playing the factory girls, were in place. They looked at her, wondering what had taken her so long. One of the tallest of the girls—Leigh was her name—reached out and squeezed her hand. "*In bocca al lupo*," she whispered.

In the mouth of the wolf.

Sofia smiled at her and walked to the spot from which she would strut in mere minutes. As she passed each woman, each wished her the same: "*In bocca al lupo*."

Suddenly she was shaking. Was it from nerves? Or was it from the shocking meeting with Federico? She smoothed a hand down her throat and breathed deep through her nose. She was all at once calm, not nervous. For what she was about to do, on stage and off, there couldn't be any nervousness. What she was doing was right.

The bell heralding the entrance of the cigarette girls rang; they began to pass by her and move onto the stage. "*We watch the smoke drifting...*" The soldiers, already onstage responded, "*Don't be cruel, listen to us...*"

Sofia crossed herself, as she did before every performance. Hand on the railing of the steps, she listened for her cue, watched the prompter, who stood beside her, headset on, libretto in hand, a frown of concentration on his face until he raised his hand and sent her. She went.

"*Here is Carmencita!*" the soldiers sang.

And here she was. At last. Singing the role she was meant to sing. She filled her mind with the soul and spirit of Carmen. In the instant her feet touched the stage, she became Carmen: not the gypsy, Carmen, not the flirt, Carmen, nor the cruel tormenter of men. She became Carmen, the woman who made herself free to do what she wanted with her life. Singing *Carmen* was more than a part. It was more than the *Habanera* and the *Seguidilla*. Singing *Carmen* made her Sofia.

As the notes of the *Habanera* died away, Car applauded like a maniac. He didn't think, though, there was another person in the theater who was doing what else he was doing: sweating. Sofia had planned something, only he didn't know what. That scared him half to death.

"Sofia is amazing," Dawg said, keeping up a slow, rhythmic pounding of one huge hand against the other.

"She's beyond amazing," said Tina, who sat on Dawg's other side.

"You think they do this every half-time?"

"Eric...!"

"Dawg...!" Car spoke over Tina. "It's not football and it's not even the end of Act One. So chill."

"I was just asking," said Dawg, his voice aggrieved.

The applause died and people began to settle back. Lupino raised his hands to set the orchestra playing again.

"So what's next?" whispered Dawg.

With a hand cupped around his mouth Car whispered, "Break's over so the girls are going back into the cigarette factory. The trouble's about to start."

"*Ssh!*" Came a loud, sibilant warning from behind them.

Dawg gave that person a little nod. "Who's the guy in the green uniform?"

"That's Don José. He kills Carmen at the end of the

opera."

"How come?"

Car gave him a disgusted look.

Dawg raised an eyebrow and settled back.

On the stage Lorenzo—Don José—was speaking in some kind of opera-talk to Corporal Zuniga. Right on time, the shrieking came from inside the stage's cigarette factory.

"What's that about?" whispered Dawg.

"Shut up," whispered both Car and Tina.

"How am I going to know what's going on, if you guys won't explain?"

Car pointed to the supertitles, flashing across the top of the proscenium. "Read. You'll figure it out."

"I can't keep going back and forth. I want to watch Sofia."

Pandemonium reigned on stage and Carmen was dragged out of the factory. She admitted to stabbing a girl. Zuniga told José to arrest her and take her down to the lockup.

Don José-Latte moved into place beside Sofia, as she stared straight out into the audience, her hands in front of her, waiting for him to tie her hands with a rope.

On Carmen-Sofia's face was a smirk that said she was bored, and the rope José bound her with to take her to jail was no big deal.

"Listen now," Car whispered. His mouthy Sofia was going to lash Don José with her tongue. She was going to enjoy doing it in front of all these thousands, because it was Lorenzo she wanted to lash.

"What am I listening to?"

Car couldn't answer Dawg. The music was carrying them forward: the libretto too. Don José had taken Carmen into the staged jail and he was pacing back and forth, pretending not to listen to her taunts and teasing.

They were coming to the place where Carmen gets José to untie the ropes around her wrists. José came up behind her and cupped her shoulders, admitting at last how she had bewitched him.

Car took a deep breath, and braced himself in his seat. Whatever it was Sofia was about to do, it was coming now. He could feel it. Sofia looked out into the audience as she had before, and sang her words of defiance. But this time her gaze touched here and there. She was looking for him. And found him.

For a moment, their eyes locked. She raised one eyebrow in a salute, and then whirled around, the white slip beneath her black skirts showing. Facing away from the audience, standing in front of Don José, she did something Car couldn't see. Instantly the blouse sagged, pooling around her hips. There was a gasp from the man behind Car. Not that he could see anything but Sofia's beautiful back, with the defined bones of her spine marching up from her narrow waist to where her hair fell around her shoulders.

Check that. Someone did see something: Lorenzo. He was gawking. Mouth dropped open, he forgot to sing. The moment passed and Lorenzo recovered himself, pretending he was horrified by Carmen's boldness.

Before Car could work out how Sofia would keep the audience from seeing what she didn't want them to see, she held out her hands to Lorenzo, who loosened the rope. With one motion, she pulled up the front of her blouse, singing the rest of the scene, the fabric she'd torn tied in a knot at her waist, so all anyone could see was the slender gap between her breasts.

"Was that part of the opera?" asked Dawg. Car gave him a quick glance. Even in the light cast from the stage into the darkened theater, it looked like Dawg was blushing.

"I don't know." But he did.

"*Ssh! Ssh! Ssh!*"

They were going to have to deal with the guy behind them when the curtain went down at the end of Act One.

Chapter Twenty-Five

"What did you think you were doing," whispered Lorenzo in English, as the three of them—Carmen, José and Micaela—bowed to the audience at the end of Act One. Lucilla Sebastiani, who was singing the part of Micaela, and whose English was poor, couldn't understand a word.

"What is the matter, Lorenzo?" Someone backstage had given Sofia a pin so the blouse wouldn't open further. She put a hand over her heart and gave the audience a deep curtsy. You did not like that I took my blouse off? You prefer to do the taking off?"

"Are we back to that again? Will you ever let me forget?"

Sofia blew a kiss to a crazy man who was jumping up and down in the second row, joy spread across his face. "Until the moment you say, 'I am so sorry, Sofia, that I forced the sex on you in the dressing room in Florence.' No, I will not let you forget."

"Talk about forgetting... you made me forget my place, you little idiot."

The bravos continued, the clapping, if anything, became wilder. Sofia looked for Car, but couldn't find him among the people who had rushed toward the front to get close to the stage. "But Lorenzo. They are only breasts. Breasts are nothing new to you. For many years I have known you are the expert on breasts."

"What nonsense is this?" He bent to pick up a single rose and presented it to her. His implants gleamed in the house lights.

She took the rose and blew him a kiss. "It is not

nonsense. I see you many times when you think no one is looking. You are in corners backstage with the girls from the chorus, who want the great tenor, Lorenzo Latte, to notice them."

"What is wrong with that?"

"You are testing them, the breasts I mean," she said as if he hadn't asked the question. "You are weighing them with your hands." Her eyes continued to seek out Car. She saw Tina. Her pulse quickened. Car must be nearby.

"You watch me? You are a voyeur?" He forgot to bow to the audience.

On Lorenzo's other side, Lucilla pulled on his hand. He put his big smile back in place. He bowed, took the shako from under his arm, and with a flourish, extended it toward the audience. "You watch me?" he ground out, his smile now cemented on his face.

"You make it easy. You do not hide."

At last the applause began to die and they walked behind the curtain.

"What's going on between you two?" Lucilla asked in Italian. "If I didn't know any better, I'd think you were having an argument."

"Nothing to worry about," said Sofia, answering her in Italian. "We were talking about a miscue."

Stage hands rushed around them, moving the jail away, and wheeling the inn of Lillas Pastia into place for the beginning of Act Two. Sofia skirted around them, Lorenzo on her heels.

"There better not be any more surprises," he said, putting a hand on her shoulder to slow her.

She shrugged his hand away. "No more surprises." She was exhausted. Adrenalin had carried her through Act One. Now it was gone. "Please excuse me, Lorenzo. I must go to my dressing room to prepare for the next act." She hurried her steps away from him.

High in the first tier, in the center box in the horseshoe ring built with her father's money, Victoria Mosbacher watched Sofia de' Medici bring down the house. As the curtain descended at the end of the first act, the audience surged to its feet. Their applause was deafening.

Victoria's father sat beside her in his wheelchair, smiling and clapping. In his lap was the note she had sent. *She*, the bitch everyone in the audience adored tonight. She'd begged them to come back stage at the end of Act One. She had an important question to ask them. Her father wanted to go, to pay his respects to the new diva, and to answer the question, if he could. Victoria hadn't been able to change his mind.

She risked a glance at Brent, who sat on the other side of her father. Tears were running down his face. Did he love Sofia this much he would cry to hear her sing?

She was filled with renewed hate. Before the night was out, she would destroy Brent. She would destroy Car, and she would destroy Sofia. She would destroy them all.

The wonderful Brunello Chelsea had ordered, stood on the dressing table, amid the pots of powder and grease sticks. Sofia counted the wine stems: six. More than enough.

Chelsea stood next to the door, ready to leave. "Maybe you want to wait until afterwards to do this?"

"It must be now. This is when I have the advantage." Sofia opened the tiny closet door and took out a blouse to replace the one she ripped.

"That little Janet Jackson action was priceless." Chelsea's eyes filled with admiration. "Even from backstage I could see Lorenzo almost fall over." She made little clapping motions. "Yay you."

"*Grazie*, Chels. But this is no Super Bowl silliness. It was the agreement I made with the Maestro. Lorenzo would be surprised, because Don José would be surprised.

The Maestro liked that." She picked up the bottle of wine and opened it. "Soon they will come. Do you think I am ready?"

Chelsea took the cork from her and put it in the pocket of her black trousers. "You're ready. I assume you want me to keep your father out."

Only a second did Sofia not know to which father Chelsea referred. "Ah, yes. Please keep Federico away. Although I do not think, he will want to see me again."

There was a knock on the door.

"That's my cue," said Chelsea. "Consider me gone." She slipped past the crowd standing outside Sofia's dressing room: Brent and Victoria Mosbacher, a woman in a black dress—the person Americans called a caregiver, such a nice word—and the man in a wheelchair. Wellington Sotheby Kirk.

Sofia took a deep breath; this was it. "*Avanti*...come in." She had met *Signore* Kirk when she sang Cherubino in Verona during a summer festival. He had come with Brent, her father.

She was excited—and scared—that night. Her first big role, her then-father had stared at her from the first row the entire night. She hadn't known if she was singing well or if she was singing poorly. For once, he said, she'd sung well.

This was why she didn't have a firm memory of Brent's father-in-law, only of a stooped old man with a cane, a sweet smile, and sparkling eyes. Brent told her Signore Kirk had a reputation for being hard, but she remembered thinking how could this man be hard?

Tonight Signore Kirk had that same sparkle in his eyes, that same sweet smile. She went to him as if he were her beloved grandfather, almost forgetting why he was here.

"I would like to give you a kiss, but you will be covered with my makeup. May I kiss you later?"

His laugh sounded broken. But the look on his face wasn't. "I will be most pleased to get that kiss. The makeup hides your beauty."

"Dad, why you thought we needed to do this I don't know, but let's make it fast. Intermissions don't last long."

Signore Kirk turned his head to look at his daughter, who was standing by his chair. Tonight the *Signora* wore a deep navy silk pantsuit, with sequins at the lapel and on the slits on her trousers. On her neck, at her wrists, and at her ears were rows and rows of diamonds.

Sofia said, "We do not need much time, but thank you for reminding me, *Signora*."

"You begged for a word with my father. Why now? Why not after the performance?" asked the *Signora*.

Sofia pulled the dressing table stool closer to Mr. Kirk's wheelchair and sat in front of him. "*Signore...*"

She sensed Brent leaning forward, as if he wanted to help her. He couldn't. She must do this herself.

Heart hammering against her lungs, she forced herself to remain calm. "I ask you to come here because I must have your advice to know what I must do next."

Concern darkened his eyes. With bony hands, he reached out and took Sofia's in his. "What is it? How can I help?"

She looked at Brent and then at the *Signora*, who glared back, with poison-filled eyes. The *Signora* pushed the caregiver aside and grabbed the wheelchair's handles. Jerking them backward, she said, "Forget it, Dad. She's just a girl who wants you to help her career." She turned her head in Sofia's direction. "You don't need help or advice, do you? Not after that stunt you pulled in the jail scene."

Signore Kirk looked at his daughter and frowned. "Victoria." Just the one word. A warning.

The *Signora* heeded it. Her hands dropped from the handlebars. She pinched her lips together.

"I did not want to do this stunt in the jail scene. I do not like to show my breasts to the world. Maestro Lupino and I, we discuss it. He is the boss." Sofia heaved a sigh so loud it almost created an echo in the tiny room.

"While I don't like it, I know there is a move toward more *realismo* in opera productions. It's the twenty-first century, after all," said Signore Kirk.

Sofia sighed again, as if she had accepted this fact. "But..."

There was a knock, the door opened, and Car came in. Sofia had wanted him to stay away. For his own sake. But she knew he'd come. It was why she wasn't surprised to see his beloved self in the doorway. She passed him a message with her eyes, hoping he'd understand. "I am just the smallest bit afraid of one thing," she said, her voice a little loud to draw everyone's attention back to her.

The *Signora* opened her mouth to speak. *Signore* Kirk laid a hand on his daughter's arm. "Let her finish, Victoria." He gave Sofia an encouraging smile. "What are you afraid of?"

"I am afraid of too much *realismo*."

"What's too much?" asked *Signore* Kirk.

She peeked at the *Signora* to make sure she was paying attention. Then she sighed again for the sake of the story. "Baring the whole body. My body is too fat. That is too much *realismo*."

There was a deafening silence in the room.

Signore Kirk cleared his throat as if something had choked him. "Are you saying you are being expected to bare yourself on stage? Completely?"

Sofia knew she must not over-play this next part. It was necessary if she were to succeed with this farce. She let her hands hover over her face. "I... I..." She made her voice sound tearful.

"This is ridiculous," said the *Signora*. "At no time did I ever tell Antonio to have Sofia bare everything. Never."

"But *Signora*," said Sofia after a long beat. "I do not understand. You have told me from the beginning. All decisions about the operas, it is the Maestro who makes them. You do not interfere."

Brent coughed.

A frown crossed *Signore* Kirk's pale forehead, his smile gone. For the first time since he'd come into the room, there was steel in his eyes. He looked at both men and then at his daughter. "What's going on, Victoria?"

"Nothing at all." She tried for a laugh and failed. Her

face turned blotchy.

Signore Kirk looked over his shoulder to the caregiver, who had stood motionless through everything. "Nelda, please turn my chair so I can face these people. There's something I need to understand."

Once she did, *Signore* Kirk fixed his daughter with a stare and said, "One thing I know: whatever's going on, it's not nothing. You either tell me yourself, or I'm going to ask Brent. Or Car. I get the feeling they both know."

"Dad!" The *Signora* held out a beseeching hand toward him. "I thought we were going to be a team from now on. Just you and me."

His eyes softened and then hardened again. "We are a team. But unless there's honesty between us..."

"Dad!" She looked first at Sofia, then Car, and finally at Brent. Her nostrils flared. "You! You lied to me from the beginning."

Brent leaned forward, a hand held out to the *Signora*. "I tried to make it up to you."

Sofia didn't think the *Signora* heard. "If only you could have figured out a way." Tears spilled from her eyes, her face now showed the anger and misery of the life she had chosen to make unhappy. "If only you could have figured out a way," she repeated, "to have your whore of a daughter, my father's money, and the team, you would have."

"Victoria, stop." *Signore* Kirk looked up at his daughter. "You're embarrassing yourself."

"You said you would never betray me, Brent. But you did." the *Signora* continued, as if her father had not spoken. "You're no better than any thief on the street. Only difference is you didn't steal my wallet; you stole my self-esteem."

"Nobody can steal anyone's self-esteem, Victoria," Brent said.

She put her hands over her eyes, as if shutting out her pain. "You told me you didn't want children after we had Louise, that there wouldn't be anyone else in your life except me."

"I didn't know I had another child. Not then."

"What do you mean, not then?" She swiped at the

tears on her cheeks. "When we were supposed to be on our honeymoon?"

"Victoria," whispered her father, the look of steel gone, replaced by consternation.

"You knew for years," the Signora said, rushing onward. No, don't tell me. I don't care how many years." She pointed at Car. "Everything changed, Brent, when you told *him* all the sordid details. "You shamed me by telling a stranger. I'm within my rights to do what I'm doing."

"What are you doing?" Her father gripped a skeletal hand around the arm of his wheelchair.

"I..." Now it was the *Signora's* turn to be tongue-tied.

"I'll tell you, Wells," said Brent. "I did something when Victoria and I were on our honeymoon, something I shouldn't have done. I broke the vows I made in the marriage ceremony. I was with another woman, there in Florence, until the day Inez called to say you'd had that stroke." He looked straight at *Signore* Kirk. "The result of what I did I'll never regret." He held out a hand to Sofia. Sofia took it. "Say hello to my daughter," Brent said, and smiled at her with love.

"You bastard," whispered the *Signora*.

Brent gave her a quick look. "I hope you're referring to me and not Sofia."

Signore Kirk stared at Sofia. "Did you know this?"

"I did not," Sofia said. "Not until last night."

Brent let go of Sofia's hand. "If I had to guess, Sofia made up this tale about having to appear onstage nude to save the team."

A momentary frown knotted *Signore* Kirk's forehead.

"I do not make up the story entirely," Sofia exclaimed. "If the Maestro and the *Signora* want me to sing with the bare body, I must."

The *Signora* made a sound of disgust. "That was never going to happen. Who'd want to see your naked body?"

Car, who had been so quiet, laid a hand on Sofia's shoulder. "I think you better stop while you're ahead, Victoria."

"Tell your father what you're planning to do with the guys who are free agents this year, Victoria," said Brent. "You know, the ones whose contracts are coming up for renegotiation, and the ones every team, in both leagues, are dying to get their hands on, the ones you're willing to trade away to get back at me to destroy what your father and I have built up these last years."

"Is that true?" Signor Kirk's eyes filled with confusion.

"What do you care anymore what happens to the Federals?" the *Signora* asked, now looking at her father with defiance.

"Do you think because I'm in this wheelchair I don't care? That's foolish of you, Victoria."

"Daddy, Brent betrayed me." The pleading came back into the *Signora*'s eyes.

"He did, but it happened a long time ago. Why haven't you let it be in the past so you could live in the present?"

"Because he never said he was sorry."

Signore Kirk sighed. "Sometimes you must make do without the words." He turned to Brent. "It pains me to hear these things, Brent. I hope all these years of us working together for the good of the team, the feeling you displayed toward me, the camaraderie between us, was not false?"

Brent took the old man's hand and said, "If it was false in the beginning, it didn't last. I had respect for you, and yes, more than respect."

There was a knock on the door. "Fifteen minutes, Miss de' Medici," a voice called.

The *Signora*'s face had turned to marble. "Well, that settles that."

Signore Kirk said, "Victoria, I'll want to have a discussion with you about what your plans were for my team. I'll want Brent to be part of the discussion."

My. The word of possession, and there on *Signore* Kirk's face, inflexibility. Sofia had sympathy for the *Signora*. The *Signora* wanted her father to pay attention to her, perhaps because when she was a child he didn't. But he wouldn't give it to her now, not the way she wanted it, not if she would destroy something he loved.

There was no flurry of activity. No congratulations on a well-sung First Act. No hand-kissing. The woman, named Nelda, wheeled *Signore* Kirk's chair out the door. The *Signora* followed. Brent held Sofia's gaze for one moment, and left.

Only Car remained. "Sweetheart," he whispered, laying his hands on her shoulders. "That was dangerous. So much of it could have gone wrong."

Sofia patted his chest. "I made sure I thought only of success, not failure."

He smoothed one of the curls she had flattened in front of her ears. "It's always good to have a positive attitude. But inviting Mr. Kirk, out of the blue, to come to your dressing room before the end of the opera... Brent told me people don't do it. Victoria could have prevented it, and then where would you be?"

She grinned. "You do not see my beautiful note to *Signore* Kirk. It was fantastic. He could not say no."

Car ran a finger across her bodice, just as he had before her audition. "And the blouse. You gave Lorenzo an eyeful."

"The blouse was nothing. The Maestro liked the idea, even if he did not know why I did it. For everything I did now, I would do it again."

He towered over her, his face solemn with concern, his eyes, a deeper green-blue than usual.

"You saved the team." He grinned at her. "I think the fans, if they ever find out, will be very grateful. Maybe they'll even start buying tickets for the opera."

"And I will gladly sing for them." Sofia wanted to melt into Car's arms in relief that her plan had worked and now all she had to do was sing. But how could she? She didn't want to get makeup all over him. "Act Two begins and I must be on stage and you must be in your seat."

He smiled. "I know now I'm not supposed to say break a leg. I'm supposed to say in boke... in boke, um."

She smiled up at him. "*In bocca al lupo*, you say. In the mouth of the wolf."

He grinned. "Later. We're celebrating."

Chapter Twenty-Six

The word, after the performance, was Lorenzo sang an adequate Don José, Lucilla Sebastiani shone as Micaela, and the baritone singing Escamillo was bombastic in his performance of, as Dawg called it, the Toreador thing.

Every reviewer, especially Gareth Silver, went into raptures for Sofia de' Medici, her voice, shockingly sublime for someone so young, her presence and yes, her ability to act the part of Carmen to an exquisite level, unseen in decades.

Nobody could talk of anyone, but Sofia, during the dinner at the hotel after the performance, courtesy of the hotel itself. All her friends were present, and the performers—except Lorenzo, who said he had somewhere else to go. Dawg came with Tina. So did a bunch of the guys from the team. Even the Maestro made an appearance, although he didn't stay.

Car watched Lupino retreat to the bar after only a few minutes. Something about how the Muni's general manager stared at him made Car think he should join the man for a drink.

Lupino's beverage of choice was vodka on the rocks with a twist of lemon. Car signaled the bartender to hit him with the same. "She was something else, wasn't she?"

Lupino gave him a half smile. "Do you know how something else she was?"

Car's drink came. He swirled it once, then raised it to his lips. "Enough."

Lupino shifted on his stool. "I'll tell you this. That young woman has the makings of the best mezzo of this generation."

"The makings?"

"Yes."

"But?"

"But I'm not sure it's what she wants."

"That makes no sense," Car said.

"She wanted to sing *Carmen*. I don't know how many other roles interest her the same way."

"I still don't understand."

Lupino lifted the glass to his lips and took a deep swallow. He was silent for a long time. "Well, I must be going. It's been a long night."

He wasn't going to spell it out. That was as clear as the vodka in Car's glass.

Lupino reached out a hand. "It has been a pleasure. Thank you for taking me to batting practice. Perhaps we can do it again next season." With a sparkle in his eyes, he added, "It was wonderful, too, how the lady in charge of the tickets for the All-Star game was able to send me a pair. If she should be able to do so again, I'd like that too."

Lupino had been on to him that night at Vauxhall on the Hudson. He grinned. "Give me a call. I'll set it up."

Lupino began to walk away and then stopped. He turned back. "One thing." He studied the revelers before focusing on Car. "I always wanted Sofia for my *Carmen*. But..." He stroked his upper lip. "Did you know Victoria paid for the production? No? No one did. It was a secret between us, because at the last minute, two of my benefactors fell victim to the economy. If she hadn't stepped up to the plate—pardon the baseball reference—I would not have been able to go forward. And if I hadn't been able to go forward, I wouldn't have had a job."

Car narrowed his eyes at Lupino. "Why, then, did you choose Sofia?"

"When she came to sing for me that day, I knew. There was no Carmen for me but her. This is what I told Victoria. She could fire me then if she wanted. But the plans for the performance were too far along. She had no choice but to go along with everything." Lupino smiled. "I thought you might want to know."

Car watched him make his way down the length of the

bar and push the door open to the lobby.

He turned this piece of knowledge over in his mind. At last he let himself smile. "Son of a bitch," he said under his breath. It was never Sofia's looks. It wasn't her clothes, and it wasn't the damn teeth. It was Victoria. All the time.

For Car, the mid-season break came and went. He was playing lights out, hadn't been on top of his game like this since the early years of his career. At first he told himself it was Sofia who was responsible. She had been. But like he'd told the reporters the night he hit for the cycle, he just needed to get his rhythm back. He needed to let his body alone to do its thing. No longer was he thinking about retiring. Eventually, a couple of years down the road, he would. But now, he'd play and enjoy every minute.

Things were good with Noah. They bought Spiderman sheets and a set of yellow ones because yellow was Noah's favorite color. The living room, which if Car had let his decorator loose, would have looked good enough for a spread in one of those design magazines, now resembled the set of a disaster movie. Car learned the hard way to turn the lights on before entering the living room at night. He was getting used to reading bedtime stories more than once; twice, he'd have thought he got off easy.

As the summer progressed, he found it worked better to take Noah with him when the team was on the road. Invariably one of the wives was more than willing to keep Noah with her in the wives' box during the game. Before and after the game, he and Noah always found something to do. When they played the Angels, they took in Disneyland; in Baltimore, they hit the Aquarium, in Boston, they rode the duck boats.

The custody case ended with a meeting in Louise's lawyer's office, some signing of papers, a couple of handshakes, and done. Who would have thought it would end with a whimper after all the drama?

Only one thing was missing, or rather one person: Sofia. There'd been a round of celebrating after the performance. Sofia had basked in the adoration that came her way. Car enjoyed it. He'd especially enjoyed it that night after the performance.

For a little while, he'd watched the celebration. When he had his fill of watching, he joined it. Sofia gave him a no-holds-barred smile, stood on her tiptoes and kissed him softly on the mouth. "This is a good night, yes?"

"Yes. It's the best night." He slid an arm around her waist. "How much longer do we have to celebrate? I have an idea of how we can have a celebration of a different kind."

The smile slipped. "Oh Car, tonight I cannot come to you. I promise Brent I will meet him later. He wants to spend some time with me. And I? I would like to spend a little time with my real papa."

She reached up and stroked his face. "Can we be together tomorrow night?'

He didn't react, knowing how small it would make him if he whined about her spending time with the father she had just discovered. "Sure. No problem." He stuck around for another little while, but his pleasure was diminished. After a while, he gave her another kiss and said he needed to retrieve Noah from the Huggins' house.

With the next night came an invitation to appear on The Tonight Show with Jimmy Fallon. Sofia was charming, her English almost as broken as it had been when they'd first met. Car grinned, knowing how nervous she was from the way she mangled her sentences. Fallon was charmed.

She was too tired to come over after the taping. "I will go right to the bed." She did sound exhausted.

"Why can't you go to bed at my place?" he asked, a little uncomfortable with her for the first time in a long time.

"Car, please do not make the pressure."

He felt a twinge of anxiety. "It's not pressure."

Her weary eyes softened. "I know this. But it is a strange time. I must do things you cannot do with me." She patted his cheek. "We will be together later."

Later came and went and she was off doing interviews

for some big classical radio station in Chicago and a public TV station in Boston. A picture of her as Carmen, all defiance and fire, appeared on the front page of USA Today. He read about her online and in the magazine—*Opera News*—he was now subscribed to. She was out of New York more than she was in.

It took him a while to realize he was getting the brush off. When he did, he wondered how he hadn't seen it coming. He was the first man on whom she'd had a crush. He was the first man who told her she was beautiful. He was the first man who told her he loved her. Perhaps just as she thought he'd confused sex with love, she'd decided what they had wasn't truly love.

He thought back to that strange conversation with Lupino. He hadn't known what he meant about Sofia wanting to sing other roles. From what he could tell that was all she wanted. She wanted what Brent wanted for her: to be a prima donna.

He wasn't surprised when he got a call from her one afternoon, telling him she was in San Francisco to discuss a contract to sing *Carmen*. At last he knew. She was gone.

"Where's Sofia?" Noah asked him one morning.

"I'm not sure, sport." Which was true. He didn't know where she was. Not with him was all he did know. The knowledge left a terrible empty feeling in him. But he'd been empty before, so he figured he'd get used to it again. Besides, now he had Noah and that was a good thing.

"When is she coming back?"

The empty feeling suddenly filled with grief. "I'm not sure."

"You say that a lot."

"That's because I don't know when she's coming back. Maybe she'll be gone for a long time."

"I don't think so."

Car wished he could have had Noah's confidence. He

didn't.

The knock startled him. Oscar, or whoever was on at night, never let anyone up without notifying him, not after the fiasco with Louise and Jensen. Whoever was out in the hallway had to be a resident of the building. But he had no friends among his neighbors.

He opened the door.

Naturally, nobody would announce her. The doorman would let her up if she arrived in the dead of night with an entourage of horses and elephants from the Triumphal March at the end of Act One of *Aida*.

Because she was so short, the oversize shopping bag dangling from her fist grazed the floor. "I have brought the special cookies," Sofia announced, as if they'd just been talking on the phone and told him she was bringing them over. He stepped back to let her in. She didn't look at him. "Noah, he is here?"

"Yes, but sleeping. Been sleeping for an hour."

"Oh."

Was that disappointment in her voice? Was she here to see his son and not him?

She gave him an uncertain smile. "The game today, I watched it on TV." Again she shifted the bag.

He came to in a flurry of activity. "Is that heavy?" He reached for it. "Let me take it from you."

"It is not heavy. Only bulky." She lifted it in both hands a little, to show him.

He took the bag anyway. She didn't protest, only followed him into the kitchen.

"Should I put them in the refrigerator?" He lifted the first box from the bag.

"It is not necessary. Noah will eat them at once."

He lifted the second and third boxes out. Each one was decorated with Transformers stickers. All Noah's favorites: Jazz, Bumblebee, and of course, Optimus Prime; on the sides, she'd included some of the Decepticons. It had taken her more than a little time to decorate these boxes. He placed each box on the counter, one on top of the other. "What's this about, Sofia? Why are you making cookies for Noah?"

"I cannot make cookies for him?"

He held onto his patience. "Yes, you can make cookies for him. What you can't do is come waltzing back into my life without any explanation. And especially after you left it that same way."

She looked shamefaced. "I did not do that."

"What?" He could feel his ears turning red.

"I went away for a little while."

He opened his mouth to answer and snapped it shut. After he knew he'd controlled himself enough not to yell, he said, "You're not getting it, or you're evading it. I was looking for the explanation. Ex-pla-na-tion."

"You do not have to make the fun of my English," she said, all dignity.

"I'm not making fun of your English," he said, his voice rising anyway. "I want to know why you left."

"I was afraid."

Of all the answers he expected from her, this one came dead last. "Of me?"

"Not you. Me."

He thumped back hard against the counter and upset the boxes. The top-most one began to shift. Car whirled around at the same moment Sofia leapt forward. Their hands tangled. She leapt back the moment they touched, as if he'd burned her.

With slow and deliberate motions, he set the box back on the counter next to the others. Like the box almost did, it all came crashing down on him: the pain and doubt he'd lived with the weeks they'd been apart. "Are you afraid to touch me?"

He felt the press of her hand in the center of his back.

"You do not listen to me," she said, her voice low. "For sure it does not mean I am afraid to touch you. This time I am away, I long for you to be with me, but I know it cannot be because you are playing baseball."

He turned around. Slowly. "You longed to be with

me?"

She was looking up at him like she used to, way back at the beginning. Like he didn't get it. Like he was a jerk.

"Yes, I wanted you more than anything. I wanted you to hold me when I was scared, which was a lot, and when I negotiate with the men at the San Francisco Opera I was, believe me, scared, and when I decide I must have an agent to do the negotiating. And a lawyer." She fanned herself. "Thanks be to God I have Chelsea for my assistant. But she did not hold me like you would have held me."

He felt hope rise. "You could have had me. All you had to do was ask."

She bit her lip. "But I could not."

Hope faltered. "Sofia." There was an urgency in his voice he did nothing to hide. "You're killing me. What's going on?"

Taking a deep breath, she said, "I must tell you a story. Will you listen?"

"Of course I'll listen."

She hesitated. Then she said, "You know already. My whole life I love to sing. And I tell you how when I was a little girl it made me feel..." She waved a hand vaguely in the air. "Singing is my natural state. Federico—I have decided to call him *Federico*—I was his puppet.

"I did not know this when I was a child. I did not imagine my life was different than other girls' lives. And so I take the lessons. Every day, even sometimes on Sunday. Because he convinces me, I tell myself it is what I want.

"But sometimes, when I am tired, I think perhaps the singing does not make me feel so natural. But I do nothing about it. I continue performing, until at last I am singing as a professional. I sing the roles one expects of the young mezzos."

She stopped. But he'd be patient. He wouldn't push her to continue until she was ready.

She sighed again. "I tell Federico I want to perform *Carmen*. He does not like it. I tell him the reasons why. They are not good reasons for him. I argue, yes, they are; he does not know what is inside me. He says no. I say yes. Then he forbids me. I argue. He forbids me some more. But I do not let go of the idea. In secret I learn the role.

"Maria Torelli, who one day when she is no longer able to sing, will be a teacher of the highest order, tells me my instrument—my voice—is a beautiful oddity and that I am ready to sing *Carmen* even as young as I am. I continue to practice at the opera house when Federico is not there. At last, he breaks his leg."

Car took her by the hand and urged her to sit. Pulling out a chair, he sat too. "I already know this part of the story."

She gave him a tiny smile. "You do not know the best part of the story." She took a deep breath. "I discover something when I argue with the music director at the San Francisco Opera about what roles besides *Carmen* I will sing for him two and three years from now." She opened her eyes wide. "Did you know this is how the plans are made? Two and three, and perhaps even more years into the future? In four years I will be twenty-eight."

He smiled. "Not very old."

"You will be thirty-eight. Not so old either. But if that year we have our oldest child, you will be fifty when our child is twelve."

Silence.

He reached out and took her hand. It was ice cold. "Let me understand. You want to have children with me?"

She had paled. Her eyes, always so big, got bigger. "It is what I am saying. Do you want to have children with me?"

Car's heart swelled, his breath quickened, and his head began to pound.

He yanked her off the chair and onto his lap. Winding his arms around her shoulders, pressing her against his chest, burying his face in her luxuriant hair, he whispered, "I want them. With you, you crazy woman."

He leaned back. Tunneling his fingers into her hair, he tilted up her face, and kissed her. A hard, demanding kiss. A no-holds-barred kiss.

After a moment, they were both breathing hard. Car knew where this evening was going to end. Since he knew, he could take his time, find out what else was going on in his Sofia's circuitous mind. "What's really caused this change of heart? Does wanting to have kids with me—and I assume you want us to marry—mean you're going to sing less?"

She swatted him on the arm. "Most assuredly I want us to marry! What is the matter with you? Maybe I do not go to Confession in many years, but I do not say I want children with you that will be born bastards."

"Well that's one thing settled."

Snuggling closer to him, winding her arms around him, holding him closer, she said, "Yes, it is settled."

"But what about the rest? Your career?"

"Ah, this is an interesting part. When I was in San Francisco, for the first time in my life there was no Federico to tell me what to do. There was no Brent, my new papa. There was no you to catch me if I fall. So I must have the reliance on myself. I tell myself I want this reliance." She shifted to sit up. She stroked his cheek, her gaze roaming his face. "At first I think I like this. I am making decisions for my life by myself. Like Carmen. Even the decision to hire an agent and a lawyer, I make myself."

She paused, but a very short pause.

"It was then I realize something strange. I was *becoming* Carmen."

He blinked.

She laughed. "No, I am not going to stab the *Signora*—although in my dressing room that time when she calls my papa a bastard I want to. Also I do not want to make you my Don José. I have become Carmen in the way a woman makes her choices, because she can without a man to make them for her. And I discover I could be that woman." She put a hand to her lips. "*Mi dispiace...* I am sorry. I did not have to let Federico make the choices for me. I do not have to let you make choices for me.

"But here is the thing." She was back to petting him. "I want to make the choices with you. I want to decide when and yes, where I will sing. With you. Because we are partners and partners make the decisions together."

She slid off his lap. Standing in front of him, she said, "I am here not so much to bring Noah the cookies, but to ask you if you want this too. The discussion, the decisions, the children, and the life together."

He grinned up at her, not too far up, her being the

little thing she was. Little, but so powerful. "You were sure of me, weren't you?" It was no question, just a statement of fact, because at the end of this story of hers, Car knew he'd been played. But hadn't he been played in the most outstanding way. He was looking forward to a lifetime of being played.

"Well, I was not so sure." She held up a hand, forefinger and thumb held straight and parallel to each other. "I was *this* sure."

He stood. Walking over to the counter, he opened one of the boxes and lifted out a cookie and got his first look at its shape. He started to laugh. "It's Optimus Prime." He looked into the box. "They're all Transformers." He pulled her toward him. "I'll accept your proposal of marriage and all that other stuff that goes along with it on one condition."

She arched an eyebrow at him. "Yes? What is the condition?"

"That from now on when you make cookies for Noah, I get my share too."

She stood on tiptoes and kissed him. "With me, you will always get the first share of everything."

The End

Made in the USA
Monee, IL
26 February 2020

22220557R00171